**Expecting Lone**
by Mauree

ﭏﭏﬦﬦ

## *"I'm pregnant."*

Laying both hands protectively against her flat abdomen, she whispered, "Don't worry about a thing, little guy. You'll be okay. I promise."

Even as she said the words, she felt a flicker of unease as she thought about telling Sam her news. He wouldn't be happy; she knew that already. He was so determined to keep his heart locked away, he would see this baby as an invitation to pain.

Her brain raced with thoughts and wishes and half-baked dreams she knew didn't have a chance at becoming reality. Silently she admitted a secret she'd been hiding not only from Sam but from herself.

She loved Sam Lonergan. She loved everything about him and knew she couldn't keep him.

But at least when he left, she'd have his child.

# The Sins of His Past
## by Roxanne St Claire

ᗑᗄᐟᐠᗧ

# *Praise for award-winning author Roxanne St Claire*

# Expecting Lonergan's Baby
## MAUREEN CHILD

# The Sins of His Past
## ROXANNE ST CLAIRE

MILLS & BOON®

Desire™

*MILLS & BOON and MILLS & BOON with the Rose Device
are registered trademarks of the publisher.*

*First published in Great Britain 2007
Harlequin Mills & Boon Limited,
Eton House, 18-24 Paradise Road, Richmond, Surrey TW9 1SR*

The publisher acknowledges the copyright holders of the
individual works as follows:

Expecting Lonergan's Baby © Maureen Child 2006
The Sins of His Past © Roxanne St Claire 2006

*ISBN: 978 0 263 85010 9*

51-0307

*Printed and bound in Spain
by Litografia Rosés S.A., Barcelona*

# EXPECTING LONERGAN'S BABY

by
Maureen Child

## MAUREEN CHILD

is a California native who loves to travel. Every chance they get, she and her husband are taking off on another research trip. The author of more than sixty books, Maureen loves a happy ending and still swears that she has the best job in the world. She lives in Southern California with her husband, two children and a golden retriever with delusions of grandeur.

For my family—for always being there.
I love you.

# One

Sam Lonergan had expected to find a ghost at the lake. He *hadn't* expected a naked woman.

Given a choice, he much preferred this view. He knew he should look away, but he didn't. Instead he focused his gaze on the long, lean woman slicing through the dark, moonlit water.

Even in the pale wash of moonlight her skin glowed tan and smooth. The water she displaced slipped behind her with hardly a splash. Her arms made long strokes through the water, carrying her from one edge of the small lake and back again to the other. A part of him saw her as a trespasser on holy ground—but another part of him was grateful she was here.

While he watched her, he told himself he shouldn't have come. This lake, this ranch, held too many memories. Too many images that crowded his mind and made remembering an exercise in pain.

Abruptly he squeezed his eyes shut, took a deep breath and slowly released it before opening his eyes again. She'd stopped swimming and was now treading water, watching him watch her.

"Seen enough?" she asked.

"Depends," he told her. "You have anything else to show me?"

Her mouth worked as if she were biting down on words she wouldn't allow herself to say.

"Who are you?" she finally demanded, her voice more angry than worried.

"I could ask you the same thing," he pointed out.

"This is private property."

"Sure is," he agreed, hitching one hip higher than the other and folding his arms over his chest. "So I have to wonder what you're doing on it."

"I live here," she replied, swinging a long, wet fall of dark brown hair back from her face.

Water droplets arced around her head and dropped to the lake like raindrops. It took a minute or two, but her words hit home.

"You live here? This is the Lonergan ranch."

A ranch that had been in his family for generations. Since the early days of the gold rush, when

Sam's great-great-whatever had decided that the real fortune to be found in California was the land—not rocky cold streams where the occasional nugget was discovered.

That Lonergan had settled here, raising horses and a family. A family that now consisted of one old man, one ghost and three Lonergan cousins: Sam, Cooper and Jake.

His grandfather, Jeremiah Lonergan, had lived alone for the last twenty years. Ever since his wife, Sam's grandmother, had died. Now, if a naked woman was to be believed, he had a roommate.

"That's right," she said, warming to her subject. "And the owner of this ranch is *very* protective of me. And *vicious.*"

Sam wanted to laugh. His grandfather was maybe the most gentle-hearted man Sam had ever known. But to hear this woman tell it, Jeremiah was a mad dog.

"Well, he's not here right now, is he?"

"No."

"So since it's just the two of us and we're getting so friendly…mind telling me if you go skinny-dipping often?" he asked instead.

"You spy on naked women often?"

"Whenever I get the chance."

She scowled at him and pushed one hand through her wet hair. She dipped a little lower in the water, and he figured her legs were getting tired of the constant kicking to keep afloat.

"You don't sound ashamed of yourself."

He gave her a lazy smile that didn't go anywhere near his eyes. "Lady, if I *didn't* watch a naked woman when given the opportunity, that'd be something to be ashamed of."

"Your mother must be so proud."

He chuckled. Probably not, but the old man would have been.

She glanced around her and he knew what she was looking at. Emptiness. Except for the oak trees standing like solitary guardians around the ring of the lake, they were alone. The ranch was a good mile east of here, and the highway ten miles south.

"Look," she said and dipped again, the water lapping at the tops of her breasts. "You've had your peep show, but it's cold and I'm tired. I'd like to get out now."

"Who's stopping you?"

Her eyes went wide and dark. "Hello? I'm not getting out of this water with you watching me."

Something like guilt nibbled at the edges of a conscience that was already too noisy. But he ignored it. Yes, he should look away, but would a starving man turn down a steak just because it was stolen?

"You could turn your back," she said a moment later.

One corner of his mouth lifted. "Now, if I do that,

how do I know you won't hit me over the head with something?"

"Does it *look* like I'm carrying a concealed weapon?"

He shrugged. "A man can't be too careful."

She nodded, dipped low enough to have the surface of the water lap at her throat, then muttered, "Perfect. I'm naked and *you're* the one threatened."

A wind kicked up out of nowhere, rustling the leaves on the oaks until it sounded as if they were surrounded by a whispering crowd. She shivered and dipped even lower in the water, and another ping of guilt echoed inside Sam.

He tipped his head back to look at the star-studded sky before looking at her again. "It's a nice night. Maybe I'll camp out right here."

"You wouldn't."

"No?" Beginning to enjoy himself, he pretended to consider it. "Maybe not. But the question remains. You getting out of the lake or do you know how to sleep while treading water?"

She huffed out a disgusted breath and slapped one hand against the water. "I'm getting out."

"Can't wait."

"You're a real jerk, you know that?"

"That's been said before."

"Color me surprised."

"You're still in the water." He unfolded his arms

and stuck both hands into the back pockets of his jeans. "Must be getting pretty cold about now."

"Yeah, but—"

"Told you I'm not going anywhere."

She gave another quick glance around at the dark country surrounding them, as if hoping to catch a glimpse of the cavalry riding to her rescue.

"How do I know you won't attack me the minute I get out of the lake?" she asked, eyes narrowed on him.

"I could give you my word," Sam said, "but since you don't know me, that wouldn't be worth much."

She studied him for a long minute and he had the weird sensation that she was looking far more deeply than he would like. But after another long minute she said, "If you give me your word, I'll believe you."

Frowning, he pulled one hand from his pocket and scrubbed the back of his neck. A beautiful, naked trespasser trusted him. Great. "Fine. You have it."

She nodded, but another long minute or two ticked past before she started in toward shore. Something inside him quickened. Anticipation? Excitement? It had been long enough since he'd felt either, he couldn't be sure. But the moment came and went so fast, he couldn't explore it or even take a second to enjoy it.

Moonlight dazzled on her wet golden skin as she walked out of the water and up the short incline to where her clothes were stacked in a neat little pile.

He watched her and felt a hot, pulsing need rush through him with enough force to stagger him.

She was tall and lean, with small, firm breasts, narrow hips and a tan line that told him she didn't usually skinny-dip. He could only be grateful that she'd chosen to tonight. Somehow those tan lines made her nudity that much more exciting. Paler strips of skin against the honey-brown tempted a man to define the edges of those lines.

Desire stirred and heat pooled inside him.

She was magical in the moonlight, and it took everything he had to keep from grabbing her up and pulling her close. It was like watching a mermaid step out of the sea just long enough to tempt a man.

"You are amazing."

She faltered slightly, then lifted her chin and stood tall and proud, no embarrassment, no hesitation. And Sam knew he should feel guilty for staring at her, taking advantage of the situation.

But damned if he could.

In seconds, she'd yanked on a T-shirt and stepped into a soft-looking cotton skirt that swirled around her knees as she bent to pull on first one sandal and then the other.

Hell, he should be thanking her. She'd taken his mind off the past, made facing this lake and the memories again much easier than he'd expected.

"Look," he said as she straightened up, "I'm sorry

for giving you a hard time, but seeing you here surprised me and—"

She slugged him in the stomach.

Didn't hurt much, but since he was unprepared, all his air left him in a rush.

"*I* surprised *you?*" Maggie Collins grabbed her long brown hair, held the mass off to one side and quickly wrung the excess water from it before flipping it all over her shoulder again.

Amazing. He'd called her *amazing*.

She could still feel the flush of something warm and delicious as he watched her. It was as if she'd felt his touch, not just his gaze, locked on her. And for just one brief moment she'd *wanted* him to touch her. To feel his hands sliding over her wet skin.

Which only made her madder. She looked him up and down dismissively, then lifted her chin. "You rotten, self-serving, miserable…" Oh, she hated when she ran out of invectives before she was finished.

Inhaling sharply, she threw her shoulders back and gathered up her tattered pride. She'd about had a heart attack when she'd first seen him, standing on shore, watching her in the darkness. But the initial jolt of fear had subsided quickly enough the longer she'd looked at him.

Maggie'd been on her own long enough to develop a sort of radar that told her when she was safe and when she was in danger. And none of her internal warning bells had gone off, despite the fact that he hadn't been gentleman enough to either leave or turn around.

He wasn't dangerous.

At least not physically.

Emotionally—now that might be a different story. He was tall and gorgeous—already worrisome—and then there was the gleam in his dark eyes. Not just the flash of desire she'd seen and noted—but an undercurrent of something sad and empty. Maggie'd always been attracted to wounded guys. The ones with sad eyes and lonely hearts.

But after getting her own heart bruised a few times, she'd decided that sometimes there was a *reason* men were alone. Now all she had to do was remember that.

She stood her ground, glaring at the man who'd intruded on her nightly swim. Just a few years ago she might have skittered away quickly, trying to disappear. But not now. In the last two years things had changed for her. She'd found a home. She *belonged* on the Lonergan ranch, and no one—let alone a surly, good-looking stranger—would scare her off.

"You've got a good right jab," he conceded.

"You'll live." She started past him, headed for the line of trees and the path beyond that would lead her back to the ranch house.

He stopped her with a hand on her arm. Instantly

her skin sizzled and her blood bubbled in her veins. She yanked free of his grasp and took a step back just for good measure.

"Hey, hey," he said, his voice soothing as he lifted both hands in mock surrender. "It's okay. Relax."

The quick jolt of adrenaline she'd felt at his un-expected touch was already dissipating when she glared at him. "Just…don't grab me."

"No problem." he said, "Won't happen again."

She blew out a breath and willed herself to calm down. It wasn't just the fact that he'd surprised her by taking hold of her arm—it was the sudden flash of heat that had dazzled up her arm only to ricochet throughout her body. She'd never felt that punch of awareness before and wasn't sure she liked it much. Better to just get away from the man. Fast.

"It's going to take me about ten minutes to walk back to the house," she said when she was certain her voice wouldn't quiver. "I suggest you use that time to get gone."

He shook his head. "Can't do it."

"You'd better. Because the minute I get to a phone, I'll be calling the police to report a trespasser."

"You could," he said and fell into step beside her as she once again started for the tree line. "But it wouldn't do any good."

"And why's that?"

"Because," he said, coming to a stop, "I went to

high school with half the police force in town. And I think Jeremiah Lonergan might just object to you having me arrested."

A sinking sensation opened in the pit of her stomach, but Maggie asked the question anyway. "Why would he object?"

"Because I'm Sam Lonergan, and Jeremiah's my grandfather."

# Two

Everything else faded away but a rush of anger that nearly strangled Maggie. She'd known, of course, that all three of Jeremiah's grandsons were arriving this summer, but she hadn't expected one of them to sneak in under the cover of darkness and then turn out to be a Peeping Tom.

"If I'd known who you were," Maggie snapped, "I would have hit you harder."

"Lucky for me I kept quiet then."

"How could you do this to him?" she demanded, planting both hands on her hips.

"Do what?"

"Stay away," she snapped. "You—*all* of you. Not

one of the three of you has so much as visited your grandfather in two years."

"And you know this how?"

"Because I've been here," she said, slapping one hand to her chest. "Me. I've been taking care of that sweet old man for two years and I don't remember tripping over any of you in the house."

"Sweet old man?" His laughter shot from his throat. "Jeremiah Lonergan is the most softhearted, crustiest old goat in the country."

"He is *not*," she shouted, infuriated by his amusement at the expense of an old man who had been even lonelier than she had when she first met him. "He's sweet. And kind. And caring. And *alone*. His own family doesn't care enough to come and see him. You should all be ashamed of yourselves. Especially *you*. You're a *doctor*. You should have come home before this to make sure he was all right. But no. You wait until he's…" God. She couldn't even bring herself to say the word *dying*.

She couldn't think about losing Jeremiah. Couldn't bear the thought of losing him and the home she'd come to love so much. And here stood a man who took all of that for granted. Who didn't appreciate the love that was waiting for him. Who didn't care enough about that sweet old man to even *visit*.

New fury pumped through her and she narrowed

her eyes on the man who only moments before had stirred her blood into a simmering boil.

His laughter faded away and a scowl that was both fierce and irritated twisted his features. "Just who the hell are you anyway?"

"My name's Maggie Collins," she said, straightening up to her full five feet four inches. "And I'm your grandfather's housekeeper."

And she had that position because the "crusty old goat" had taken a chance on her when she'd needed it most. So she wasn't about to stand by and let *anyone,* even his grandson, berate the old man she loved.

"Well, Maggie Collins," he said through gritted teeth, "just because you've been taking care of Jeremiah's house doesn't mean you know squat about me or my family."

She leaned in at him, not intimidated in the slightest. In the last two years she'd watched Jeremiah flip through old photo albums, stare at home movies, lose himself in the past because the grandsons he loved didn't care enough to give him a present.

And it infuriated her that three grown men who had the home she'd always longed for didn't seem to appreciate it.

"I know that though the man has three grandsons, he's *alone*. I know that he had to take in a *stranger* to keep him company. I know that he looks at pictures of the three of you and his heart aches."

She poked him in the chest with her index finger. "I know that it took his being near death's door—" her breath hitched and she hiccupped "—to get you all back here to see him this summer. I know *that* much."

Sam shoved one hand through his long dark hair, looked away from her for a slow count of ten. Then, when he turned his gaze back to her, the anger had left him. His eyes were dark and shadowed.

"You're right."

She hadn't expected that and it took her aback a little. Tipping her head to one side, she studied him. "Just like that? I'm right?"

"To a point," he admitted and his voice dropped, wrapping the two of them in a kind of insular seclusion. "It's...*complicated,*" he said finally.

So much for being surprised into feeling just a tiny bit of sympathy for his side of the story. Disgusted, she shook her head. "No, it's not. He's your grandfather. He loves you. And you ignore him."

"You don't understand."

"You're absolutely right." She folded her arms across her chest, tapped her foot against the rocky ground and waited.

His eyes narrowed. "I don't owe you an explanation, Maggie Collins, so don't bother waiting for one."

No, he didn't, though she desperately wanted one. She couldn't understand how anyone with a home, a family, could deliberately avoid them. "Fine. Maybe you don't owe me anything, but you certainly owe your grandfather."

That scowl deepened until it looked as though it had been carved into his face. "I'm here, aren't I?"

"Finally. Have you seen him yet?"

"No," he admitted, shoving both hands into his pockets as he shifted his gaze to the lake behind them. "I haven't. I had to come here first. Had to face this place first."

And just like that, Maggie's heart twisted. She knew what he was seeing when he looked at the small lake. She knew what he was remembering because Jeremiah had told her everything there was to know about his grandsons. The good, the bad and the haunting.

"I'm sorry," she blurted, wishing she could pull at least *some* of her harsher words back. "I know how hard this must be for you, but—"

He cut her off with a look. "You don't know," he said tightly. "You *can't*. So why don't you go back to the house. Tell my grandfather I'll be there soon."

He walked away to stand at the water's edge, staring out over the black, still surface of the lake. His pain reached out to her and she flinched from it. She didn't want to feel sorry for him. Didn't want to give him the benefit of the doubt. Though even if he did have his reasons for avoiding the Lonergan ranch, she thought, that didn't make it all right for him to avoid the old man who loved him.

Her sympathy evaporated and Maggie left him there, alone in the shadows.

Jeremiah just had time to shove the blood-curdling horror novel he'd been reading under his covers before Maggie opened his bedroom door after a brief knock. He watched the girl he'd come to think of as a granddaughter and smiled to himself. Her dark brown hair was wet, trailing dampness across her T-shirt. Her long, flowing skirt was wrinkled and dotted with dried bits of grass, and her sandals squeaked with the water seeping into the leather.

"Been down to the lake again, eh?" he asked as she came closer and straightened the quilt and sheet covering him.

She smiled but couldn't quite hide the flash of something else in her dark eyes.

"What is it, Maggie?" He grabbed her hand, making sure to be as feeble as possible, as she reached for the glass pitcher on his bedside table. "Are you all right?"

"I'm fine," she said, pulling her hand free and giving him a pat before carrying the carafe to the adjoining bathroom to fill it with fresh water. She stepped back into the bedroom and walked quickly back to his side. "I met your grandson, that's all."

Jeremiah's heart lifted, but he remembered just in

time that he was supposed to be a dying man now. Keeping his voice quiet, he asked, "Which one?"

"Sam."

"Ah." He smiled to himself. "Well, where is he? Didn't he come back with you?"

"No," she said, frowning as she turned the bedside lamp with the three-way bulb down to its lowest setting. Instantly the room fell into shadows, the pale night light hardly reaching her, standing right at his bedside. "He said he wanted to stay at the lake for a while first."

Jeremiah felt a twinge of pain in his heart and knew that it was only a shadow of the pain Sam must be feeling at the moment. But damn it, fifteen years had gone by. It was time the Lonergan cousins put the past to rest. Long past time, if truth be told. And if he'd had to lie to get them all to come here, well, then, it was a lie told with the best of reasons.

"How'd he look?"

Maggie fidgeted quickly with his pillows, then straightened up, put her hands on her narrow hips and said thoughtfully, "Alone. Like the most *alone* man I've ever seen."

"Suppose he is." Sighing, Jeremiah let his head fall back against the pillows that Maggie had plumped so neatly. He should feel guilty about tricking all of his grandsons into coming home. But he didn't. Hell, if you couldn't be sneaky when you got old, what the hell good were you?

"It's not going to be easy," he said. "Not on any of 'em. But they're strong men. They'll make it through."

Maggie gave the quilt covering him one last tug, then leaned down and planted a quick kiss on his forehead. "They're not the ones I'm worried about," she said, then stood up and smiled down at him.

"You're a good girl, Maggie. But you don't need to worry about me. I'll be fine once my boys are home."

Sam entered the house quietly, half expecting the old man's bodyguard to leap at him from the shadows, teeth bared. When there was no sign of Maggie Collins, though, he surrendered to the inevitable and glanced around the room he'd once run wild through.

Two lamps had been left burning, their soft glow illuminating a room he would have been able to find his way through blindfolded. Nothing had changed. Oak floors, scarred from years of running children and booted feet, were dotted with faded colorful throw rugs. Four dark brown leather sofas sat arranged in a huge square, with a table wide enough to be a raft in the dead center of them. Magazines were stacked neatly in one corner of the table and a vase of yellow roses sat center stage.

Had to be the bodyguard's doing, he told himself, since he knew damn well Jeremiah wouldn't have thought to cut fresh flowers. Maggie Collins's face rose up in his mind, then faded away as Sam looked around the house, familiarizing himself all over again with his past.

A river-stone hearth wide and high enough for a man to stand in dominated one wall, and a few embers still glowed richly red behind a fire screen of scrolled iron. The walls were adorned with framed family photos and landscapes painted by a talented, if young, hand. Sam winced at the paintings and quickly looked away. He wasn't ready just yet to be smothered by ghosts. It was enough that he was here. He'd have to swallow the past in small gulps or he'd choke on them.

Dropping his duffle bag by the door, he headed for the stairs at the far end of the room. Each stair was a log, sawn in half and varnished to a high sheen. The banisters looked like petrified tree trunks, and his hand slid along the cool surface as he mounted the stairs to the bedrooms above.

His steps sounded like the slow beating of his own heart. Every move he made took him closer to memories he didn't want to look at. Yet there was no going back. No avoiding it anymore.

At the head of the stairs he paused and glanced down the long hall. Closed doors were all that greeted him, but he knew the rooms behind those doors as well as he knew his own reflection in the mirror. He and his cousins had shared those rooms every summer for most of their lives. They'd crashed up the stairs, slid down the banisters and run wild across every acre of the family ranch.

Until that last summer.

The day when everything had changed forever.

The day they'd all grown up—and apart.

Scowling, he brushed away the memories as he would a cloud of gnats in front of his face and walked to the door at the head of the stairs. His grandfather's room. A man he hadn't seen in fifteen years.

Shame rippled through him and he told himself that Maggie Collins would be proud if she knew it. She was right about one thing. They shouldn't have stayed away from the old man for so long. Should have found a way to see him despite the pain.

But they hadn't.

Instead they'd punished themselves, and in the doing had punished an old man who hadn't deserved it, as well.

He knocked and waited.

"Sam?"

The voice was weaker than he'd thought it would be but still so familiar. Apparently the house-keeper/bodyguard had spilled the news about his arrival. He opened the door, stepped inside and felt his heart turn over in his chest.

Jeremiah Lonergan. The strongest man Sam had ever known looked...*old*. Most of his hair was gone, his tanned scalp shining in the soft lamplight. A fringe of gray hair ringed his head, and the lines that had always defined his face were deeper, scored more fully into his features. He looked small in the wide bed, covered in one of the quilts his wife had made decades ago.

Sam felt the solid punch of sorrow slam him in the gut. Time had passed. Too much time. And for that one startling moment he deeply regretted all the years he'd missed with the man he'd always loved. For some reason, he hadn't really expected that Jeremiah would be different. Despite the phone call from the old man's doctor saying that he didn't have much time left, Sam had thought somehow that his grandfather would be unchanged.

"Hi, Pop," he said and forced a smile.

"Come in, come in," his grandfather urged, weakly waving one hand. Then he patted the edge of the bed. "Sit down, boy. Let me look at you."

Sam did and, once he was close enough, gave his grandfather a quick once-over. He was thinner, but his eyes were clear and sharp. His tan wasn't as dark as it had been, but there was no sickly pallor to his cheeks. His hands were gnarled, but they weren't trembling.

All good things.

"How you feeling?" Sam asked, reaching out to lay one hand on his grandfather's forehead.

Jeremiah brushed that hand away. "Fine. I'm fine. And I've already got me a doctor to poke and prod. Don't need my grandson doing it, too."

"Sorry," Sam said with a shrug. "Professional hazard." As a doctor, he could respect another doctor's territory and not want to intrude. As a grandson, he wanted to see for himself that his grandfather was all right. Apparently, though, that wouldn't be as easy as it sounded. "I spoke to Dr. Evans after I talked to you last month. He says that your heart's in pretty bad shape."

Jeremiah winced. "Doctors. Don't pay them any mind."

Sam laughed shortly. "Thanks."

"Don't mean you, boy," the old man corrected quickly. "I'm sure you're a fine doctor. Always been real proud of you, Sam. In fact, I was telling Bert Evans that you might be just the man to buy him out."

Sam stood up and shoved both hands in his pockets. He'd been afraid of this. Afraid that the old man would make more of this visit than there was. Afraid he'd ask Sam to stay. Expect him to stay. And Sam couldn't. Wouldn't.

But his grandfather either didn't notice his discomfort or didn't care. Because he kept talking. And with every word, guilt pinged around inside Sam just a little bit harder.

"Bert's a good doc, mind. But he's as old as me and getting ready to fold up shop." He smiled up at Sam and winked conspiratorially. "The town needs a doctor, and seeing as you don't have a place of your own—"

"Pop, I'm not staying." Sam forced himself to say it flat out. He didn't want to hurt his grandfather, but he didn't want the old man holding onto false hopes either. Guilt tore at him to see the gleam go out of his grandfather's eyes. "I'm here for the summer," he said softly, willing the old man to understand just what it had cost him to come home again. "But when it's over, I'm leaving again."

"I thought…" Jeremiah's voice trailed away as he sagged back into his pillows. "I thought that once I got you back here, you'd see it's where you belong. Where all of you belong."

Pain rippled through Sam in tiny waves, one after the other. There was a time once, when he was a kid, that he would have done anything to live here forever. To be a part of the little town that had once seemed so perfect to him. To know that this house would always be his.

But those dreams died one bright summer day fifteen years ago.

Now he didn't belong anywhere.

"I'm sorry, Pop," he said, knowing it wasn't enough but that it was all he had to offer.

The old man looked at him for a long time before finally closing his eyes on a tired sigh. "It's a long summer, boy. Anything might happen."

"Don't make plans for me, Jeremiah," Sam warned, though it cost him to hurt the man again. "I won't stay. I can't. And you know why."

"I know why you think that," he said, his voice a weary sigh. "And I know you're wrong. All of you are. But a man's got to find his own way." He slipped down farther beneath the quilt. "I'm feeling tired now, so why don't you come see me tomorrow and we'll talk some more."

"Jeremiah…"

"Go on now," he whispered. "Go down and get yourself something to eat. I'll still be here in the morning."

When his grandfather closed his eyes, effectively ending any more tries at talking, Sam had no choice. He turned and headed for the door, let himself out and quietly closed the door behind him. He'd been in the house less than fifteen minutes and already he'd upset an old man with a bad heart.

Good job.

But he couldn't let his grandfather count on him staying. Couldn't give Jeremiah the promise of a future when the past was so thick around Sam he could hardly see the present.

He'd long since become accustomed to living with memories that haunted him. But he'd never be able to live here again—where he'd see a ghost around every corner.

# Three

Maggie sat in her living room and stared across the yard at the main ranch house. No more than twenty feet of ground separated the two buildings, but at the moment it felt like twenty *miles*.

In the two years she'd lived at the Lonergan ranch she'd never felt more of an outsider. Never felt as *alone* as she had that first day when her car had finally gasped its last and died right outside the main gate.

*Tears were close. Maggie was out of money and now out of transportation. Though she had nowhere in particular to go, up until five minutes ago she'd have been able to get there.*

*Staring up and down the long, empty road,*

*edged on both sides by open fields, she fought a rising tide of despair that threatened to choke her. The afternoon sun was hot and reflected back off the narrow highway until she felt as though she were standing in an oven. No trees shaded the road, and the last sign she'd passed had promised that the town of Coleville was still twenty-five miles away.*

*Just thinking about the long walk ahead of her made her tired. But sitting down and having a good long cry wouldn't get her any closer to town. And feeling sorry for herself would only get her a stuffed-up nose and red eyes. Nope. Maggie Collins didn't waste time on self-pity. Instead she kept trying. Kept searching. Knowing that someday, somewhere, she'd find the place where she belonged. Where she could plant herself and grow some roots. The kind of roots she'd always wanted as a child.*

*But to earn those roots she had to get off her duff. Resigned, she opened up the car door and grabbed her navy-blue backpack off the floor of the passenger seat.*

*"Looks like that car's about had it."*

*She hit her head on the roof of the old car as she backed out and straightened up all in one motion. The old man who'd spoken stood just a few feet from her, leaning against one of the whitewashed posts holding up a sign that proclaimed Lonergan. She hadn't even heard him approach, which told her that either he was more spry than he looked or she was even more tired than she felt.*

*Probably the latter.*

*He wasn't very tall. He wore a battered hat that shaded his lined, leathery face and his watchful dark eyes. His blue jeans were faded and worn, and his boots looked as if they were older than him.*

*"It just die on you?" he asked with a wave of one tanned hand at the car.*

*"Yeah," she said after seeing the quiet glint of kindness in his dark brown eyes. "Not surprising, really. It's been on borrowed time for the last few hundred miles."*

*He looked her up and down—not in a threatening way, she thought later, but as a man might look at a lost child while he thought about how to help her.*

*Finally he said, "Can't do anything about that car of yours, but if you'd care to come up to the house, maybe we can rustle up some lunch."*

*She glanced back down the road at the emptiness stretching out in either direction, then back at the man waiting quietly for her to make up her mind. Maggie'd learned at an early age to trust her instincts, and every one she had was telling her to take a chance. What did she have to lose? Besides, if he turned out to be a weirdo, she was pretty sure she could outrun him.*

*"I can't pay you for the food," she said, lifting her*

*chin and meeting his gaze with the only thing she had left—her pride. "But I'd be happy to do some chores for you in exchange."*

*One corner of his mouth lifted and his face fell into familiar laugh lines that crinkled at the edges of his eyes. "I think we can work something out."*

Maggie sighed at the memory and leaned her head back against the overstuffed cushion of the big chair. Curling her legs up beneath her, she looked around the small cottage that had been her sanctuary for the last two years. A guesthouse, Jeremiah had offered it to her that first day. By the end of the lunch she'd prepared for them, he'd given her a job and this little house to call her own. And for two years they'd done well together.

She turned her head and for the first time saw a light other than the one in Jeremiah's bedroom burning in the darkness. And she wondered what Sam Lonergan's arrival was going to do to her world.

The scent of coffee woke him up.

Sam rolled over in the big bed and stared blankly at the ceiling. For a minute or two he couldn't place where he was. Nothing new for him, though. A man who traveled as much as he did got used to waking up in strange places.

Then familiarity sneaked in and twisted at his heart, his guts. The room hadn't changed much from when he was a kid. Whitewashed oak-plank walls, dotted with posters of sports heroes and one impossibly endowed swimsuit beauty, surrounded him. A desk on the far wall still held a plastic model of the inner workings of the human body, and the twin bookcases were stuffed with paperback mysteries and thrillers sharing space alongside medical dictionaries and old textbooks.

He threw one arm across his eyes and winced at the sharp jab of pain as memories prodded and poked inside him. A part of him was listening, half expecting to hear long-silent voices. His cousins, shouting to him from their rooms along the hall. It had always been like that during the summers they spent together.

The four Lonergan boys—as close as brothers. Born during a three-year clump, they'd grown up seeing each other every summer on the Lonergan ranch. Their fathers were brothers, and though none of them felt the pull for the ranch where they'd grown up, their sons had.

This was a world apart from everyday life. Where the land rolled open for miles, inviting boys to hop on their bikes to explore. There were small-town fairs, and fireworks and baseball games. There was working in the fields, helping with the horses Jeremiah had once kept and swimming in the lake.

At that thought, everything in Sam seized up. His heart went cold and air struggled to enter his lungs. It was harder than he thought it would be, being here. Seeing everything the same and yet so different.

"Shouldn't have come," he muttered, his voice sounding scratchy and raw to his own ears. But then, how could he *not?* The old man was in bad shape and he needed his grandsons. There was simply no way to deny him that.

Fifteen years he'd been gone and this room looked as though he'd left it fifteen *minutes* ago. It's a hard thing for a grown man to come into the room he'd left as a boy. Especially when he'd left that room under a black cloud of guilt and pain.

But none of this was making it any easier on him.

"Not supposed to be easy," he muttered, tossing the quilt covering him aside so he could stand up and face the first day of what promised to be the longest summer of his life.

From downstairs came the homey sounds of pans rattling and soft footsteps against the hardwood floor. The aroma of coffee seemed thicker now, heavier, though it was probably only that he was awake enough now to really hunger for it.

Had to be the water nymph in the kitchen.

Jeremiah's housekeeper.

The woman he'd seen naked.

The woman he'd dreamed about all night.

Hell. He ought to thank her for that alone. With her

in his mind, his brain had for once been too busy to torture him with images of another face. Another time.

Grabbing up his jeans, he yanked them on, then pulled on a white T-shirt and shoved his arms through the sleeves. Not bothering with shoes, he headed down the hall, pausing briefly at his grandfather's closed bedroom door before continuing on toward the kitchen.

He needed coffee.

And maybe he needed something else, too. Another look at the mermaid?

His bare feet didn't make a sound on the stairs, so he approached her quietly enough that she didn't know he was watching her. Morning sunlight spilled through the shining windowpanes and lay like a golden blanket across the huge round pedestal table and the warm wood floor. Everything in the room practically glistened, and he had to admit that as a housekeeper, she seemed to be doing a hell of a job. The counters were tidy, the floor polished till it shone and even the ancient appliances looked almost new. The walls had been painted a bright, cheery yellow, and the stiffly starched white curtains at the windows nearly crackled in the breeze drifting under the partially opened sash.

But it was the woman who had Sam's attention. Just as she had the night before. She moved around the old kitchen with a familiarity that at once pleased and irritated him.

Not exactly rational, but it was early. A part of Sam was glad his grandfather had had this woman here, looking out for him. And another completely illogical side of him resented that she was so much at home on the Lonergan ranch when he felt...on edge.

Her long dark hair was gathered into a neat braid that fell down the center of her back, ending at her shoulder blades. A bright red ribbon held the end of the braid together and made a colorful splash against the pale blue shirt she wore tucked into a pair of the most worn, faded jeans he'd ever seen. Threadbare in patches, the jeans hugged her behind and clung to her long legs like a desperate lover.

An old Stones tune poured quietly from the radio on the counter, and as Sam watched, the mermaid did a quick little dance and swiveled her hips in time to the music. His breath caught as his gaze locked on her behind and he found himself praying that one of those threadbare patches would give way, giving him another glimpse of her tanned skin.

Then she did a slow spin, caught a glimpse of him. And the smile on her face faded.

"Do you always sneak up on people or am I just special?"

Sam scrubbed one hand over his face, as if that would be enough to get his brain away from the tantalizing thoughts it had been entertaining.

"Didn't want to interrupt the floor show," he said

tightly, hoping she wouldn't hear the edge of hunger in his voice. He walked past her and headed straight for the coffeepot on the counter.

As the Stones song drifted into an R&B classic, he filled a heavy white mug with the coffee, took a sip, then turned around to face her. Leaning back against the counter, he crossed one bare foot over the other and asked, "You always dance in the kitchen?"

She huffed in a breath and tightened her grip on the spatula she held in her right hand. "When I'm *alone.*"

"Like the skinny-dipping, huh?"

Glaring at him, she said, "A gentleman wouldn't remind me of that."

"And a gentleman wouldn't have looked," he reminded her as the image of her wet, pale, honeyed skin rose up in his mind. "I did. Remember?"

"I'm not likely to forget."

One eyebrow lifted as he swept his gaze up and down her quickly, thoroughly. "Me, neither."

She opened her mouth to speak, then shut it again and took a deep breath. He could almost see her counting to ten to get a grip on the temper flashing in her eyes. Eyes, he noticed, that in the morning light weren't as dark as he'd thought the night before. They were brown but not. More the color of good single-malt scotch.

He took another gulp of coffee and told himself to get a grip.

"You're deliberately trying to pick a fight," she said. "Why?"

He frowned into his coffee. "Because I'm not a nice man."

"That's not what your grandfather says."

He looked at her. "Jeremiah's prejudiced. And a hell of a storyteller. Don't believe half of what he tells you."

"He told me you're a doctor. Is that right?"

"Yeah." Frowning still, he took another sip of really superior coffee. "I am."

"Did you—" she paused and waited for him to look at her "—examine him last night?"

He laughed, and that short burst of sound surprised him as much as it did her. "Me? Not a chance. Jeremiah still thinks of me as the thirteen-year-old kid who slapped a homemade plaster cast on his golden retriever."

"You didn't."

He smiled to himself, remembering. "I really did. Made it out of papier-mâché. Just practicing," he said, remembering how Jeremiah's golden, Storm, had sat patiently, letting Sam do his worst. "Pop took it off before it had a chance to dry."

She was smiling at him and her eyes looked... shiny. Something in him shifted, gave way, and uncomfortable, Sam straightened up and gulped at his coffee again. "Anyway, the point is, Jeremiah won't let me touch him. I'll talk to his doctor, though. Get what information I can."

"Good." She nodded and turned to stir the eggs, a golden foamy layer in the skillet on the stove. "I mean, it's good that you can check. I'm worried. He's been so…"

"What?"

She turned around to look at him again. "It's not something I can put my finger on and say, *There. That's different. That's wrong.* It's just that he's not the same lately. He seems a little more tired. A little more…fragile somehow."

"He's closing in on seventy," Sam reminded her and scowled to himself as he realized just how much time had slipped past him.

"And up until two weeks ago," she said, "you wouldn't have known it. Up at sunrise, doing chores, driving into town to have lunch with Dr. Evans, square dancing on Friday night."

"Square dancing?" Another surprise and another flicker of irritation that this woman knew so much more about his grandfather than *he* did.

She waved one hand at him while she stirred the eggs. "He and some of his friends go to the senior center in Fresno on Fridays." She paused and sighed. "At least, he *used* to."

"Maybe it's nothing," he said, and wasn't sure which of them he was trying to console.

"I hope so."

He heard the hope in her voice and was touched that she cared so deeply. "You really love him, don't you?"

"I really do." She turned her back on the stove and faced him. "Look, *Sam*." She said his name firmly, as if forcing herself to make a connection that she really wasn't interested in. "You're here to see your grandfather and I'm glad. For *his* sake."

He shifted, pushing away from the counter to stand on his own two feet. "But…?"

"*But…*" she said, turning for the stove and the pan that was beginning to smoke, "I think that we should try to stay out of each other's way while you're here."

"Is that right?" He stepped up alongside her and he *felt* tension ripple between them. Damn it. He didn't need this. Didn't want it. And he'd had every intention of steering clear of the little housekeeper. Until she'd suggested it.

Maggie stirred the scrambled eggs quickly, flipping them over and over again in the cast-iron skillet until they were a golden-brown and dry, just the way Jeremiah liked them. She tried to keep her mind on her cooking, but with Sam standing so close, it wasn't easy.

She'd made up her mind last night that the one sure way to protect her place on this ranch was to stay out of the way this summer. She didn't want to give any of the Lonergan cousins reason to think that their grandfather would be better off with someone other than her taking care of him.

She'd lain awake in her bed most of the night, thinking about this place and what it meant to her. About the old man who had become her family.

And if she were to be completely honest, sometime around dawn she'd thought about Sam. About the way she'd felt when he'd looked at her walking naked from the water.

About the swirl of heat that had swept through her, making the chill wind nothing more than a whisper. And she'd wondered what it would feel like to have him touch her, smooth his hands over her skin, dip his fingers into her—

"The eggs are burning."

"What?" She blinked, stared at the pan and instinctively used her free hand to push it off the flame.

Instantly pain bristled on her palm and she dropped the spatula to cradle her left hand against her chest. Tears clouded her eyes and a whimper squeaked past her lips.

"Damn it!" Sam set his coffee cup on the stove, grabbed her left hand, looked at it, then dragged her with him across the kitchen to the sink. He turned on the cold water and held her hand beneath the icy stream. Instantly the pain subsided and she sighed.

"What the hell were you thinking?"

"I don't know," she said, wiggling her fingers in an effort to pull her hand free of his tight grasp. It didn't work. "I just—"

"Doesn't look bad," he said, smoothing his fingers over the palm of her hand with a tenderness that touched something deep inside her. "Hold still and let me be sure."

The doctor in him took over, she noticed, as the cranky man became suddenly all business.

Then something shifted. Something changed.

His touch became less professional and more... personal. He turned her hand beneath the flow of water, inspecting every inch of her skin. And Maggie closed her eyes against the twin sensations rushing through her. The cold of the water numbed her even as the heat of Sam's touch engulfed her. Her breath staggered a little as she felt his fingertips glide across her wet skin with a gentleness that she'd never known before.

She opened her eyes to find him staring at her. Their gazes locked and a thread of something warm and unspoken drew tight between them. Her breath staggered out of her lungs and her heartbeat thundered in her ears. After what felt like a small eternity, she couldn't bear the tension-filled silence anymore. Mouth dry, voice croaking, she asked, "Is my hand okay?"

"You were lucky." His voice was a low growl of sound that seemed to reverberate around the room. "There's no blistering."

"Good," she managed to say while she locked her knees so they wouldn't wobble and give out on her. God. Was the air really hot? Or was it just her own blood boiling? Oh, yeah, going to keep her distance this summer. Nice start to that plan.

His fingers continued to stroke and soothe her skin and she felt that touch all the way to the center of her. Strange. She'd never experienced anything like this before. A simple touch shouldn't turn her insides to mush.

At last, he turned off the water and reached for a dish towel. Holding her hand in his, he used the soft linen to blot her skin dry. Then he lifted his gaze to hers again, and Maggie felt a jolt of something amazing pass between them just before he dropped her hand as if it was a rattler and took a step back.

"You'll be fine," he said, pushing one hand through his hair. "Just be more careful, okay?"

"I usually am."

"Right." He paused, took a breath and said, "Look, about last night—"

Her head snapped up and her gaze locked with his. "What?"

He studied her for a long minute before lowering his gaze. "Nothing. Never mind. Probably better all around if we just forgot last night ever happened."

Sure. Pretend he hadn't seen her naked. No problem. "Probably would."

"Yeah." He tossed the towel to the counter, then shoved both hands into the back pockets of his jeans, as if unwilling to risk touching her again. "I'm thinking you're right about something, too. Better if we just stayed out of each other's way this summer."

"Okay." Maggie was still struggling to even out her breath and convince her heart to slide down back into her chest where it belonged. Apparently, though, Sam Lonergan had much quicker recuperative powers. Because he could pretend all he wanted— she *knew* he'd felt something as powerful as she had.

"Fine. Then we're agreed." He glanced around the room as if he didn't remember where he was. Then, shaking his head, he crossed the room and grabbed up his coffee cup. Stalking to the counter, he refilled it, then passed her on his way out of the room. He stopped in the doorway and looked back at her. "I'm going to grab a quick shower. Then I'm headed into Coleville. Want to talk to Jeremiah's doctor."

She nodded, but he was already leaving the room with steps so quick his feet might have been on fire. Apparently she wasn't the only one a little flustered by what had just happened.

She'd thought that Sam Lonergan could be a threat to the home she loved so much.

But she hadn't expected him to be an entirely different kind of threat to her sanity.

# Four

He took an ice-cold shower.

It didn't help.

Damn it, things were going to be hard enough this summer without worrying about the sexy little housekeeper with whiskey-colored eyes and fragile hands.

Slathering shaving cream on his face, Sam stared into the mirror and dragged his razor across his cheeks, losing himself in the feel of cold steel against his skin. And still he could feel Maggie's hand cupped in his. He hadn't expected this. Hadn't expected to find a woman who made him feel a little too much and want a little too much more.

Finished shaving, he bent his head, scooped water

over his face, then stood up and glared at his reflection. Water cascaded down his neck and ran along his chest, but he hardly noticed. His hands gripped the cold edges of the sink and he leaned his head forward until his forehead rested against the mirror.

Coming home was turning out to be even harder than he'd thought it would be.

Jeremiah waited until he heard the Jeep leave the ranch yard, its engine becoming little more than a distant purr. Just twenty minutes later Maggie's old heap of a car jumped into life, and within minutes it, too, was gone off down the road. Then, quietly, Jeremiah threw back the quilt covering him and jumped to his feet.

As he stretched the kinks out of his back and legs, he gave a low, deep-throated sigh of pure pleasure to be up and out of that bed. Saturday mornings on the ranch, he could count on one thing absolutely: Maggie would be gone for at least two hours. She'd have lunch with her friend Linda, who worked in the Curl Up and Dye hair salon, then do the grocery shopping for the week.

"Thank God Sam picked today to go visit Bert," Jeremiah muttered as he did a few deep knee bends, then touched his fingertips to his toes. "One more hour in that bed and I just *might* become an invalid."

An active man, Jeremiah hated nothing more than

sitting still. And lying down just wasn't in his game plan. A man of almost seventy knew only too well that soon enough he'd have an eternity to lie down. No point in hurrying things up any.

Grinning to himself, he hotfooted it to the bedroom door and turned the old brass key in the lock. Just in case. Then he slipped over to the bookcase, pulled down a copy of *War and Peace* and reached behind it for his secret stash.

"Ah..." He pulled out one of three cigars he had tucked away, then quickly found a match and lit it. A few puffs had him sighing in pleasure. Then, before he could forget, he walked to the bedside table and picked up the phone.

Punching in a few numbers, he puffed contentedly while he waited for his old friend to answer the phone. When he did, Jeremiah said, "Bert? Good. Wanted to warn you. Sam's headed your way."

"Damn it, Jeremiah," the good doctor complained, "I don't like this at all. Told you when you first thought it up it was a harebrained scheme, and nothing's changed."

It was an old song and Jeremiah knew the words by heart. Bert had been against this plan from the beginning. It was only their long-standing friendship that had finally convinced the doctor to go along with it.

Jeremiah tucked the cigar into the corner of his mouth and talked around it. "There's no backing out now, Bert. You signed up for this. And blast it, man, you know it was my only choice."

"Telling your grandsons you're *dying* is your only way to get 'em home?"

Jeremiah scowled into the shaft of sunlight spearing through his bedroom window. Reaching out, he lifted the sash high so that a brisk breeze flew in, dissipating the telltale cigar smoke. Did Bert think faking his own demise was a piece of cake? It sure as hell wasn't. Doing nothing but lying around sighing all day was making him sore all over. And pretending to be old and feeble irritated the hell out of him. Plus, he didn't care for the fact that he was worrying Maggie, either.

But despite how it went against the grain to admit it, the truth was there staring at him, so no point in avoiding it. "Yes, it was the only way. The boys haven't been back since…"

A long pause fell between the two old friends as they both remembered the long-ago tragedy that still haunted the Lonergan boys. Finally Bert Evans broke it with a sigh of resignation. "I know. Fine, fine. In for a penny…"

Jeremiah grinned and tried to remember where he'd stashed his spare bottle of bourbon. It might be early in the morning, but he felt as if a toast was in order. Things were moving right along according to plan.

"Thanks, Bert. I owe you."

"You surely do, you old goat."

When he hung up, Jeremiah chuckled, took a long drag of his cigar and blew a perfect smoke ring in quiet celebration.

Coleville hadn't changed much.

Sam drove down the narrow main street and let his gaze slide across familiar storefronts. Early on a Saturday morning, there were plenty of people filling the sidewalks and almost no parking spaces.

A small town, Coleville was fifty miles from Fresno, the closest "big" city. To keep its citizens happy, the town boasted a supermarket, a theater and even one of the huge national chain drugstores. And sometime over the years, Sam noted, it had also acquired one of the trendy coffee shops that were dotting nearly every corner of every street in the country.

The schools were small, as they'd always been, populated by the children who lived both in town and on the surrounding farms and ranches. And the only doctor worked out of a small clinic at the edge of town. Emergencies were handled here first and then, if needed, the patient was either driven by ambulance or airlifted into Fresno and the hospital.

Sam pulled his grandfather's Jeep into the clinic parking lot and shut off the engine. The sun blasted down on him out of a brassy sky, and he squinted at the squat building in front of him. Bert Evans, M.D.

was written across the wide window in florid gold script that was peeling at the edges. The whole place needed a good coat of paint, but there were terra-cotta tubs on either side of the double front doors overflowing with bright flowers, and the walkway and porch were swept clean and tidy as a church.

He climbed out of the Jeep, shoved the keys into his pocket and headed for the door. As he walked, memory marched with him.

He saw himself as a kid, running into the clinic and badgering Dr. Evans with hundreds of questions. The doctor had never lost patience with him. Instead he'd answered what he could and provided old medical books so that Sam could discover other things on his own.

It was in this little clinic that Sam had first decided to become a doctor. Even as a kid, he'd known he wanted to be able to fix people. To help. He'd had grand plans back then. He'd wanted to be the kind of doctor that Bert Evans was. A man who knew his patients as well as his own family. A man who was a part of the community.

Well, things changed. Now he did what he could, when he could, and tried not to get involved.

A bell over the door jangled cheerfully when he stepped into the blessed cool of air-conditioning. Three kids and their tired mother sat on the green plastic chairs in the waiting room. The mom gave him a tired smile and an absent nod while two of her kids tried to kill each other.

Behind the reception desk a young woman sat typing on a computer keyboard, and Sam flinched inwardly because he'd half expected to find Dr. Evans's old nurse still enthroned in this office. But the woman had been at least a hundred when he was a kid.

"Can I help you?" The young woman looked up from her task and gave him a smile that offered a lot more help than he required at the moment.

"I'd like to see Dr. Evans for a minute," he said. "Tell him Sam Lonergan's here."

She stood up and smoothed her hands down her pale cream-colored slacks while somehow managing to showcase her truly spectacular breasts, hidden behind a light blue sweater. "If you'll have a seat…"

He didn't, though. When she left the room, he wandered around, looking at all of the framed photos on the wall. What Dr. Evans had always called his "trophies." Babies he'd delivered, kids he'd treated, adults he'd cared for in life and seen into death. Dozens—hundreds—of faces smiled at him, but Sam only saw one.

That familiar grin slammed a well-aimed punch to Sam's gut, but he couldn't seem to look away. The boy in the photo was only sixteen—and would never get any older. Sam's hands fisted at his sides. The sounds of the squabbling kids behind him faded into nothing and he lost himself staring into the face of the one person he should have saved and hadn't.

"The doctor will see you now." A tug on his shirt-sleeve got his attention when the soft voice didn't.

"What?" He stared at the doctor's assistant, shook off the memories clouding his brain and reminded himself why he was here. "Thanks."

Without another glance at her he stalked across the room, opened the door into the back and headed down the long hallway to Dr. Evans's office. Much like the rest of the clinic, the office looked as though it had been caught in a time warp. Not a single thing was different.

The walls were still crowded with floor-to-ceiling bookshelves. There was a standing scale in one corner, and on the edge of the wide, cluttered mahogany desk, a glass jar of multicolored lollipops still stood ready for the doc's younger patients.

"Sam!" The older man leaped to his feet and came around his desk with a smile on his face. Doc Evans took Sam's hand in both of his own and shook heartily. His blue eyes were still soft and kind, but his hair was almost snow-white now. "Good to see you. Been too long, boy. Way too long."

"Yeah," Sam admitted, though it cost him another pang of guilt. "Guess it has."

"Sit down, sit down." The doctor waved a hand at the deep leather chairs opposite his desk, then took his own seat, folding his hands atop a manila file folder. "So you've been to the house? Seen your grandfather?"

"Yeah. I got in last night."

"Good, good," the older man crowed. "Then I expect you've met Maggie."

"Yes, I—"

"Fine girl, that one. Why, she's been the best medicine Jeremiah could ever ask for. Just keeps the old coot smiling all the time now." He steepled his fingertips. "Yes, she's a fine girl."

"She seems…nice," Sam said because he had to say something and he couldn't very well tell the older man that she looked great naked. Besides, he hadn't come here to talk about Maggie. In fact, Sam was doing all he could to not even think about her. So he quickly shifted the conversation back to where he wanted it. "But about my grandfather—what exactly is Pop's condition?"

Dr. Evans grumbled something unintelligible, then leaned back in his chair, stroking his chin as if he still had the beard he'd shaved off twenty years ago. "Well, now, that's, uh… You say you talked to Jeremiah?"

"Yeeesss…" Suspicion curled in Sam's mind and he narrowed his gaze on his grandfather's oldest friend. "He said that you were taking good care of him and that I shouldn't bother."

"Well, then," Dr. Evans said, trying another smile.

"Sounds like good advice to me, Sam. No point in you worrying yourself. Yessiree, it's good to see you, son."

"Uh-huh." Sam leaned in even closer to the older man, keeping their gazes locked. Didn't surprise him in the slightest when Doc Evans broke contact first, glancing first at the ceiling, then at his desk and finally settling for staring blankly out the window. "What is it you're not telling me, Doc?"

"Now, Sam," the older man whined, "you know all about doctor-patient confidentiality…."

Sam's eyes narrowed thoughtfully. "I'm not asking you to break a confidence," he said. "But as one doctor to another, you could throw me a bone here. Have you done an EKG? What're his cholesterol levels? Blood pressure? Has he had a stress test lately?"

Dr. Evans smiled and stood up, coming around the edge of his desk to pat Sam on the back as if he were a schoolboy acing his latest test. "All good questions, son. Glad to see you've become the kind of doctor I always knew you would be."

"Thanks," Sam said and let himself be nudged out of his chair and toward the door. "But you haven't really answered any of those questions and—"

"Don't you worry about a thing, Sam. Your grandpa's in good hands."

"I know that," he assured the older man. "I only wanted to—"

"Best thing for you to do," Doc Evans said,

opening the office door and ushering Sam out, "is to visit with Jeremiah. He's missed all of you."

Guilt reared up again and this time took a huge bite out of Sam. "I know. We never meant to—"

"Hell, boy," the doctor said, patting Sam's shoulder, "I know that. So does Jeremiah. But years go by and a man misses seeing his family."

"But his heart…?"

Doc Evans winced a little and glanced away. "I've been doctoring folks longer than you've been alive, Sam. Don't you worry any about Jeremiah's treatment. I'm on top of things." He gave Sam another pat, then started to close the door. "Thanks for stopping by. Good seeing you again."

Sam slapped one hand against the door, holding it open. "Why do I get the feeling you're trying to get rid of me?"

Doc Evans's blue eyes went wide and innocent behind his steel-rimmed glasses. "Why, no such thing. But I've got patients waiting for me and more in the waiting room. I'm a busy man, Sam. Busy, busy."

"Uh-huh." Sam couldn't quite put his finger on what was wrong here, but there was definitely something up. "If you don't mind, I'd like to examine my grandfather myself."

The doctor blustered a minute or two, then his features went stiff and stern. "No call for that, Sam. Don't think Jeremiah would allow that anyway. Appreciate that you're worried, boy. But you'll just have to trust me when I say things are as they should be." He swung the door closed again, pushing hard against Sam's restraining hand. "Now, if you'll excuse me…"

Sam let the door close and stood there frowning at it for a long minute before shaking his head and heading back down the hall.

Inside his office Bert Evans leaned back against the door and blew out a long breath. Dipping one hand into the pocket of his white office coat, he pulled out a handkerchief and used it to wipe his brow. Sam hadn't been fooled, he knew. But he'd done what he could.

Lying didn't come easy for Bert—mostly because he'd never been any good at it. His oldest friend, on the other hand, had a real gift for it. "Jeremiah, you old bastard," he whispered. "You really owe me for this."

Maggie walked briskly down Main Street, nodding to the people she passed, but her mind wasn't really on visiting. Which was why she was just as glad Linda had had an emergency appointment and couldn't make their standing lunch date.

Better this way, she told herself. She didn't really like leaving Jeremiah alone these days. Not when he was feeling so badly. And at that thought, her mind went to Sam and what he might be finding out from

Dr. Evans. Worry twisted inside her. Jeremiah had refused to talk to her about what he was feeling, brushing off her concern even while taking to his bed.

Frowning, she turned her thoughts from Jeremiah to Sam, and from there confusion reigned supreme. She'd known the man only twenty-four hours and already he was taking up way too much of her thoughts. But how could she not think about him?

"For heaven's sake, Maggie," she muttered, "give it a rest. You've already agreed to keep your distance. It's not like he's demanding his grandfather fire you or anything."

But he *could* if he wanted to.

A whole different kind of worry spiraled through her despite Maggie's determination to look on the bright side. It wasn't fair that she had to worry about both Jeremiah's health and her own home.

With her brain still churning, she stepped off the sidewalk and glanced around quickly before walking across the crowded supermarket parking lot. Cars came and went, but she hardly noticed. Focused on her errands, she hit the entrance and stepped into the air-conditioning with a grateful sigh. The sun was already high in the sky and blasting down with a heat that promised even higher temperatures soon.

Muzak drifted from the overhead speakers and from somewhere in the store a child's temperamental wail sounded out. Wrestling a single cart free of the others, she dropped her brown leather purse in the front section. Then she started into the produce department, muttering a curse as the front wheel of the cart wobbled and clanged with her every step.

"Do they *make* those things broken?" A deep familiar voice came from right behind her, and Maggie nearly jumped out of her sneakers.

Whipping around, she lifted her gaze—quite a bit—to look into Sam Lonergan's dark eyes. "You scared me half to death."

He shook his head, pushed her aside and curled both hands around the cart handle. "I called your name three times when you were walking in from the parking lot. Called out to you again," he said as he pushed the cart and clearly expected her to keep up, "as you were picking out this great cart."

She frowned. "I didn't hear you." She'd been too busy *thinking* about him to actually *see* him. What did that say about her?

"Clearly." He shrugged and stopped alongside the bin of romaine lettuce.

"What're you doing here?" she asked.

"Getting groceries, apparently." He bagged first one, then two heads of lettuce, then moved on to inspect the fresh green beans.

Maggie shook her head as she watched him pick through the beans carefully. "I'm perfectly capable of shopping on my own, you know."

He glanced at her. "You seem awfully territorial over a handful of green beans."

She inhaled sharply and blew the air out in a huff. Yes, she was being territorial. But this was *her* life he was intruding on. She'd been taking care of Jeremiah for two years and it sort of rubbed her the wrong way to think that he was implying in some way that she hadn't done a good job of it.

But then again, maybe getting snippy with the man wasn't the way to handle things either. "Fine," she said, congratulating herself on the calm, even tone of her voice. "We can do it together." Then she reached out and took the bag of beans from him before dumping its contents back into the bin. "And you should know, your grandfather doesn't like green beans."

He frowned, then turned toward her and shrugged again as his frown slowly faded into a half smile. "You're right. I'd forgotten. My grandmother used to make them for my cousins and I, but Pop never touched 'em."

Maggie smiled, too, and felt a whisper of something almost comfortable spin out between them. "He does like cauliflower," she suggested, in an attempt to continue the truce.

"And broccoli, too!" He laughed at the memory, and something dazzling flashed in his eyes, stealing Maggie's breath.

"You should do that more often," she said when she was sure that her voice wouldn't quiver.

"What's that?" he asked, already grabbing up a head of cauliflower and dropping it into a plastic bag.

"Smile."

He dipped his head, looked up at her, then tossed the vegetable into the basket before answering. "I just left Dr. Evan's office."

Maggie walked beside him, picking up a few lemons, a couple of grapefruits and several bunches of green onions. She didn't speak right away and she knew it was because she was afraid of what Sam was going to say. What he'd found out from the doctor.

Jeremiah hadn't spoken much about his sudden illness, and frankly she hadn't asked for information. Cowardly or not, she simply didn't want to have to face any dire truths that would have the capacity to break her heart.

"Aren't you going to ask what I found out?" He came closer and Maggie could feel the heat of his body reaching out for her.

She swallowed her own fear, told herself she couldn't hide from the truth forever and forced herself to nod. "What is it? What's wrong with him?"

"Not a clue."

"What?"

"*Excuse me.*" An overweight woman in a tight

flowered dress stared at them both. "If you don't mind, I'd like to buy some oranges."

"Sorry." Sam frowned again, took Maggie by the arm and used his free hand to guide the limping cart away a few feet. When he stopped, he released her and said, "Doc Evans wouldn't tell me anything."

"Oh, God." Maggie covered her mouth with her hand and stared up at him as terrifying thoughts wheeled through her mind. If the doctor didn't want to tell Jeremiah's grandson what was wrong with him, that could only mean the older man was desperately ill. "That can't be good. He must not want to worry you."

He folded both arms across his chest and thought about that. "Could be the reason, I suppose, but I don't think so." Shaking his head, Sam muttered, "No. There's something going on."

"What do you mean?"

"I mean," he said, "Jeremiah and Doc Evans are up to something and I want to know what it is."

Instantly defensive, Maggie said, "Are you trying to say that Jeremiah's *not* sick? Because if you are, that's ridiculous. He wouldn't do that."

"Maybe," Sam allowed, but clearly he wasn't convinced. Maggie reached for him, laying one hand on his forearm and somehow ignoring the sizzle of heat that erupted between them. "Jeremiah is a wonderful man. He would never worry his family unnecessarily. You should know that even better than I do."

He glanced down at her hand on his arm and slowly Maggie withdrew it.

"You could be right," he said finally. "But I want you to keep an eye out."

"You're asking me to *spy* on your grandfather?"

"Spy's a harsh word."

"But appropriate." Maggie shook her head and stepped out of the way as a tall man squeezed past her to get at the table full of bananas. Sam frowned, took her arm again and pushed the cart farther out of the produce section, away from most of the crowd.

He glanced around as if to make sure that no one was close enough to overhear them. Then he bent his head toward hers. "I'm not asking you to betray him. I'm only asking you to help *me*."

"Not two hours ago," she reminded him in a fast whisper, "you agreed that we should keep our distance from each other this summer. Now you're asking me to work with you against a man who's been nothing but kind to me."

He scraped one hand across his face, then grabbed her upper arms and pulled her close. She sucked in a gulp of air and held it as his face came within a breath of hers. Her heart pounded and she heard the rush of her own blood in her ears. Her gaze dropped to his mouth, then lifted to his eyes again.

"Things change, Maggie," he said, his voice low and fast. "And now I'm saying that I need your help.

I'm worried about Jeremiah. So are you." His gaze moved over her face like a caress. He licked his lips, pulled in a breath, then let her go suddenly and took a step back. "The question is, are you willing to work with me to find out what's going on around here?"

# Five

Three days later an uneasy truce had been declared. She tried to stay out of Sam's way and he kept butting into her life. Okay, so the truce was only on *her* side.

The man seemed to pop up everywhere. If she was outside gardening, he showed up, leaning casually against the side of the house, watching every move she made. If she was cooking, he found his way to the kitchen, interrogating her on his grandfather's diet. If she was cleaning, he was close at hand, as though making sure she wasn't going to steal the family silver or something.

And at *all* times she felt his dark gaze on her as she would a touch.

In fact, the only time she felt as though she wasn't being watched was the evenings, spent in her own little house. But even then there was no peace. Because her dreams were full of him.

His dark eyes. His well-shaped mouth, long fingers and leanly muscled body. In dreams he did more than watch her. In dreams he held her, kissed her, tasted her, explored her body with his own and every morning she woke up just a little bit more tense than she'd been the day before.

Every nerve in her body felt as though it were on fire from the inside. There was a coiled tension within her that made every breath a labor and every heartbeat a victory.

Up to her elbows in hot, soapy water, Maggie swished the scrubbing sponge over a mixing bowl, rinsed it out, then set it carefully in the drainer. Shaking her head, she yawned, blinked tired eyes and whispered, "It's only been three days. If this keeps up, by the end of summer I'll be dead."

"What?"

She jumped, splashing a small wave of hot water onto the front of her pale pink T-shirt. When the adrenaline rush ended, she sighed, glanced down at herself, then lifted her gaze to Sam, standing in the doorway. "You have *got* to stop sneaking up on me."

A brief half smile curved one corner of his mouth, then was gone before she could get a good look at it.

"You would have heard me if you weren't talking to yourself," he pointed out.

"Right." She used the tips of her fingers to pull her wet shirt away from her abdomen, then gave it up and reached into the water for the next dish. "Before you ask," she said while she swiped a plate, rinsed it and set it to dry, "Jeremiah ate a big breakfast. Eggs. Bacon. Toast and juice."

"Cholesterol Surprise for a heart patient. Good thinking."

Turning her head to glare at him, she said, "We've been through this before. It's *turkey* bacon, egg *substitute* and *wheat* toast. Perfectly healthy."

Frowning, he walked into the room and stopped alongside her. Turning, he leaned one hip against the counter, folded his arms across his chest and said, "Sorry."

"Wow," Maggie countered. "An apology. This is so exciting."

He sighed and shook his head. "Guess I owe you more than one apology, huh?"

Turning off the rinse water, Maggie grabbed up a flowered dishcloth, dried her hands and faced him. If he was suddenly in the mood to talk, she'd take advantage of the situation.

"You've been following me around for days," she said quietly, trying to keep the ring of accusation out of her voice. "It's like you're *trying* to find something wrong with me and what I do for your grandfather. I want to know why."

Sunlight pouring in from the kitchen windows played across his features and spotlighted the worry gathered in his eyes.

"Because this is making me crazy," he admitted finally with another shake of his head. "Pop won't talk to me. Said he's got nothing to say until my cousins Cooper and Jake get here."

More Lonergan cousins to keep an eye on her. Yippee.

"When will that be?" she asked.

He pushed away from the counter, shoved his hands into his jeans pockets and walked across the room, his boot heels clacking noisily against the linoleum. "I don't know. Jake was in Spain at some road rally when the old man sent for him. And Cooper...well, he locks himself away when he's working. God knows if he's even gotten the message yet."

"I've read a couple of his books," Maggie said.

He turned to look at her. "What'd you think?"

"They terrify me," she admitted with a small smile. The last Cooper Lonergan thriller she'd read had forced her to leave her bedroom light on all night for nearly a week. The images he created were so real, so frightening, she didn't know how the man himself slept at night. "He must be one scary man— because he's got a really twisted imagination."

A sad smile raced across Sam's face. "He never used to," he said. "Cooper was always the funniest one of us. The one nothing bothered. At least until—" His voice faded away and even the echo of that smile disappeared from his eyes. "Things change."

Maggie's heart ached for him.

For all of them.

Even though a part of her wanted to shout that it had been fifteen years. Long enough to come to terms with a tragedy.

Instead, though, she only said, "You could try talking to Doc Evans again…."

He snorted a laugh. "Yeah, that'll be helpful. He just keeps muttering about doctor-patient confidentiality. No. Whatever's going on here, Jeremiah and the doc are in it together. And they're both too stubborn to break."

"Stubborn must run in your family."

"Yeah?" One dark eyebrow lifted.

"Well," she said, tossing the dish towel over her left shoulder, "you've already admitted they're not going to tell you anything and yet you don't stop trying. What's that if not stubborn?"

"Dedicated?"

She laughed and she saw a flash of appreciation dart across the surface of his eyes. And in response, a sweep of something warm and delicious rushed through her. Her hands trembled, so she pulled the dish towel off her shoulder again and wrapped it through her fingers. She pulled in a couple of short, uneasy breaths and told herself to get a grip.

"Who's that?" he asked suddenly and Maggie's head snapped up.

She looked out the kitchen window and saw one of their neighbors, Susan Bateman, rushing across the yard, her four-year-old daughter Kathleen cradled in her arms.

"It's Susan," Maggie said, already moving for the back door. "She and her family live on the ranch down the road. And something's wrong."

She threw open the door and Susan raced inside, her features taut, her blue eyes wide in a face gone pale. Blood blossomed on her white collared shirt, and the little girl in her arms whimpered plaintively. She hardly looked at Maggie, instead turning her gaze directly on Sam. "You're a doctor, aren't you?"

"Susan," Maggie said, "what—"

"I heard in town," the other woman kept talking, "that you're a doctor. You are, right?"

Sam stared at her and looked as though he wanted to deny it. But the sense of desperation clinging to Susan—not to mention Kathleen's muffled whimpering—was impossible to ignore.

"Yeah," he said tightly. "I am."

"Thank God," Susan said. "Katie cut herself on a postholer, and you were so much closer to town that I just came here right away."

At that, the little girl lifted her head from her mother's chest and turned big, watery blue eyes on Maggie and Sam. "I got a owie and it's all blooding."

"Aw, baby," Maggie cooed, stepping forward instinctively to smooth back the fringe of light blond hair on the little girl's forehead. "You'll be okay. Sam can fix it. You'll see."

She looked at Sam, mouth quivering. "Does it gonna hurt?"

Sam's mouth worked. He scraped one hand across his face and then said gruffly, "You should take her into town. She'll need a tetanus shot."

"No shots, Mommy!" The wail lifted the hairs at the back of Maggie's neck, and she winced as the child's voice hit decibels only dogs should have been able to hear.

Susan, though, ignored her child's distress and focused on reaching the doctor still staring at her. "We can take care of that later. She's hurt. She needs help *now*."

Maggie sensed his hesitation and wondered at it. She could see Sam leaning toward the girl, instinctively moving to help, but there was a distance in his eyes he couldn't hide.

"Fine," he said abruptly, and though a sense of detachment still remained in his eyes, he reached out both arms for the little girl. "Maggie," he said quickly as he examined the slice across the child's forearm, "go upstairs. There's a medical bag in my room."

"Right." She left the kitchen at a dead run and was back downstairs again a moment or two later.

He had the little girl sitting on the counter beside a now-empty sink while he carefully held her small arm under a stream of water from the faucet.

"It's still bleeding," Katie cried, kicking her heels against the wood cupboards beneath the counter.

Sam smiled at her. "That's because you have smart blood."

"I do?" She sniffled, wiped her red eyes with her free hand and stared at him.

"Yep. Your blood's cleaning your cut for us. Very smart blood."

"Mommy," she said, delighted to know how intelligent her body was, "I'm smart."

"You bet, baby girl," Susan said, watching every move Sam made.

"Here's your bag." Maggie stepped up close and set the bag down beside the little girl. Then she lifted one hand to smooth silky-soft hair off the child's cheeks.

She watched Sam, impressed and touched by his gentleness with the little girl. She'd been around him for three days now and this was the first time she'd gotten a glimpse of his heart.

"Thanks," Sam said and pulled a paper towel off the roll, gently patting the cut dry. "Katie, you just sit right here for a second and we'll fix it all up."

"'Kay."

He delved into the bag, pulled out a small package and opened it up. "These are butterfly bandages," he said as he pulled the backing off the tiny adhesive patches.

"Butterflies?" More curious now than afraid, Katie watched him as he pulled the skin of her wound together and carefully applied the bandages.

His fingers smoothed over the edges of the bandages, carefully making sure they weren't too tight, weren't pulling too closely. Then he lifted his gaze to hers and smiled into her watery eyes. "All finished," Sam said. "You were very brave."

"And *smart,*" she added with a sharp nod of her head that sent a tiny pink barrette sliding toward her forehead.

"Oh," Sam said despite the warning twinge of danger inside him, "*very* smart."

She flashed him a smile that slammed into him like a sledgehammer, and Sam had to remind himself to emotionally back up. It was the little ones that always got to him. The helpless ones. The ones with tears in their eyes and blind trust in their hearts.

At that thought, he straightened up, lifted her down from the counter and set her onto her feet.

Then he closed his bag and glanced at the child's mother. "She'll be fine. But you should still get her in to Doc Evans for that tetanus—" He broke off with a glance at the girl, then finished lamely, "For the other thing I talked about earlier."

"I will," she promised, gathering up her daughter and holding her close. "And thank you. Seriously."

"It wasn't bad," Sam assured her, uncomfortable with the admiring stares of both Susan and Maggie.

"She's my baby," the woman said, hugging the girl tightly. "Which means, everything is serious to me."

"I understand." And he did. All too well. Which was exactly why he needed the emotional distance that was, at the moment, eluding him.

When they were gone, Katie waving a final goodbye from the safety of her mother's arms, Sam felt Maggie's curiosity simmering in the air.

"You're very good with children," she said.

He forced himself to glance at her and saw the shine of interest in her eyes. Ordinarily having a woman like Maggie look at him like that would be a good thing. But not now. Not when they'd be in close quarters for the summer. Not when he'd be leaving in three months and she'd dug her own roots deep into the Lonergan ranch.

"I almost never bite," he said, choosing to make a joke out of her observation.

She tipped her head to one side and studied him.

"Jeremiah told me that you work with Doctors Without Borders."

"Sometimes," he said, trying to head her off at the pass before she started making what he did into some kind of heroics.

"And," she continued, "he said when you're not doing that, you work in hospital E.R.s around the country."

True. He kept on the move. Never staying in one place long enough to care about the people he treated. Never making the kind of connection that could only lead to pain somewhere along the line.

Frowning, Sam only said, "Jeremiah talks too much."

"What I don't understand," she said softly, keeping his attention despite the voice inside telling him to leave the room, "is why someone like you doesn't want to settle down in one place. Build a practice."

His chest tightened and his lungs felt as though they were being squeezed by a cold, invisible fist. Of course she didn't understand. The woman had been at the ranch less than two years and she'd already put her stamp on the place.

Little touches—flowers, candles—decorated the big rooms. The house always smelled of lemon oil, and every stick of furniture in the place gleamed from her careful attention. She'd nested. Put down roots here in the land that had nurtured him in his youth. Of course she couldn't comprehend why he wouldn't want the same things.

And if things had been different, he probably would have. But he'd learned early that loving, caring, only meant that you could be hurt, torn apart inside by a whim of fate. So now he chose to stand apart. To keep his heart whole by keeping it locked away.

"I like to be on the move," he said and heard the gruffness of his own voice scratching at the air. Here, in this kitchen that shone and glistened in the morning sunlight, a part of him wished things were different. Wished *he* were different.

But no amount of wishing could turn back time.

"Before," she said, apparently unwilling to let this conversation end and allow him an escape, "you told me that you weren't a nice man."

He stilled, his hands atop the medical bag that went with him everywhere. "It's the truth."

"No," she said softly. And he couldn't help it—he had to look at her.

The sun shining in behind her silhouetted and lined her form with gold. Their gazes locked. She looked deeply into his eyes, and Sam wanted to warn her that what she would see in his soul wasn't really worth a long look.

"It's not the truth at all," she was saying, her gaze on his, a small smile curving her lips. "I think you'd like to believe it's true, but it's not."

"You don't know me," Sam countered and deliberately forced himself to break the spell somehow linking them. He grabbed up his bag and took the few steps to the doorway leading out of the kitchen.

Her voice stopped him.

"Maybe not," she said quietly. "But maybe *you* don't know you very well, either."

"You shouldn't come here alone."

Maggie's rhythm was shattered and she came up out of her swim stroke to look at the man standing at the lake's edge. Under the light of a nearly full moon he looked...*amazing*.

All day she'd been thinking of him. Didn't matter that he'd managed to keep out of her way, busying himself with tasks around the ranch yard. He'd mended fences, repaired a loose board on the back porch and cleared out the empty stables where Jeremiah used to keep horses.

And when he hadn't known she was watching, Maggie had taken the opportunity to indulge herself with a good stare. He worked like a man trying to keep himself too busy to think. In the heat of the afternoon he'd stripped off his black T-shirt, and Maggie'd been mesmerized by the sight of his tanned flesh, muscles rippling with his every movement.

Heat had settled deep inside her and didn't show any signs of dissipating. She'd moved through the rest of her day in a fog of confused lust. Not that she was confused *about* the lust. That was really clear. Gorgeous man, dark, haunted eyes, deep voice, gentle hands. What woman wouldn't be tied up in knots over him?

The confusion resulted from the fact that she *knew* he wanted her, too—and was doing everything he could to avoid her. But then, hadn't they made a pact to do just that? Steer clear of each other?

So why was he here now?

Treading water, Maggie kicked her legs and waved her arms through the cool water, keeping herself afloat as she watched him. "I've been coming here alone for two years now. I'm perfectly safe."

"I came here every summer of my life. Only took the one time."

"Sam…" If they were going to have this talk, she wouldn't do it while treading water. Giving a good strong kick, she headed for shore, and as soon as the water was shallow enough, she walked across the silty bottom, sand pushing up between her toes. Water rained off her body and she wrung her hair out before tossing it over her shoulder as she moved up onto the shore, coming to a stop right in front of him.

His gaze swept up and down her quickly, thoroughly. "No more skinny-dipping?"

She glanced at the black one-piece bathing suit she

wore, then lifted her gaze to his. Smiling, she shrugged. "I'm being a little more careful these days."

Instantly the humor in his eyes disappeared and he reached for her, curling his fingers into her shoulders as he pulled her close. His eyes even darker than usual, his voice was raw. "I hope you are. You don't dive here, do you? Jump in from the ridge?"

"No," she said quickly, responding to the fear in his eyes more than to the dictatorial note in his voice. "I just come here to swim. To cool off."

She shifted her gaze to the moonlit water behind her. She tried to see it through his eyes, through the veil of a memory that clearly still shadowed him. But all she saw was the beauty. As always, being in this spot soothed her, filled her in a way that nothing else ever had. The sigh of the wind through the trees and across the open fields. The cool ripple of the water against her skin. The wash of pale light streaming down from the sky.

"It's beautiful here," she said softly, almost reverently.

"It is," he agreed almost reluctantly, his grip on her shoulders easing but not releasing. "I'd forgotten."

"Sam." She looked up at him and waited for his gaze to meet hers. "I...*know* what happened here fifteen years ago. I know why you and your cousins left and never came back."

In a heartbeat his hands tightened on her shoulders again, and she wasn't sure if he was holding on to her to keep her there or to keep himself steady.

Shaking his head, he looked down at her and sucked in a deep, long breath. "You can't know. You can't know what it's like to be so young and to lose everything."

She reached up and cupped his cheek in her palm. Heart aching for him as she saw old pain blossom in the shine of his eyes, she said, "I know what it's like to have *nothing* to lose. I know that you still have so much—but you're determined not to see it."

He pulled her even closer and loomed over her. Maggie met his gaze and wouldn't look away. The desire that had pumped inside her so fiercely came back to the forefront and made her nerve endings fire. Something fluttered in the pit of her stomach and she swallowed hard against the knot of need lodged in her throat.

"You pull at me," he admitted, his gaze sweeping over her face. "And if I could stop it, I would."

Her heartbeat galloped and her mouth went dry. "I know." She wasn't stupid. She knew it was a mistake to get involved with a man whose very presence might be a threat to her remaining at the ranch she loved. But it had been so long since she'd felt this sense of…*wanting*. And she'd *never* known the near electrical surge in her body that being close to Sam engendered.

"I've told you, I'm *not* a nice man," he said. "You have to believe me."

"I don't."

He closed his eyes and rested his forehead against hers for a heartbeat of time. Warmth spiraled through her, like ribbon falling unfettered from a spool.

"You will, Maggie," he said. "God help me, you *will* believe me."

There was that confusion again.

Then he took her mouth with his and all thought stopped. She didn't want to think. She only wanted to feel. He wrapped his arms around her, pressing her cold, wet body to his, and Maggie could have sworn she felt steam rise up between them.

When he broke the kiss, she felt bereft, unsteady on her feet and hungry for more. Every cell in her body was awake and demanding attention. She watched him swallow hard and shudder as a matching need coursed through him.

He lifted his head, stared down into her eyes and whispered, "This is a mistake."

"Probably."

"I want you," he admitted. "More than I should."

Struggling for air, Maggie smiled up at him, still stunned to her soul with the power of that kiss. "I want you, too, Sam. Mistake or not."

"Thank God."

# Six

Warning bells went off in Sam's mind, clanging loudly enough that he should have reacted to them. He should have let her go, taken a huge step back and then spent the rest of the night trying to forget the taste of her. The scent of her. The feel of her.

But that wasn't going to happen.

He deepened the kiss, sweeping his tongue into her warmth, feeling the shudder that wracked her body and tasting the sigh that slipped from her mouth into his. Her arms came up around his neck, her fingers smoothing through his hair, nails dragging along his scalp. A chill raced along his spine and danced with the blood boiling in his veins.

Those warning bells came louder, but still Sam tuned them out. He couldn't walk away from this. Couldn't turn his back on a need, a hunger, that was suddenly stronger than anything he'd ever known.

A hot summer wind wrapped itself around them and Sam dived deeper into the wonder that was Maggie. Lifting her off her feet, he staggered away from the bank, laid her down on the cool, green grass and levered himself over her.

Tearing his mouth from hers, he shifted, kissing the line of her jaw, trailing his lips along the curve of her neck to the dip of her shoulder. He inhaled her scent, the lingering trace of floral shampoo in her hair, the clean, fresh scent of the lake water clinging to her skin. And he felt heat pool inside him, swamping him with a raw hunger that clawed at him.

She sighed, slid her hands up and down his back, and even through the fabric of his T-shirt he felt the warmth of her touch singeing his skin. Sam shuddered, lifted his head and stared down into eyes as dark as his own. Moonlight flashed in her eyes and highlighted the desire shining there. When she took his face between her palms and pulled him down for a kiss, her mouth met his with a tenderness he hadn't expected. A gentleness that rocked him more thoroughly than the need clamoring inside.

Then her teeth tugged at his bottom lip, her tongue

touched the tip of his and gentleness was forgotten. A nearly electrical jolt of something amazing shot through Sam, stealing his breath as it pushed his hunger to an overwhelming pitch.

He groaned and swept one hand down the length of her body, feeling every curve, enjoying the cool dampness of her bathing suit and the heat waiting for him at her center. He cupped her, and even through the fabric separating his flesh from hers, he felt that heat pulling him in. For days he'd thought about this moment. He'd dreamed about touching her, the feel of his skin against hers. The brush of her lips, the sigh of her breath.

In the few days he'd known her, Maggie had invaded his every thought. While a part of him worried over his grandfather and the consequences of returning to the ranch, there was another completely separate part of him that hadn't been able to keep from thinking about her. From the moment he'd met her there'd been *something* simmering in the air between them. Something he'd never felt before. Something he really didn't want to think about.

At the moment it was enough to have her. To touch her.

She gasped and arched into his touch, her legs separating, parting to give him easier access.

It wasn't enough.

He needed more.

Wanted more.

Still kissing him, tantalizing him, her hands dropped to his belt and tugged at his shirt, pulling the hem of it free of his jeans and then pushing it up over his chest. Her palms splayed against his skin and it felt as though she were branding him—and he wanted to feel her hands all over him.

Instantly he sat up, ripped off his shirt and tossed it to one side. He watched her and his breath strangled in his throat as she pushed first one strap of her suit, then the other off her shoulders. The tops of her breasts peeked up from the edge of the suit, straining against the stretchy fabric as if trying to escape. When she would have slid the suit farther down though, he stopped her.

Heart pounding, throat tight, he grabbed her hands, stilled them and whispered, "Let me."

She licked her lips, nodded and then closed her eyes as he pushed the bathing suit down and off her until she lay naked in the moonlight. Her tan lines gleamed pale against her honey-colored flesh, and he found himself wishing she'd worn the bikini that had created those lines.

"Went for a one-piece tonight," he murmured, lips curving.

She smiled and lifted one hand toward him. "I thought it would be…safer to be covered up, just in case I ran into you out here."

His smile faded as he watched her eyes. "Do you want to be safe?"

She shook her head. "No. I want *you*."

"Glad to hear it." He dipped his head and took first one of her nipples and then the other into his mouth.

Her soft sighs scalded him. "Sam…"

"I've been thinking about doing this since that first night," he admitted, lifting his head as he stroked one hand down her chest, between her breasts, past her navel to the soft, dark curls at the juncture of her thighs.

"Me, too," she said and reached for him, running her fingertips down his chest, scraping her thumbnails across his flat nipples.

He groaned again, fighting for air. For control. But it was a hopeless battle. With this woman naked before him, control wasn't something he was really interested in. All he wanted, all he could think about, was burying himself inside her, feeling her heat surround him, surrendering to the hunger.

Standing up, he toed off his boots, ripped off his jeans and then knelt down on the cool, soft grass in front of her. She sucked in air like a drowning woman and reached out her arms to him.

"Don't wait," she said, planting her feet, lifting her hips and rocking them in silent invitation. "Don't wait another minute."

"No. No waiting." He stretched out over her,

bracing himself on his hands at either side of her head. His gaze locked with hers as he entered her.

"Tight."

"*Good*," she whispered, arching her head back, keeping her gaze on his as he filled her. "Oh...*Sam*..."

Better than good, he thought, biting back another groan of desperation. *Essential.* With one hard thrust he shoved himself all the way home, and she gasped, drawing her legs up, wrapping them around his hips, pulling him closer, deeper.

He rocked his hips against hers, moving in and out of her heat with a rhythm driven by an overpowering need. She moved with him in a frantic dance fed by the flames devouring them both. Together they slid into a vortex of need that erupted around them, growing even as the demands of their bodies were met. The rest of the world dropped away and it was only the two of them—wrapped in a cocoon of desire that stripped away thought, logic, caution.

Lost in the sigh of the wind and the call of a night bird, they raced toward completion. The blanket of grass their bed, the star-filled sky their roof, they were locked together in the darkness, lost in each other.

Maggie stared up into Sam's eyes as he took her, as his body claimed her, pushing her higher and faster than she'd ever been before. His body pushed into hers, and a delicious friction erupted within, sparkling through her veins like shaken champagne exploding from the bottle. She held on to him tightly, her arms and legs wrapped around his hard, strong body. She felt his breath on her cheek, saw the tempest in his eyes and knew she shared it.

Breathless, she clung to the edge of sanity and fought for the wild release just out of reach. She arched into him again and again, trying to take him even deeper inside, struggling toward the soul-shattering end waiting for her.

"Sam...Sam..." Her voice, broken, shattered the quiet.

"Come for me," he whispered, his voice rumbling through her like a freight train.

"It...feels..." She couldn't define it. Couldn't explain it. Could only enjoy it and hope she survived it. And in the next second her body splintered in a fiery burst of sensation that nearly blinded her in its raw fury. She screamed, arching into him, quivering with the slam of pleasure that rocked her right down to her soul. She trembled and held on to him as if it meant her life while wave after wave of ecstasy rippled through her again and again.

Body dissolving, a whimper clogged in her throat, Maggie still found the strength to cradle Sam when he emptied himself into her with a groan torn from the depths of his soul.

Sam lay atop her and thought that even if it had meant his life, he wouldn't be able to move. Heart thudding in his chest, he felt the rapid-fire echo of her heart beating in time with his and knew she'd been as shaken as he. Gathering his strength, he pushed himself up onto his elbows and looked down into her eyes. "You okay?"

She licked her lips, blew out a short laugh, then moaned as their bodies moved together again. "I should be fine," she said. "Once the paralysis goes away."

"I hear that." Smiling, he brushed his palm across her breast and relished the hissed intake of her breath at the contact. She squirmed beneath him, her hips twisting, and he felt his body swell within her again.

She must have felt it, too.

"I see you're not completely immobile."

"Apparently not." He rocked his hips against hers, enjoying her quick inhalation of air and the way her body responded to his intimate invasion.

Her arms dropped to her sides, then swept along the grass until they lay stretched out behind her head. She looked like an Earth goddess. Moonlight pale on her skin, the long, green grass enveloping her, her still-damp hair spread out around her, her eyes glazed with a quickening need that he felt, too.

"Maggie," he whispered, bending his head to taste her mouth, to mate her tongue with his, to give her his breath and swallow hers.

"Sam," she whispered, stretching, twisting, writhing beneath him, "we're going to do it again, aren't we?"

"Oh, yeah. *Again.*"

Sliding his hands beneath her back, he lifted her as he went to his knees. She took him deeper and groaned as she straddled him and he dropped his hands to her hips.

Throwing her head back, Maggie stared blindly up at the night sky as she rocked on him, taking him so deep inside that she felt as though he was touching the tip of her heart. Her arms wrapped around his neck. She clung to him and ground her hips against him, creating the friction that sizzled deep within.

He guided her every movement with his strong hands and held her steady even when she felt as though she were about to fly apart. Lifting her head, she looked into his eyes and dived into their darkness, drowning in their depths, losing herself in the heat, the need, the tantalizing sensations of wickedness that rippled through her and around her.

And this time when the end came hurtling toward them, they reached it together and clung to each other like survivors of a storm.

Time drifted by, and Maggie wasn't sure if minutes or hours had passed when she finally drew a deep breath and lifted her head from his shoulder. "I think that paralysis may be permanent this time."

"Better not be," he said, his voice muffled with his mouth against the base of her neck. "It gets cold out here in the middle of the night. Even in summer. We could freeze."

"Well," Maggie said, laughing slightly, "that would be embarrassing, wouldn't it? Naked ice statues discovered by some poor rancher."

He didn't respond and Maggie's smile slowly faded. Carefully he lifted her off him and she sighed with loss as his body slipped from hers. Without the sexual heat surrounding them, the kiss of the wind felt icy on her sweat-dampened skin and she shivered.

He noticed and leaned to one side, grabbed up the summer dress she'd worn over her swimsuit and handed it to her. "You should get dressed."

She frowned a little as she pulled her dress over her head and wiggled into it. Her gaze followed him as he snatched up his jeans and stepped into them, tugging them up his long, muscled legs. He buttoned them up, then turned to look down at her.

"I'm sensing the magic is over," she said and held out one hand toward him. He took it and pulled her to her feet in one smooth move.

"Maggie…" Scrubbing one hand across his face, he shook his head, bent and scooped up his T-shirt from the grass. Fisting it in one hand, he looked at her and said, "I don't want you to think that—"

"Hold that thought," she said, lifting one hand for silence and was almost surprised when she got it. "If you're going to start telling me that this—" she waved one hand at the now-flattened patch of grass "—doesn't mean anything, don't worry. I'm not expecting a proposal or something."

Her heart twisted a little. She didn't do this kind of thing lightly. She'd been with exactly one other man in her life, and then it was because she'd thought she was in love. And really, wasn't *thinking* you were in love the same as *being* in love? But even then she hadn't felt the same...*need*, that she'd felt for Sam from the beginning. Tonight had been inevitable. Where it went from here was still in question.

"Yeah, but—"

Maggie cut him off, speaking up quickly. "And you know, I don't usually sleep with a man I've known less than a week." Before he could open his mouth again, she said, "It was just..."

"I know," he said quietly. "You kind of hit me hard, too."

"Really?"

He gave her a brief one-sided smile. "You've been making me nuts for days."

"You, too," she admitted with a sigh, then clarified, "I mean, you've been getting to me, too."

"You should know," he said tightly as he pulled his T-shirt on, shoving his arms through the sleeves, "I didn't come down here tonight for this—" he paused. "I mean, that wasn't the plan."

"What was the plan then?"

"Damned if I know." He shrugged, frowned into the distance, then shifted his gaze back to hers. "Guess I wanted to see you."

"I'm glad you did."

"Me, too, but—"

"But…?"

"It's a little late to be asking," he said, "and as a doctor, I sure as hell should have known better…" He shook his head and stabbed both hands through his hair impatiently. "Can't believe I didn't think. Didn't consider—"

"What?"

He turned a flat, emotionless stare on her. "I didn't use anything." When she didn't say anything, he added, "A *condom*?"

"Oh." She thought about it for a second, then realization dawned like a hammer to the head. "Oooh."

"Crap." He closed his eyes, sighed heavily, then opened them again to look at her. "I'm guessing from your reaction that you're not on the Pill."

"No reason to be," she said and slapped one hand to her abdomen as if she could somehow protect it belatedly. "I mean, until you—tonight—well, it's been…a long time."

Oh, she really had been way too wrapped up in the heat of the moment. Her stomach did a slow swirl and dip as the ramifications of what they'd done hit home. They might have made a *baby* tonight.

"Damn it." He leaned over, grabbed his boots and straightened up again, his features tight, his eyes shuttered. "Stupid. I was stupid. Sorry doesn't seem like enough."

"We were both stupid," she reminded him. "I was there, too, so you don't get to take the whole blame. It's not as if you took advantage of me or something. I'm a grown-up and I make my own choices."

"Somehow that doesn't make this any easier."

"Maybe not," she said, "but this is just as much my fault as yours, so no point in wasting a perfectly good apology."

She tried to think. Tried to figure out where she was in her cycle. Then she gave it up because she'd never been good with math anyway. She crossed her fingers for luck and said, "I'm sure it'll be fine."

His eyes narrowed. "You're sure."

"It was only the once."

"Twice."

"Right." She blew out a breath and told herself not to panic. No point in panicking yet. She swallowed hard and nodded as if convincing herself as well as him. "It'll be fine. You'll see."

"I hope you're right," he said, his gaze still narrowed and thoughtful on her. "But you'll tell me. Either way."

"Of course," she said. "There won't be anything to tell, but if there is, I'll tell you everything."

"Good. Good." He nodded firmly, as if that settled the matter. "And just so you know, I'm healthy."

"Oh, I am, too," she assured him and wished that sex in the twenty-first century could be a little less clinical and a little more fun. Although, they'd *had* fun and now look where they were.

After that an awkward silence stretched out between them. An owl hooted in the distance, and with a push from the wind the lake lapped at the shoreline. Leaves rustled overhead, and from the next ranch came the sound of a barking dog, eerie in the darkness.

"I don't want to hurt you, Maggie," he said suddenly, his voice hardly louder than the soft, papery rustle of the leaves.

Her heart fisted in her chest and Maggie sensed him pulling even further away from her. There was misery in his eyes and a loneliness in his voice that tore at her.

"What makes you think you will?"

He shifted his gaze from her to the dark surface of the lake. He stared hard, and Maggie had the distinct impression that he was looking at the lake not as it was now but as it had been on a long-ago summer day. And almost to himself he said, "There's just no other way."

# Seven

Over the next week Jeremiah sensed a change between Sam and Maggie. He couldn't put his finger on it, but he was pretty sure there was more going on between them than they were saying. Every time one of them came into the room, the other one started getting jumpy.

He was old.

Not stupid.

When his bedroom door opened, Jeremiah lay back against his pillows weakly, just in case. Sunlight lay across him in a slice of gold. He opened one eye, spotted his friend Bert and sat straight up. "About time you got here. Did you bring it?"

Bert winced and closed the bedroom door with a quiet snick. "For God's sake, keep it down. Yes, I brought it—and it's the last time," he added as he stalked toward the bed.

Bert's face was flushed, and guilt shone in his pale blue eyes so clearly it was easily readable even from behind the thick glasses he wore.

"Now, Bert," Jeremiah said, swinging his legs off the bed, "no reason to start losing your nerve now."

The other man set his black leather medical bag on the edge of the bed and gave the tarnished bronze clasp a quick twist. Then he delved one handed into the bag and pulled out a bottle of single-malt scotch. Scowling fiercely, he handed it over. "It isn't about nerve, Jeremiah. It's about what's right. I don't like lying to Sam."

Frowning himself, Jeremiah studied the bottle of scotch. "Well, come to it, neither do I. But I had to get them all home *somehow*."

"Yes, but he's here now. Tell him the truth."

"Not yet." Jeremiah shook his head and fought his own feelings of guilt. He didn't like worrying his grandsons, but once they were all here, back where they belonged, he'd tell them the truth together. Resolve strengthened, he nodded firmly and asked, "Say, Bert, when you were downstairs, did you happen to notice anything between Sam and Maggie?"

At the abrupt change of subject, Bert blinked, then

thought about it for a long minute. "Nope. Can't say that I did. Though Maggie wasn't in the house. Sam let me in." Giving his head a slow shake, he said, "Tried to talk to him about sticking around. Buying my practice."

Jeremiah perked up at that. "What'd he say?"

"Same as always," Bert said on a sigh and sat down on the edge of the mattress beside his friend. Tiny dust mites danced in the sunlight, tossed by the brush of wind slipping under the partially opened sash. "He's not staying. Not interested in sticking around. Wants to practice medicine on *his* terms."

"Disappointing," Jeremiah said on a matching sigh as he twisted the cap on the scotch bottle, breaking the seal. He lifted the bottle, took a sip, then handed it off to Bert. "The boy's a hardhead, no doubt about it."

Bert snorted, took a quick pull on the scotch and said, "Wonder where he got *that* trait?"

Maggie walked along the line, pulling the wooden clothespins free and taking down the now-dry sheets and pillowcases. Carefully she folded each item as she went and set it in the basket at her feet. When she'd finished one item, she kicked the basket along and moved on to the next.

Sam stood on the back porch, one shoulder leaning against the newel post as he watched her.

With Bert upstairs keeping Jeremiah occupied, he'd followed his instincts—which had brought him here.

To Maggie.

He didn't like admitting that, even to himself, but there it was. Without really wanting to or even trying, he'd found a connection with this woman. He was already used to seeing her every day. To hearing her sing to herself when she thought no one was around. To seeing the way she cared for his grandfather and this place.

God, he'd missed the ranch. When he was a kid, the summers he'd spent here had meant more to him than anything. This place, this ranch, had been more home to him than any of the military bases he'd grown up on. His parents had always been too wrapped up in each other to take much notice of him—so the summers with his grandparents and cousins had shone golden in his mind. He'd always known that this place was here for him. This town. This ranch.

His gaze shifted briefly away from Maggie to encompass the ranch yard. The barn/stable needed a good coat of paint, and there were a few weeds sprouting up at the edges of the building and along the fence line. In the old days, weeds had never had a chance. But times had changed.

Too much had changed.

At the thought, his gaze drifted back to Maggie. Completely oblivious to him, she kept moving along the line of clean clothes she'd pegged out to dry hours ago. She wore white shorts that hit her midthigh and a tiny yellow tank top. Her white sneakers were old and worn, and her shoulder-length dark hair was drawn back into a ponytail that swayed with her movements like a metronome.

When he found himself smiling at the picture she made, he worried.

"If you're going to stand out here anyway," she called out, never turning her head, "the least you could do is help fold."

He straightened up and blew out a disgusted breath. So much for being the stealthy type. Taking the steps to the grass, he wandered over to her side. "How'd you know I was there?"

She swiveled her head to glance at him. "I could feel you watching me."

He quirked one eyebrow at her.

She grinned briefly. "Okay, *and* I heard you come outside. The screen on the kitchen door still squeaks." Shrugging, she added, "Then there was the sound of your boot heels on the porch—not to mention that tired-old-man sigh I heard just a minute or two ago."

Her fingers never stopped. She plucked off clothespins, dropped them into a canvas sack hanging from the line and then folded the next item.

"You're too observant for your own good," he said, taking the edge of the sheet when she held it out to him.

"Oh, I am," she agreed, folding one edge of the sheet over the other, then walking toward him to make the ends meet. "Just like I've *observed* that you've been avoiding me all week."

Sunlight played on her hair, dazzling the streaks of blond intermingled with the darker strands. She squinted up at him, and he noticed for the first time that she had freckles sprinkled across the bridge of her nose. Not many. Just a few. Just enough to make a man want to count them with kisses.

Which was, he told himself, *exactly* why he'd been avoiding her all week.

Because that night with her was never far from his mind. Because with every breath he wanted her again. And again. And again.

Shaking his head, he blew out a breath. Damn it. Having her should have taken the edge off the hunger. Instead he now knew just what he could find in her arms and it was taking everything he had to keep from trying to have it again. "Like I said. Observant."

Silently he took the gathered edges of the sheet, folded them neatly and dropped them onto the stack already in the basket. When he was finished, Maggie handed him a pillowcase and took one for herself.

"Hmm," she quipped with a glance at him, "not even going to try to deny it?"

"Not much point in that, is there?"

"So want to tell me *why* you've been avoiding me?"

"Not particularly," he admitted and took the pillowcase she handed him.

"Okay, then why don't *I* tell *you?*"

"Maggie…" He dropped the pillowcase onto the stack of clean laundry.

"See," she said, cutting him off neatly, "I think you don't want to talk about that night because it *meant* something to you. And that bothers you."

He stiffened, narrowed his gaze on her and watched as she quickly plucked two more clothespins off the line, gathering up a sheet as she went. "I already told you, I don't want to hurt you."

"Yes," she said, nodding, "we've already covered that."

"So why don't we just leave it alone?"

"Can't," she said, turning to face him.

"Why am I not surprised?"

She gave him a sad smile. "Is it really so hard for you to admit that what we had that night was special?"

"No." He huffed out a breath. "It *was*. I can admit that. But I can't give you anything else."

"I didn't ask for anything else," she reminded him with a patient sigh.

"Yeah, but you will," he said, meeting her dark gaze with his own. "It's in your nature."

She laughed and the music of it slammed into him, rocking him on his heels.

"My nature," she repeated. "And you know this how?"

He waved one hand, encompassing the ranch yard, the house and *her.* "You're a nester, Maggie. Look at you. I can see the curtains you hung in the guesthouse from here. You've burrowed your way into the very place that I've been steering clear of for fifteen years."

"But you're here now."

"For the summer," he clarified, in case she'd missed him saying it in the last week. "Then I'm gone again."

"Just like that?" she asked. "You can leave again, even knowing how much your grandfather needs you? Loves you?"

Sam shifted uncomfortably. Guilt pinged around inside him like a marble in the bottom of an empty coffee can. "I can't stay," he said finally through gritted teeth.

She shook her head slowly and he followed the motion of her ponytail swinging from side to side behind her head. "Not *can't,*" she said, *"won't."*

"Whichever." He sounded as irritable as he felt, but apparently the tone of his voice had no effect on her. Because she only looked at him with that same sad smile, half disappointment, half regret.

"Fine. But even if you're leaving at the end of summer, you're here *now,*" she reminded him.

Yeah, he was. And he wanted her. *Bad.* For one

brief instant his body tightened and his breath staggered in his lungs. Then he came back to his senses. "You're not a 'right now' kind of woman, Maggie. And I can't make you promises."

"You keep forgetting that I didn't ask for anything from you." She stepped toward him, cupped his cheek in her palm and stared directly into his eyes. "What? Only men are allowed brief, red-hot affairs?"

He caught her hand in his, stilling the feel of her fingertips against his skin. "What about the other?"

"Hmm?"

"The chance of pregnancy?" Couldn't believe he had to remind her about *that*.

Realization dawned on her features, but she said, "I don't know yet. But since there's nothing we can do about it at the moment, no point in worrying about that until we know for sure, is there?"

"Guess not." Though he knew damn well a corner of his mind would be worrying about that small chance nonstop until he knew one way or the other.

"And we could be careful."

Her voice brought him back from his thoughts, and as he looked down into her eyes, he felt his resolution to keep his distance fading into nothingness. If they were careful, if she didn't expect more from him than he could give…

It would be crazy.

Stupid.

Great.

When he didn't speak, she shrugged. "Either way," she mused, still giving him that half smile, "still got to get the laundry in."

With the abrupt shift in subject, Sam felt as if he'd just been shown a safe path through a minefield. As she walked along the line to take down the next sheet, he studied the sway of her hips, despite knowing that he'd be better off ignoring it. "Why don't you just use the dryer on the service porch?"

"This way things smell better," she said, lifting one shoulder in a half shrug as she reached up to the line. The hem of her tank top pulled up, displaying an inch or two of taut, tanned abdomen. Just enough to tempt him. "The wind and the sun…at night, you can sleep on sheets that make you dream of summer."

That'd be good, he thought, shoving his hands into his jeans pockets. But then, *anything* would beat the kind of dreams he normally had.

"Besides," she was saying as she tossed him one end of a pink-and-blue floral sheet, "when I was a little girl, I always wanted my own clothesline."

He chuckled, surprising both of them. "That's different."

She glanced at him, then looked down at the sheet they were folding. "There was a house down the street from where I lived and this woman would be out there almost every day." Her voice went soft and hazy and he knew she was looking at a memory. "She had this big golden dog who followed her all around the yard and she'd laugh at him while she hung out clothes to dry. Sometimes," she added, smiling now, "her kids would go out there, too. And they'd all play peek-a-boo in the clean clothes and it all looked so...*nice.*"

"So your own mom wasn't the clothesline type, huh?"

Maggie's features stiffened and a shutter dropped over her eyes. "I don't know what my mother preferred," she said and heard the wistfulness in her voice. "I never knew her."

She glanced at Sam and saw his wince. "Sorry."

She shrugged again and reached to push up the strap of her tank top that had slid down her arm. "Not your fault. You didn't know."

"And your father?"

She forced a smile. "He's a mystery, too. They died when I was a kid. I went into the system and stayed there until I was eighteen. That neighbor I told you about? She lived down the street from the group home."

"You weren't adopted?"

"Nope. Most people want babies. But don't get that sympathy look on your face," Maggie warned. She hadn't needed anyone's pity in a long time and she sure didn't want it from Sam. "I did *fine.* There were a couple of foster parents along the way and the group home was a good one." Wanting to throw up roadblocks on memory lane, she changed the subject fast. "Anyway, now that there's a clothesline nearby, I get to indulge myself."

Thankfully he didn't ask anything else about her childhood. It hadn't all been popcorn and cotton candy, but it hadn't exactly been a miserable Dickensian childhood or anything, either. But that was the past and she had the present and future to think about.

"Indulge yourself even though this way it's more work."

"Sometimes more work makes things better."

"Not your average attitude these days."

She smiled at him. "Who wants to be average?"

"Good point." He finished folding the sheet, glanced around the yard. "You know, there's something still missing from your laundry recreation. Pop used to have a dog."

"Bigfoot." Maggie nodded sadly. "I know. He died last year."

*"Last year?"* Sam whistled as he did the math. "He had to have been nearly twenty years old."

"Almost," Maggie agreed, "and pretty spry right up to the end. Jeremiah was brokenhearted when that dog died. He said it was his last link to you and your cousins."

He slapped one hand to his chest and rubbed it hard, as if her words had hit him like a dart.

"You shouldn't have stayed away so long," she said.

His gaze slid to hers. "I couldn't come back. Couldn't be here…be surrounded with memories. Couldn't do it."

"But you're doing it *now*."

He snorted. "Just barely."

"Maybe it'll get easier the longer you're here."

"No, it won't."

"You could try. For *his* sake." She nodded in the direction of the house.

"It's only for *his* sake that I'm here at all." He reached up, closed one hand around the nylon clothesline and hung on as if it were a life rope tossed into a stormy sea.

"It wasn't your fault." She said it without thinking, and the minute those words came blundering out of her mouth, Maggie knew they'd been a mistake.

His features froze over. His jaw clenched. She watched him grind his teeth together hard enough to turn them to powder. And his gaze—dark, filled with pain—stabbed hers. "You don't know anything about it."

"You could talk about it. Tell me."

Another harsh, rasping laugh shot from his throat as he shook his head. "Talking about it doesn't change anything. Talking about it doesn't help. It just brings it all back."

"Sam," Maggie said softly, "you don't *have* to bring it back. It's with you all the time."

"God, I know that." He blew out a breath, seemed to steady himself, then started talking again, forcing a change of subject. "So how'd you come to be here on the Lonergan ranch, working for Jeremiah?"

Maggie nodded, silently agreeing to the shift in topic, and she was pretty sure she caught the flash of relief in his dark eyes. Then she took down the next sheet and handed one end to him. They had a rhythm now, working together as a team, and a part of her wished that that teamwork could spill over into other areas.

"My car broke down," she said. "Right outside the front gates." Pausing to remember, she added, "*Broke down* doesn't really cover it. More like it fell apart."

One corner of his mouth lifted and Maggie wondered what he looked like when he was *really* smiling. Or laughing.

"Anyway," she said, getting her mind back on track, "Jeremiah invited me in, made me lunch, called a mechanic. And by the time Arthur's Towing Service arrived to take my car away to heap heaven, your grandfather had offered me a job as his housekeeper."

"That explains how you got here," he agreed, folding the sheet and setting it down on top of the rest. "Now tell me why you're *still* here."

Nodding, Maggie straightened up and looked around beyond the ranch yard and the outbuildings. To the now golden-brown fields stretching out for miles all around them, the acres of blue sky overhead and finally to their closest neighbor, the Bateman ranch house that was no more than a faint smudge of red in the distance.

Finally she looked back at him. "Why wouldn't I be?" she asked. "It's beautiful here. I like the small town. I love your grandfather—and I owe him a lot. He gave me a place to belong."

A simple word and yet it meant so much to Maggie. It probably meant more than Sam would ever be able to truly understand. No one who'd had a home and a family could ever really know how lonely it was to be without those things.

"And," she said, "working for Jeremiah gives me plenty of time to take classes at the community college in Fresno."

"What kind of classes?"

"Nursing. I…*like* taking care of people."

"According to Jeremiah and Doc Evans, you're good at it, too."

"Thanks."

"You're welcome."

The conversation was dwindling pretty fast. But maybe that was because they were through working. There was nothing else to focus on but themselves. Each other.

Afternoon sunlight streamed down from a brassy sky, and heat radiated up from the pebble-strewn dirt. A halfhearted puff of wind stirred things up a bit without cooling them off.

And seconds continued to tick past.

He looked down at her, a thoughtful expression on his face, and Maggie wondered just what he was thinking.

More than that, she wondered if he was ever going to kiss her again. Heartbeat suddenly thundering in her ears, she was painfully aware of every shallow breath panting in and out of her lungs. Her mouth was dry, her throat tight.

He continued to stare at her. His dark, shadow-filled eyes drew her in. She couldn't have looked away even if the notion had occurred to her. There was something about this man that touched something in her no one else had ever come close to.

And, oh, God, she wanted his mouth on hers again.

As if he were reading her mind, his gaze dropped briefly, hungrily, to her mouth. Maggie's stomach did a nose dive and heat pooled somewhere even farther south.

When he reached for her, she leaned in toward him, and her breath caught as his hands closed around her upper arms.

Lowering his head to hers, he whispered, "We're going to make the same mistake again, aren't we?"

She felt his breath on her face and nearly sighed. Then, looking deeply into his eyes, she said, "Every chance we get."

# Eight

His mouth came down on hers and Maggie felt herself sway into him. Her breasts pressed against his broad chest, her nipples hardened in eager anticipation.

Her lips parted under his and his tongue swept inside. She sighed and gave herself up to the intense sensations pouring through her. Deliberately she shut her brain down and ignored completely the one small, rational voice still whispering warnings in her brain.

He pulled her even tighter against him, and the combined heat from his body and the blistering warmth from the afternoon sun on her back made Maggie feel as though she were about to combust.

He growled low in his throat, and one of his hands

slid down her spine to the curve of her rear. He held her tightly to him until she felt his erection through the thick fabric of his jeans. Instantly her own body went hot and needy.

She wrapped her arms around his neck and clung to him, and when he tore his mouth from hers to lavish kisses along the length of her throat, she threw her head back and stared blindly at the clear summer sky overhead. There was a delicious haze at the edges of her vision and a distinct wobbly feel to her knees.

And she was loving every minute.

"Well. Ahem." A deep voice, then a cough, then someone said, "Excuse me, I didn't mean to interrupt."

*Oops!*

Abruptly the moment was shattered. Maggie swayed unsteadily as Sam lifted his head to reluctantly face the speaker. Doc Evans stood on the back porch, studiously avoiding looking at them by using his handkerchief to polish the lenses of his glasses.

"Hi, Doc." Sam took a step back from Maggie, though it cost him. His body was tight and hard and his vision was blurred with the desire nearly throttling him. Beside him Maggie quickly tugged the hem of her tank top down and ran one hand over the sides of her head, checking to make sure her ponytail was still straight.

"Just wanted to let Sam know I was leaving," the doc said, slipping on his glasses and stuffing the handkerchief into his pocket.

"How is Jeremiah feeling?" Maggie asked, and if her voice sounded a little breathless, Sam was probably the only one to notice.

Doc took the few steps to the yard and glanced at the watch on his left wrist before answering. "He seems…better."

Sam's eyes narrowed on the older man. With lust still pounding through his blood, he was on the ragged edge of control. This thing with his grandfather—the unidentified "illness"—was bothering him, and now seemed like as good a time as any to have some questions answered. "Have you determined just what the problem is yet?"

"Not yet. Um, still running a few tests…" He started rocking on his heels and his gaze shifted to a spot just to one side of Sam. "I'll, um, keep on top of things, though. Don't you worry."

"Doc…" Every instinct he had was telling Sam that something was definitely up. Bert Evans and Jeremiah had been best friends and fishing buddies most of their lives. There wasn't much one wouldn't do for the other. Up to and including trying to pull a fast one. He crossed the yard to the other man and looked down at him. "Is there something I should know?"

Doc ran one finger along the inside of the collar of his shirt and swallowed hard. Still not meeting Sam's gaze, he shook his head. "Nope, not a thing, boy. Everything's as it should be."

"Uh-huh." Folding his arms over his chest, Sam braced his feet wide apart and simply stood there. Waiting.

Seconds ticked past, and a strong breeze jumped up out of nowhere and rushed through the yard. The older man shifted uneasily on his feet, glanced around the yard, looking everywhere but at Sam.

"He's faking, isn't he?"

Bert's gaze snapped to his and he didn't even have to say anything for Sam to know that he'd guessed right. Guilt was stamped on the other man's features.

"Now why would you say that?" The doctor asked, deliberately avoiding answering the question outright.

"Because," Sam said, scowling now, "it occurs to me that if Jeremiah was really as desperately ill as you two want me to think, you'd have him in the hospital. Or at the very least, have a trained nurse here taking care of him."

"Maggie's here," Doc argued.

"Yes," Sam said and heard Maggie come up to stand beside him. "And she's been great with Pop. But she's not a trained nurse. Not yet anyway," he conceded, remembering that she was studying to be just that. "So I have to wonder, Doc. Is Jeremiah putting one over on me? Or *you?*"

The older man cleared his throat, rubbed his jaw, then blew out a breath. When he didn't speak, Maggie did.

"Dr. Evans," she said, aligning herself with Sam, "is Jeremiah ill or not?"

He huffed out another breath, swallowed hard, then admitted, "I never wanted to lie to you, Maggie. Or you either, Sam."

"I don't believe this," Maggie muttered.

"I do," Sam said with a shake of his head. "The old goat tricked us into coming home."

Instantly Bert's eyes fired up and his spine straightened as if someone had suddenly shoved a steel pole down the back of his shirt. Shaking an index finger at Sam as if he were still a kid and needed a good dressing-down, the older man said, "It's a damn shame that old goat *had* to trick the three of you into coming back to the ranch." He took a breath and rushed right on before Sam could try to defend himself. "You boys haven't been back since that summer, and do you think that's right? Do you think it's a fair thing to do? Cutting your grandfather out of your life?"

"No, but—" Sam shoved both hands into his pockets and backed up a step. He also noticed that Maggie's gaze was on him.

"There's no buts about it, boy," Doc Evans said. "You three mean the world to that 'old goat' in there. Not surprising he'd do whatever he had to do to get you back here, now is it?"

No, it wasn't. And if the doc's aim had been to

make Sam ashamed of himself, it had worked. But no one could understand just how hard it was to come back to Coleville. To this place that had once meant everything to him. No one could know that coming here, being here, felt as if he was somehow dismissing what had happened that summer. As if he was trying to forget.

"It was an accident," Doc said, his voice softer now. "But you three have been making Jeremiah pay in loneliness. That isn't right."

Sam didn't trust himself to speak. Guilt roared through him with a sound so thunderous it surprised the hell out of him that the others couldn't hear it. The doc was right. Jeremiah had been punished for something that wasn't his fault. Sam and his cousins had each cut this ranch and the old man out of their lives to make living with that summer easier on *themselves*. But they'd never stopped to consider how their actions affected their grandfather. And what kind of bastards did that make them?

He scrubbed one hand over his face and turned away, suddenly unable to face the accusatory glare in Doc Evans's eyes. He walked across the yard in long, hurried strides until he reached the edge of the field. Then he stopped and stared. Stretched out for miles in front of him, open land raced toward the horizon. The breeze whistled past him, lifting his hair, tossing dirt into his eyes. Midday sun beat down on him like a fist and made him feel as though he were standing at the gates of hell, feeling the heat reaching out for him.

Appropriate.

Behind him, he absently listened to Maggie thanking Bert for coming and then to the soft sounds of the doctor's footsteps as he left. Shame still rippled inside Sam and he had no defense against it. The bottom line was he and his cousins had forced their grandfather into faking a serious illness just to get them home.

"Are you okay?"

Maggie came up beside him and laid one hand on his arm. The simple heat of her touch, the gentleness of her voice, eased back the knot of pain lodged in the center of his chest.

"No," he admitted, never taking his gaze from the horizon. "I don't think I am."

She sighed. "What Jeremiah did wasn't right. He shouldn't have worried you and your cousins—or me."

Finally then Sam looked at her, caught the worry in her dark eyes and warmed himself with it. "He shouldn't have worried *you*. *We* had it coming."

"You're being really hard on yourself."

He laughed at that. "Aren't you the one who's been telling me that I should never have stayed away?"

"Yes," she said. "But if anyone should have understood what you were feeling, it should have been Jeremiah."

"No." Sam turned to face her and laid both hands on her shoulders. "He couldn't. Because he doesn't know all of it."

"Tell me," she said, reaching up to cover his hands with her own. "Tell me what happened."

His fingers tightened on her shoulders, his grip clenching as if holding on to her to steady himself. Maggie sensed the pain radiating from him and wished she could do something to ease it. But there was nothing—not unless he could talk to her. Tell her what it was that kept him in pain. Kept him from the home and the grandfather that he loved.

"Sam…"

He inhaled sharply, deeply, and blew the air out again in a rush. "Every summer we came here. There were four of us. All of us born within a year or two of each other. Our fathers were brothers and we were more like brothers than cousins ourselves."

His eyes misted, and she knew he was staring into the past, not seeing her at all, though his grip on her shoulders remained strong.

"Me, Cooper, Jake and Mac." A wistful smile curved one corner of his mouth. "I was the oldest, Mac the youngest. Not that it mattered," he admitted.

The wind kicked up again, twisting dirt into tiny tornadoes that raced across the yard in front of them.

"Mac was brilliant. Seriously smart. He was only sixteen, but he had some great ideas." Sam smiled now and Maggie felt the tension in him climb. As if talking about that last summer brought it all even closer. "That year Mac had come up with some gizmo he said would make us all rich."

"Really?" Maggie smiled up at him, trying to make this easier. "What was it?"

He smiled back at her and shook his head. "Hell if I know. Mac and Jake were big into motorcycles, though—always tinkering with some damn thing or another. And that summer the two of them said they'd come up with something that was going to improve engine performance and make us all millionaires." His smile faded slowly. "They were right. The royalties on that invention have been incredible. But Mac never lived to see them."

"Tell me what happened."

He let her go and shoved both hands through his hair as he took a step back. Distancing himself from her? Or from the memories gathering around him?

"It was a contest," he said bitterly, his mouth twisting as if even the words had a foul taste. "We took turns jumping off the ridge into the lake. We got 'points' both for how far out we were able to jump and for how long we stayed underwater before surfacing."

Maggie's stomach fisted and sympathy washed through her. She reached for him, but he shook his head.

"Just…let me get it out." He swallowed hard and

stared off into the distance again, seeing the past unroll in front of him. "It was Mac's turn. Jake had already outjumped all of us." A choked-off laugh grumbled from his throat. "Mac hated to lose. He took a running start, jumped off the ridge and landed farther out than any of us had gone before. Jake was pissed, but to win, Mac had to stay down longer than he had, too."

"Oh, God…" She knew what was coming. Knew that Mac had died that long-ago summer day and, in dying, had set his cousins on a path that had kept them from everything they'd ever cared about.

Sam kept talking as if Maggie hadn't spoken. "I was timing him. Had Jeremiah's stopwatch. Mac had been under two minutes when I started worrying."

"Two minutes? Isn't that an awfully long time?"

"Not for him. He'd done it before. But this time…" Sam shook his head. "It felt…different. Don't know why. I told Cooper we should go in after him, but Cooper wanted Mac to beat Jake, so he said to give him another few seconds. We waited. We should have gone in after him, but we waited." His eyes filled with tears that he viciously rubbed away a moment later. "Not *we*. *Me*. *I* should have gone in after him. I knew something was wrong. Knew he was in trouble. *Felt* it. But I waited."

"Sam…" Her heart ached for him. For the pain he'd carried for so long.

"I waited, stood there on the ridge *timing* him, for God's sake, while Mac was dying."

"You're being too hard on yourself. You always have been."

He snapped her a furious glare. "Weren't you listening? I *knew* he was in trouble."

"You had a bad feeling. You were a kid, too."

He brushed off her attempt at understanding and said, "I was the oldest. I should have known better. It was *stupid* to jump off that damn ridge. At two minutes and fifteen seconds, I couldn't take it anymore. I ran and jumped in. The others were right behind me. The lake water was cloudy." He squinted, as if still trying to see his cousin through the murky water. "Took us too long to find him. Took *forever.* He was lying on the bottom. We grabbed him and dragged him out. Laid him on the bank and pushed the water out of him, but it was too late. He was dead. Mac was dead."

She reached for him, taking hold of his forearm, and his tensed muscles felt like steel beneath her palms. "I'm so sorry, Sam. But it wasn't your fault."

"That's what everybody said," he told her on a sigh. "Doc Evans examined the…body. He said Mac broke his neck when he jumped in—and unconscious, he drowned. And after that nothing was ever the same again."

"You stayed away, Sam," she said, sensing somehow that he didn't want her sympathy now any more than he had before. "You made that choice. You and the others. You didn't have to. No one blamed you."

"*I* blamed me. Mac *drowned*. While we all stood there, *timing* him, he *died*."

"You're not psychic, Sam. You couldn't have known that he broke his neck."

He shook his head, refusing to hear her. Refusing to drop the burden of guilt he'd been carrying so long it had become a part of him. "I should have known he was in trouble. If I'd gone in when I first wanted to, I could have saved him."

"He broke his neck," she reminded him softly.

"He was only sixteen."

"I know…" She lifted one hand and laid her palm against his chest, feeling the thundering beat of his heart. "But does staying away from Coleville make it easier?"

"Nothing makes it easier."

"Then why stay away? Couldn't you—I don't know—honor Mac's memory by coming home? Being the doctor this town needs? By living your life and being happy?"

Hope flickered briefly in his eyes before fading away again. God, Sam would like nothing better than to agree with her. To tell her yes, he'd stay. He'd stay here in Coleville, move back to the ranch. Surround himself with everything he'd missed for so long.

But he couldn't.

He'd failed Mac.

And now he wasn't *allowed* to be happy.

She frowned up at him and he saw the disappointment in her eyes when she asked, "Do you really think Mac would want you all to be miserable for the rest of your lives? To avoid coming home to the place you all loved so much?"

"No, he wouldn't," he said softly, reaching out to run the tip of his fingers along her cheek. "But that doesn't seem to matter. Not for me. Or the others."

"So when the summer's over, you'll leave again."

He swallowed hard. "Yes."

"And not come back."

"Yes."

"No matter how far you run, Sam," she said quietly, "you'll never be able to outrun your past. I know. I've tried."

# Nine

"Mad at me, aren't you?"

Maggie turned from the chest of drawers where she was putting away the old man's clean laundry to stare at him. He looked worried. And as guilty as a child who'd stolen a cookie just before dinner.

Her heart turned over and she realized that as disappointed as she'd been in him that he'd lied to her— she was more relieved to know that he wasn't sick at all. He'd become so important to her over the last two years. This one old man had become the family she'd always longed for, and the thought of losing him had terrified her.

"Mad?" she repeated with a slow shake of her

head. "No, not now. But I *was*. When Doc Evans first told us the truth."

"I'm real sorry about that, Maggie," Jeremiah said and hung his head before glancing up at her from beneath bushy gray brows. "Didn't like lying to you, if that's any comfort."

His gray whiskers shone in the late afternoon sunlight streaming through his bedroom window. Wisps of gray hair fluttered around his head in the breeze dancing under the partially opened window. And his dark eyes glittered with the hope that he was forgiven.

Love filled her, sweet and rich, and Maggie knew she couldn't hold out against him. Smiling at him, she said, "I'm just glad you're not really sick, Jeremiah. You had me scared."

He winced and hunched his shoulders as he pushed himself off the bed and stood up. "I'm sorry about that, too, girl. It's just...I couldn't think of any other way to get my boys home."

In a weird way, she understood the desperation of his lie. But still. "You worried everyone."

"I know."

"Sam's pretty angry."

He sighed. "I figured he would be." Then, nodding, he added, "But he's *here*. That's the important thing. And he'll stay the summer. Just as the others will. They all gave me their word."

"What made you do it, Jeremiah? I mean, I know you miss them. But why now? Why *this* summer?"

He smiled again, and this time she saw that he was enjoying being secretive. "Can't tell you that yet, Maggie. I'm going to wait until all of my boys are home to spill that secret."

"You're as stubborn as Sam," she said with a slow shake of her head. Turning, she went back to the dresser and carefully stacked clean T-shirts in the top drawer.

"You like him, don't you?"

She narrowed her eyes and glanced at him over her shoulder. "Jeremiah…"

He held up both hands and grinned. "Just asking. I've been watching the two of you—and I'm not so old I can't see the sparks flare up when you're together."

She flushed and hoped he hadn't sensed just how hot those sparks had gotten. Her heartbeat quickened and heat pooled deep in her center just thinking about the single night she'd had with Sam. And it wasn't just the amazing lovemaking—it was watching him with Jeremiah, seeing him help little Katie. Seeing his tenderness and aching at his loneliness. He touched her in so many ways, but… "It doesn't matter, Jeremiah. He's still leaving."

"And you're going to let him?"

Her gaze snapped up to his. "It's not up to me, Jeremiah. You know that. Sam told me. About Mac."

The old man slumped as if someone had let the air out of his body. "It was a terrible thing, no doubt," he said, his voice a low rumble. "But it's time they all came to grips with it. Learned to let Mac go."

"I don't know if Sam can," Maggie whispered, remembering the shadows in his eyes when he'd told her the story of that summer day.

"I hope you're wrong about that, Maggie."

Hours later Sam stared out the kitchen window at Maggie's house across the yard. The summer night was clear and bright under the light of a full moon. A wind swept across the fields and rattled the leaves of the trees, sounding like a whispering crowd making bets on whether or not Sam would be able to stay away from Maggie.

Hell, even he wouldn't take that bet.

From the living room came the sound of the television, some game show with a too-enthusiastic host shouting at a contestant. Jeremiah, now that his pretense of illness was over, lay comfortably in his recliner, snoozing.

Sam frowned and shoved both hands into his jeans pockets. He'd had it out with Jeremiah before dinner, telling his grandfather just what a rotten thing he'd done by pretending to be dying. By worrying them all.

But after apologizing, Jeremiah had said in his own defense, *I'm sorry to hurt you, boy, but the day that Mac died, I didn't lose one grandson—I lost four. Can't blame me for trying to get 'em back.*

And the truth was, Sam couldn't blame him. Couldn't even be angry about being tricked into coming home. Because honestly he'd missed this ranch and that cranky old man more than he could ever say.

Opening the back door, Sam stepped out onto the porch and closed the door behind him, shutting out the drone of the television and the rumble of Jeremiah's snores. The summer night was warm, but the breeze sweeping across the open fields was cool enough. The scents of his childhood wrapped themselves around him, and he closed his eyes just to concentrate on them. Summer grass, clean, sweet air and from somewhere—probably the neighboring ranch—he caught the distinct aroma of steaks on a barbecue.

A low growl in the distance announced approaching thunder and the promise of rain sometime soon. He glanced up at the sky and watched as massive dark clouds rolled in from the coast, obliterating the moon, covering the ranch yard in deep shadow. How many storms, he wondered, had he and his cousins watched from the safety of this old porch? How many nights had they sat out here with cold sodas, watching lightning dance across the sky while they talked about girls and school and cars and every other subject so important to teenage boys? They'd all been so close. So much a part of each other.

So when Mac died, his leaving had splintered the rest of them. They hadn't known how to talk to each other anymore. There were only three of them. They were off balance. Out of sync. Like a three-legged dog trying to remember how to run, they'd stumbled and fallen and finally they'd quit trying.

A shimmer of lightning flashed behind the clouds, illuminating them briefly just before a clap of thunder rattled the window glass in the door behind him.

Sam leaned one shoulder against a porch post and shoved both hands into his jeans pockets as he shifted his gaze back to Maggie's house. It was taking everything he had in him to keep from crossing the yard, knocking on that door and begging her to let him in.

He'd been on his own for years—but he'd never been as *alone* as he was at that moment.

And for the first time in far too long, he hated it.

Across the yard Maggie's front door opened and a slice of lamplight stretched across the ground, reaching for him. She held the screen open and stepped outside. "Are you going to stay there all night?"

His heart gave one sudden hard jolt against his chest. "I was thinking about it."

She tipped her head up, glanced at the sky, then lowered her gaze to him again. "Looks like rain."

Thunder growled in the background as another flash of light shattered the dark.

"Looks like," he agreed, though he couldn't tear

his gaze from her long enough to look at the sky. She stood like a dancer, all fluid grace. Then she moved, taking another step toward the edge of her porch, letting the screen door swish shut behind her. Backlit, she looked like a dream, gilded curves and long hair loose around her shoulders.

"You'll get wet if you just stand there."

Nature's cold shower.

Not a bad idea.

But he only said, "Probably."

"It's better in here."

"But not safer," he pointed out. Though the thought of going to her, letting himself be surrounded by her warmth, was nearly enough to bring him to his knees.

"Are you so concerned with being safe?" she asked.

"I'm trying to be," Sam said. "For your sake."

She tipped her head to one side and her hair swung in a lazy arc. "And you said you're not a nice man."

"I'm not. I'm really not."

Overhead, lightning cracked and white-hot light pulsed over the yard. Thunder boomed, deafening, and the echo of it rolled through Sam until he felt his whole body shaking with it.

"I don't believe you."

"Damn it." He muttered the words as he jumped off the back porch. Frustration punched at him. Couldn't she see what it was costing him to try to do the right thing? His boots hit the dirt just as the first fat drops of warm rain splattered from the sky. He hardly noticed. His long legs carried him across the yard in a few hurried strides. He stopped at the foot of her front porch steps and stared up at her. "I'm trying like hell to stay away from you, Maggie."

She smiled. "Who asked you to?"

"*You* should be."

"See, I don't think so."

He looked up into her dark eyes while the lightning lit up the yard like a strobe light in a crowded club, and the emotions flashing in her eyes were just as wild. Just as dangerous.

"I think you're a better man than you pretend to be."

He pushed one hand through his hair, wiping the rain back and out of his eyes at the same time. "That's because you don't know me."

"Oh, I think I do," she said. "For instance, I know you volunteer with Doctors Without Borders— helping children who desperately need it."

"Because I can help them and leave," he said flatly, refusing the halo she kept trying to fit him for. "It's not noble, it's *safe*." Rain slapped at him, thunder boomed and lightning flashed. He stared up at her, rain falling into his eyes and trailing down his face like hot tears. "I do my job and then I leave. I don't hang around. Don't make friends. Don't *care*."

"Yes, you do. You care," she said stubbornly and

he wondered why in the hell she wouldn't listen. Wouldn't run. "You care more than you want to."

"You're wrong," he insisted. "I travel around the country, work different E.R.s for a couple months and then leave. I don't stay, Maggie. Not anywhere. I won't get involved again. Won't *care*. It's the only way to keep from getting my heart ripped out. Again."

She reached out to him, her fingers trailing over his cheek, wiping away the rain and smoothing his wet hair back from his face. "If you have to protect yourself, go ahead. But you don't have to protect me from you, Sam. I'm a big girl. I make my own choices."

"If you had any sense," he muttered thickly, "you'd tell me to get the hell away from you."

She smiled and shook her head. "Now, why would I do that when I so much want you to stay?"

He flinched. "I can't. Stay I mean. Don't count on that, Maggie."

She came down the steps and into his arms, wrapping her own arms around his neck and looking into his eyes. She said softly, "I meant stay *tonight,* Sam. Stay with me tonight."

The heat of her body sank into him, warming all the cold, dark places inside him. The scent of her—shampoo, soap and *woman*—filled him and Sam knew he couldn't leave. Not even for *her* sake.

He pulled her close, his gaze moving over her face like a touch. And when he couldn't stand waiting another moment, he took her mouth with his, parting her lips with his tongue, sweeping inside, tasting her, exploring her. He claimed her breath and gave her his own. He slid one hand up her spine and into her hair, threading his fingers through the thick, soft mass and holding her head still for his conquest.

She sighed and melted into him and the rain pelted them both. Thunder and lightning rattled the sky. The wind howled. And neither of them noticed. His heartbeat roared in his chest and his blood pumped fierce and wild.

He took her deeper, harder, and felt her arms tighten around his neck as she gave herself up to him. Again and again he plundered her mouth hungrily, eagerly, until finally, needing air, he tore his mouth from hers and moved to taste the length of her throat. His lips trailed heat up and down that long, slender column, and she shivered in his grasp, moaning gently and tilting her head to one side to grant him easier access.

It wasn't enough.

Would never be enough.

Groaning tightly, he pulled back long enough to scoop her into his arms. Then he stepped up onto the porch, opened the screen door and walked inside. Holding her close, he kicked the door closed and stalked across her cozy living room to the bedroom.

He knew this house as well as he knew the main

house. When he was a kid, the foreman had lived here and he and his cousins had run free through the place.

It had changed, of course, which he absently noticed as he headed for her bedroom. Soft colors on the wall, framed posters of faraway countries and, over it all, the scent of flowers and fresh coffee.

She nibbled at his neck and Sam groaned again, his body fisting, his breath laboring. He crossed the short hall and entered the only bedroom. The mattress was covered by a quilt and the edges had been turned down, as if she'd prepared it for them. He could only be grateful.

Standing her on her own two feet, he took a step back from her and yanked off his sodden T-shirt. "I need you, Maggie. Here. Now. I need you."

Her lips curved in a self-satisfied smile as she pulled her tank top up and off. She wasn't wearing a bra. His hands itched to cup her breasts. But she walked up to him and pressed herself against him, her hardened nipples branding his bare chest with twin points of heat.

He dropped his head to the curve of her neck and feasted on her smooth skin. With lips, tongue, teeth, he tasted her and felt the shivering reaction ripple through her as she sighed.

Maggie leaned in closer, needing him every bit as much as he needed her. The kiss they'd shared that afternoon had haunted her for hours. The taste of him, the feel of him, the roaring need pulsing inside her. She'd never known anything like this and she didn't care if he wasn't going to stay. Well, she cared. And wished he would change his mind. But a part of her knew that wouldn't happen. And still she had to have him.

There had been so few perfect moments in her life that she'd learned early to treasure them when they *did* show themselves. And every moment with Sam was perfect. She wanted—*needed*—to feel him inside her again. To feel his strength covering her, opening her, filling her.

And when he was gone—when he left—she would still have these moments to relive. To remember.

His hands, broad-palmed and long-fingered, stroked her spine, then slipped beneath the waistband of her shorts to cup her behind. She sucked in air, then held it as sparklers fired off in her bloodstream. She closed her eyes and concentrated on the sensations he caused. The feel of his hands on her skin—the cold sting of his belt buckle against her belly, the hard ridge of him pressed against her abdomen. Even through the thick fabric of his jeans she felt his heat, his desire, and it fired her blood until she felt as though she were burning up from the inside.

Lifting his head, he stared down into her eyes and whispered a raw confession. "I want you even more than I did the first time."

"I feel exactly the same way," Maggie admitted

and went up on her toes, despite her wobbly knees, to kiss him. Instantly he deepened that kiss, claiming her, devouring her.

He walked her backward until her knees hit the edge of the mattress. Then he laid her down on the bed and came down with her. His hands were everywhere at once. Maggie's eyes closed as she concentrated on the feel of him exploring her every line and curve. Expertly he peeled off her shorts in a matter of seconds and tossed them to the floor. Then he stood up, toed off his boots and yanked his jeans down and off to lie in a sodden heap on the old wooden floorboards.

Then he stopped.

"What?" she demanded impatiently, her body tingling, ready, eager.

"Condom. Still don't have a damn condom."

"In the drawer." She waved a hand at the bedside table and rocked her hips. "I bought some."

He grinned and yanked at the drawer knob. Grabbing up a silver foil packet, he ripped it open, sheathed himself, then came to her, still smiling. "I do like a woman who plans ahead."

His body covered hers and she lifted her hips into him, chewing at her bottom lip. "Enough talking, cowboy. Show me."

"My pleasure," he said and pushed himself into her depths.

Maggie groaned, lifted her legs to wrap them around his hips and drew him deeper, closer. He groaned, too, closing his eyes as the sweet rush of sensation poured through them, connecting them, binding them together in a surge of heat.

He dipped his head to taste her nipples, drawing and suckling her as she rocked beneath him, pulling him close and moaning as his body briefly left hers only to fill her again.

Their bodies linked. They stared into each other's eyes, and when the first shattering explosion came hurtling down on them, they held on to each other and jumped into the abyss.

# Ten

Over the next week life at the Lonergan ranch eased into a routine. Days were spent exploring the ranch Sam had known so long ago and nights were spent in Maggie's arms. He'd stopped worrying about what would happen when he left—Maggie was determined to enjoy what they had while they had it, and some of that feeling had seeped into Sam.

And now that Jeremiah's pretense was over, he and Sam spent hours exploring the ranch land together. Years had passed, but the land remained the same—with a few minor changes.

"Vegetables?" Sam asked as he parked the ranch

truck and stared out at long rows of green stretching out as far as the eye could see.

Jeremiah shrugged and squinted into the afternoon sunlight. "Cut way back on running cattle, didn't want the land laying fallow. So I rent this half of the ranch to a group of farmers for a percentage of the net profits. Dave Hemmings rents the grazing land for his dairy herd." He sighed a little and Sam turned to look at him. "I'm an old man, boy. Too much ranch to run alone."

Guilt pinged inside Sam and he tried to ignore the sour stab of it. None of the old man's sons had been interested in the ranch, instead going off to find their own paths. And his grandsons—Sam included—had made themselves scarce fifteen years ago.

Not surprising that Jeremiah would have to make adjustments in how he ran the Lonergan ranch. Still, it stung to realize how much he regretted the necessity. His gaze swept over the neatly tended fields, but in his mind he saw the ranch as it had been years ago—herds of Black Angus cattle wandering over the knee-deep grass.

But times change.

"I'm sorry," he said, still staring out at the neatly tended field of leaf lettuce. "Sorry I wasn't here to help."

Jeremiah reached over and patted Sam's shoulder. His voice gruff, he said, "Never expected you to take on the ranch, boy. It was always doctoring for you.

Will say, though, that I've missed you something terrible. Missed all of you."

"I know." He turned his head to stare at the old man who'd always been so important to him. "And I wish it could have been different. God, Jeremiah, you have no idea how many times I've wished things were different."

"It wasn't your fault, Sam," he said, tiredly. "Wasn't any of you boys' fault."

"Wish I could believe that." He took a breath, blew it out and added, "I missed you, too, you old goat."

Jeremiah's lips twitched and his bushy gray eyebrows wiggled like live caterpillars. "Well, good. Glad to hear it."

"Glad enough to tell me what's going on?" Sam asked. "Why you picked *this* summer to get us all back here?"

"Nope." He shook his head firmly. "Time enough for that once Jake and Cooper show up. Now how about we head into town? Visit Bert?"

Sam narrowed his eyes on his grandfather. "I'm not taking over Bert's practice."

"Who said anything about you?" Jeremiah demanded. "I'm talking about going to see an old friend."

"Uh-huh." Sam wasn't buying it, but he couldn't think of a reason to *not* go. So he put the truck in gear and headed off down the dirt road.

* * *

Maggie lined up all three plastic sticks on the edge of the bathroom sink and swallowed back the knot that was lodged firmly in her throat.

"Three tries," she murmured, shaking her head and staring down at the test results. "Three pluses."

She'd had to be sure. This kind of thing couldn't be trusted to just a "feeling." Though that feeling had been pretty strong. Pretty sure. She was *never* late. If there was one thing in her life that she had always been able to consistently count on, it was the fact that her cycle was as regular as clockwork.

Until this month.

She lifted her head and met her own reflected gaze in the mirror. She deliberately chose to not notice the flicker of worry in her eyes—instead she focused on the joy. All her life she'd longed for family. For someone to love. To love her.

Here at Jeremiah's ranch, she'd found her place.

And now she'd found her family.

"I'm pregnant."

Just saying the words made it all real and brought a tender smile to her face.

Laying both hands protectively against her flat abdomen, she whispered, "Don't worry about a thing, okay, little guy? You'll be okay. I promise."

Even as she said it, though, she felt a flicker of unease as she thought about telling Sam her news. He wouldn't be happy, she knew that already. He was so determined to keep his heart locked away, he would see this baby as an invitation to pain.

Turning around, she sighed and leaned back against the edge of the sink. Her brain raced with thoughts and wishes and half-baked dreams she knew didn't have a chance at becoming reality.

Maggie stared absently at the framed picture of dolphins romping in the sea with children and silently admitted a secret she'd been hiding not only from Sam—but from herself.

She loved him.

She loved Sam Lonergan.

His strength, his tenderness, his gentle touch, even his crabby streak.

She loved everything about him and knew she couldn't keep him. But at least when he left she'd have his child.

And she'd never be alone again.

The waiting room was full.

Babies wailed, harried mothers tried to cope and a tired nurse shouted out the name of the next patient, trying to be heard over the din.

And Sam's instincts were to jump in and help.

Jeremiah strode across the room toward the door leading back to Bert's office, but instead of following him, Sam stopped beside a toddler whimpering softly.

Going down on one knee, he smiled briefly at the boy's mother, then concentrated on the child watching him through wide, anxious, tear-filled eyes.

"What's your name?" Sam asked gently.

"Toby an' my 'froat hurts."

His mother smiled again and said, "He's had a fever since yesterday and I just thought it would be best to bring him in…." She glanced around the crowded waiting room and sighed.

Sam saw the fever shining in the boy's eyes but laid the heel of his palm against the child's forehead anyway. Warm but not bad. Gently he pressed his fingertips against the child's swollen glands and then ruffled light brown featherweight hair. Looking up at the boy's mother, he said, "Looks like tonsillitis. He should be fine with some children's-strength pain reliever. Just make sure he has plenty of fluids."

The woman smiled, then cocked her head to one side and asked, "I'm sorry, but you are…?"

Sam chuckled and straightened up. Not hard to figure out why she was surprised at his spur-of-the-moment diagnosis, dressed as he was in worn jeans, shabby boots and an open-throated, short-sleeved shirt. "Sam Lonergan. Don't worry. I'm an actual doctor."

"Is my 'froat all better now?" The boy's voice was shrill.

"Not yet," Sam said, "but soon." Then he

glanced at the boy's mother. "I'll tell Doc Evans you're out here and—"

She smiled, her eyes brightening even as she stood up and held out one hand. "Thank you. I'm Sally Hoover. This is my son Toby."

Sam smiled. "We've met."

"This is great," she was saying, glancing around the room as if making sure that everyone else there was listening. "You're Jeremiah's grandson, aren't you?"

"Yes…"

"I can't tell you how relieved we all are," Sally continued, rolling right over him as he tried to get in another word or two. "With Doc Evans retiring, most of us thought that we'd have to drive into Fresno to find a new doctor. Having you here is going to make everyone so happy."

Sam backed up. "No, I'm sorry, you don't understand—"

"You're the new doctor?" Another woman, holding an infant tight to her chest, stepped forward, grinning. "I'm Victoria Sanchez, and it's so nice to meet you."

"Thanks, but—"

"I'm Donna Terrino," another woman said from behind him, and Sam spun around to face her. She had twin boys of about five clinging to her legs. It was a wonder she could walk. "This is great. It's a pleasure to have you here," she said. "I can't tell you what this is going to mean to the town."

Panic clawed at Sam's throat.

As more and more of the patients in the waiting room came forward to meet him, faces blurred and names became nothing more than a buzz of conversation around him. His brain raced, his heart pounded.

He felt…trapped.

They were all looking at him as though he were a longed-for Christmas present. They wouldn't let him speak long enough to shatter their illusions, and damned if a part of him wasn't grateful. He didn't want to be here to see the disappointment on their faces. Didn't want to care that he'd be leaving the town he'd once loved in the lurch.

It wasn't his responsibility.

The welfare of the town's health care wasn't up to him.

So why then did the guilt crawling through him feel so much bigger? Stronger?

"When will you be setting up your own practice?" someone in the back of the crowd asked.

"Is he the new doctor?" a child called out.

*No*, he wanted to shout but doubted any of them would pay attention. They already had him hanging out his shingle and seeing his first patient. A yearning he hadn't quite expected darted through him, then was gone again in the next heartbeat. Just as well. It didn't matter if a part of him wished he *could* settle here, be the man they all wanted him to be.

The door into the hallway opened up behind him and Sam turned to try to make a break for it. He took one step though and stopped dead.

"Sam?" The big man coming through the door tightened his grip on the little girl at his side and marched toward Sam with long, measured strides.

Memories kicked in and Sam momentarily forgot about looking for the fastest way out. "Mike? Mike Haney?"

"Damn straight," the big man said, grinning. "Good to see you, man," he added. "It's been way too long. I heard you were back in town. Cooper and Jake here, too?"

"Not yet," Sam said, ignoring the chattering mothers and crying babies surrounding them. Mike Haney had been a good friend years ago. He was only one of the people in Coleville that Sam had missed. "Soon, though."

"This is my daughter," Mike was saying, tugging a blond girl out from behind him.

"Your *daughter?*" Hard to believe. In Sam's mind, Mike Haney and all of his other friends were still seventeen years old. Still swiping beers from their fathers' refrigerators to meet out at the lake and lie to each other about their conquests.

Proudly Mike said, "We—me and Barb—you remember Barb?"

"Sure," Sam said, still bemused by the blond-haired cutie half hiding behind her father. Then it clicked. "You and Barb got married?"

"Sure did—and this little beauty is our youngest. I've got three girls now."

"Three…"

"And every one of 'em's a heartbreaker. How about you?" Mike asked, smiling. "Wife and kids?"

"No," Sam said and suddenly felt the punch of all that he'd missed by avoiding any relationship that looked like it might grow into something important. "No family."

"Oh, well…" Mike hemmed and hawed for a moment or two, then tugged his daughter out to say hello. "Want you to meet Maxie—" He paused and added, "We named her after Mac. Maxie, honey, say hi to Dr. Sam. He's an old friend of your daddy's."

Sam stared into wide blue eyes and tried to find a smile. But the sudden thickening in his throat made it damn near impossible. Mac. The reason he'd stayed away so long. The reason he had to leave again. Soon.

"She's beautiful," Sam finally managed to say, then edged past his old friend, heading for the relative sanctuary of Bert's office. The waiting room was still filled with excited chatter. The little blond girl gave him a finger wave. "It was good to see you again, Mike."

The big man nodded, oblivious to Sam's eager

escape. "You let me know when Jake and Cooper hit town. We'll get together. Talk about old times."

"Right. Good idea." *Never gonna happen*, he thought. No way did he want to sit down and reminisce.

And he was pretty sure both Jake and Cooper would feel the same way.

Maggie waited.

All through dinner, through doing the dishes, cleaning the kitchen and even through the evening news. She held her secret close and waited until Jeremiah had fallen asleep in front of the television and she and Sam were alone.

And now that they were, she wasn't at all sure how to say what had to be said.

He sat at the kitchen table, the ranch accounting books laid out in front of him. Turning from the sink, she stared at him for a long minute and let the knots in her stomach slowly tighten.

His dark hair fell across his forehead as he bent his head to look at a row of figures. He trailed his long fingers down the line of numbers slowly as he checked and rechecked the totals at the bottom. Leaning to one side, he flipped through a stack of papers and sifted through them until he found the one he was looking for.

The quiet drone of the television played in the background, and outside, the wind tapped against the windows with chilly fingers.

Maggie sighed, dried her hands on the dish towel, then carefully hooked it over the handle on the oven door to dry. This wasn't going to get any easier. Best, she thought, to just say it and say it fast.

"Sam?"

"Hmm?" He didn't even look up. Just scribbled a notation on a legal-size yellow pad of paper to his right.

"I need to talk to you."

"Sure," he said, making another note.

"It's important."

The hesitant tone of her voice must have gotten through to him because he set his pencil down and swiveled his head to look at her. Frowning slightly, he asked, "Something wrong?"

"No," she said, though she was forced to admit that *he* might see things a little differently. What was to her a gift, Sam would no doubt consider a trap. A trap she had no intention of springing on him. "At least," she amended slightly, "*I* don't consider it a problem."

He gave her a brief smile. "Now I'm intrigued." Standing up, he crossed the room to her. Glancing into the living room to make sure Jeremiah was still sleeping in his recliner, he looked back at Maggie. "What's going on?"

She drew a deep breath, blew it out in a long rush and then tried a smile of her own. "I've been practicing all day just how to tell you this and now that I'm here—"

He cupped her face in his palms. "Just say it, Maggie."

"Right." She lifted her hands to cover his. A flutter of warmth filled Maggie as she looked up into his dark eyes. Joy and misery twisted inside her as she realized that if things had been different, this moment might have been a celebration.

She wanted to tell him how much she loved him. How much she would *always* love him. But she knew that confession wouldn't be any more welcome than the one she was about to make.

The truth was undeniable, though. She loved a man who had no intention of loving her in return. A man whose only thought was to leave as quickly as he could. Her heart ached at the knowledge of all they might have had together, all they would never share.

"You're starting to worry me, Maggie," he said, his voice a low hush of sound barely discernable over the rumble of the TV.

"Don't," she said, shaking her head. "Don't worry about me. I'm fine. Better than fine."

It didn't matter, she realized suddenly. Didn't matter if he would never love her. It was enough that *she* loved.

"Let's go outside," she said, stepping away from him and heading for the back door. She didn't want to tell him here—with Jeremiah snoring in the other room.

He followed her, and once outside, Maggie kept

walking until she was standing in the middle of the yard, with the pale wash of moonlight covering her. He stopped alongside her and said, "Okay, we're outside. Now tell me."

"I'm going to," she said and swallowed hard. "But before I do, I want you to know I don't expect anything from you. I'm only telling you because it's the right thing to do."

"Maggie…"

"I'm pregnant."

# Eleven

Sam felt like he'd been hit over the head.

*Pregnant?*

He scraped one hand across his face and tried to think of something—hell, *anything*—to say. But it was impossible with the flurry of thoughts racing through his mind. A *baby*. It felt as though a cold fist was squeezing his heart, and damned if that thought didn't make him ashamed.

He'd made a child with Maggie. Whether he'd meant to or not, the deed was done.

"You don't have to say anything," Maggie told him quickly.

He blew out a breath as his gaze fixed on her.

Moonlight draped over her like a pale cloak, and her eyes shone with it—that and a joy he hadn't noticed before. Clearly she was pleased about this pregnancy.

He wished he could be.

Instead fear grabbed the base of his throat and held on tight. Not something he wanted to admit to. Not even to himself. But it was there.

"How long have you known?" he finally managed to ask.

"Since this morning," she said, reaching out to lay one hand on his forearm. "Sam, I know this isn't something you wanted, but I'm *glad* about it. Believe me."

"I can see that." Her smile wasn't forced, but there was concern now flickering in her eyes. Concern for *him*.

"I don't expect anything from you, Sam," she said and lifted her chin proudly. "I only told you because it was the right thing to do. You have a right to know that you're going to be a father."

"God. A father." A part of him hungered for it. For the rush of expectation. For the simple pleasure of having a child. A home. And a woman like Maggie to love.

"You don't have to look so spooked," she said, forcing a smile that didn't reach her eyes. "It's not like I'm about to go into labor or anything."

"I know, it's just—"

The wind whipped past them, lifting her hair into a tangle of dark strands around her head. She pushed them out of her face and kept her gaze locked with his. "I want you to know you don't have to worry about me—or the baby. I'll take good care of him—her—it."

"I know that." He nodded while thoughts and plans ran wildly through his mind. Maggie was smart, capable, funny. She could handle anything. She'd proved that just by living her life. As a kid, she'd been given a hard road. But she'd made herself the life she'd always wanted. He had no doubt at all that she could care for their child just as well.

But she shouldn't have to.

Every instinct he possessed was telling him what to do. What to say next. "I can't let you do this alone, Maggie. This baby is my responsibility, too."

Her eyes narrowed. "Meaning…?"

*"Meaning,"* he said, straightening his spine and accepting his duty even as he inwardly worried about it, "I want you to marry me."

She staggered back a step from him, looking at him as though he'd grown another head. Safe to say he'd surprised her. Well, he'd surprised the hell out of himself, too.

*"What?"*

"You heard me. We should get married. Like you said before, it's the right thing to do." It was easier to say the second time. What did that mean? He didn't have time to search for answers. "It's my child, too, Maggie. It deserves to have its father."

The surprise etched on her features faded into sorrow as she shook her head slowly. "Oh, Sam. If I thought that was what you really wanted, I'd be so happy."

"It *is*," he said and wondered briefly if he was trying to convince her or himself.

"No," she said and unshed tears glimmered in her eyes. When she spoke again, her voice broke, but she lifted her chin as if trying to gather the strength she needed. "It's not. You don't want roots. You don't want love. You don't want me—or this baby."

"Maggie—"

"Don't, Sam," she said and took a step toward him. "Don't say something you don't really mean."

In the soft light of the moon he read regret and disappointment and *understanding* in her eyes. It almost killed him.

"We both know," she continued gently, "that if you stayed, you'd never be happy. Eventually you'd resent me and even the baby for trying to hold you."

Hard to argue with the simple truth, but God, he wanted to. Wanted to be a different man. Wanted to *feel* differently. But how could he?

"I want to say you're wrong," he said, "but I just don't know. For fifteen years," he whispered, choking the words out through a strangled throat, "I've been running from the demons chasing me. I loved Mac and I failed him and he *died*. That's something I can't change. And if I loved you and our baby and failed you the same way, I don't think I could stand it."

A small, sad smile curved her mouth as she reached up and cupped his cheek in her palm. "And that's why I can't marry you, Sam. Even though I love you."

He felt the punch of those words as he would have a fist to the midsection. Everything in him wanted to grab her, pull her close and hang on. To savor the words he'd never thought to hear. Never thought to *want* to hear. But the look on her face warned him to keep still.

"Yes, I love you. But I can't marry you, Sam, because I want our baby to be raised with love, not fear. To feel faith, not despair."

He covered her hand with one of his own and held on as if the touch meant his life. "I wish it could be different." And even while he said it, he knew the words were useless. Knew that saying it, *wanting* it, didn't make it so.

"That's the sad part," Maggie said, slipping her hand from his. "It *could* be different. You just won't let it be."

"It's not that simple."

"Yes, it is," she said. "You say you've been running from the demons chasing you—but that's not true, either."

"What?"

"It's not demons chasing you, Sam," she said, her voice soft and filled with pain. "It's only *Mac*. And he loves you."

His features tightened and Maggie *felt* him emotionally withdraw. She wanted to cry but knew it wouldn't help. She wanted to *reach* him and knew that though he was standing right in front of her, he was further away from her than ever.

And just like that, a piece of her heart died. Swallowing back the tears gathering in her throat, she said only, "I don't want a husband who thinks it's his *duty* to marry me."

"Maggie…"

"I think it's best if you leave at the end of summer, just as you planned. I don't want you to be a part of the baby's life."

He swayed as if she'd physically struck him. "It's my baby, too, Maggie."

"Yes, but you don't want him. *I* do."

"Damn it, Maggie—"

Whatever else he might have said was forgotten as a sweep of headlights sliced across the darkened yard, flashing briefly in Maggie's eyes. She turned her head and squinted at the SUV pulling into the yard and parking just a few feet from them.

The lights blinked into darkness and the engine was cut off. The driver's-side door opened and a tall man with broad shoulders and hair as dark as Sam's stepped out and walked toward them.

"Looks like I'm interrupting something," the man said, glancing from Maggie to Sam and back again. "My timing always sucked."

"Cooper," Sam said, walking toward him and holding out one hand. They shook hands, then Sam turned and said, "Cooper, this is Maggie Collins. She's…Jeremiah's housekeeper."

She winced inwardly at the distance in Sam's voice but told herself it was just as well that Cooper had arrived to stop their conversation. They only would have ended up going around and around in a never-ending cycle of pain.

"Nice to meet you," she managed to say, then tore her gaze from Cooper Lonergan to focus on Sam again. "I'll see you in the morning."

"Maggie…"

She backed up a step or two, said, "G'night, Sam. Cooper." Then she turned and hurried across the moonlit yard to her own house. Stepping inside, she closed the door behind her and leaned back against it.

Knees weak, heart breaking, she closed her eyes and gave herself up to the pain.

"So you want to tell me what's going on here?" Cooper asked after Jeremiah had gone off to bed. "I still can't believe he tricked all of us."

"Yeah, surprised the hell out of me, too." Sam took a couple of beers from the refrigerator, handed one to his cousin and motioned him down into a chair. Twisting off the cap, he took a long pull of the icy beverage, relishing the taste of the cold froth. Swallowing, he took a seat himself and explained everything he knew about Jeremiah and his pretense of dying.

When he was finished, Cooper laughed shortly and took a drink of his beer. "I'll give him this...I'm so glad he's *not* dying, I'm not even mad at him."

"Same goes."

"Who would have guessed that the old man could be that sneaky? Hell, that creative?"

Smiling wryly, Sam acknowledged, "Must run in the family." Cooper Lonergan's horror novels had been giving Americans nightmares for the last five years. Each of his books was just a little creepier than the last. And the fact that Cooper was pretty much a recluse only added to his appeal.

Leaning back in his seat, Sam cradled his beer bottle between his palms and said, "I read your latest book."

"Yeah?" Cooper asked. "What'd you think?"

"Spooky," he admitted. "Just like all the others."

A tired smile crossed Cooper's face briefly. "Thanks." He looked around the familiar room and sighed a little. "Man, nothing here has changed at all. Like stepping into a time warp or something."

"Saw Mike Haney in town," Sam offered.

"No kidding?" Cooper chuckled, remembering. "How is he?"

"Married to Barb Hawkins with three little girls."

"Man," Cooper said after another long drink. "We're old."

Sam stared across the table at the cousin he hadn't seen since they were kids. Except for getting taller and broader in the shoulders, Cooper looked pretty much the same as he had all those years ago. And in his dark Lonergan eyes Sam recognized the same shadows he faced every morning when he looked in a mirror.

Mac's death had affected them all.

"So want to tell me about the housekeeper?"

Sam stiffened, took a drink of beer and asked, "Tell you what?"

Cooper chuckled. "Don't get so defensive. It just looked like you two were talking about something…*important*."

Setting his beer on the table, Sam stood up, walked across the kitchen to the pantry and yanked the door open. Grabbing up a plastic container filled with cookies, he opened it and walked back to the table. He took a couple for himself, then shoved the tub toward Cooper.

"What kind?"

"Chocolate chip."

"With *beer?*" Cooper asked.

"Something wrong with that?" Sam demanded,

taking a bite and then washing it down with another drink of beer.

"Not a thing." Taking a bite, Cooper chewed and stared at the cookie as if it were made of gold. "These are amazing."

"Yeah." Sam grumbled the word and thought about how good Maggie had looked yesterday while she'd been baking these cookies. She'd had flour on her nose and her hair in a crooked ponytail and she'd danced a quick two-step in time with country music streaming from the radio. He'd had a hell of a time refraining from throwing her onto the floor and burying himself inside her.

Every move she made touched him like nothing else ever had. Every one of her smiles lit up his insides. Her touch was silk. Her taste intoxicating.

He wanted her with every breath.

"Hell," Cooper said, leaning forward to grab a handful of cookies from the tub, "is she married?"

*"Why?"* One word. Snarled.

"Whoa," Cooper said, holding up both cookie-filled hands in mock surrender. "Don't shoot. I was just asking."

Sam blew out a breath. "Sorry."

"So she's spoken for, then?"

"Leave it alone, will ya, Cooper?"

"Right." A couple of long minutes passed before he spoke again, and when he did, it was to offer a change of subject—for which Sam was grateful. "If Jeremiah's not dying, why *are* we here?"

"He won't say," Sam told him. "Not until we're all here. Have you heard anything from Jake?"

"I talked to him right after we got the news about Jeremiah. Said he'd get here as soon as he could. But he had some things to wrap up where he was first."

"Spain?"

Cooper shrugged. "You know Jake. He'll go anywhere for a race."

The night crouched outside the brightly lit kitchen and the wind began to whisper at the windowpanes. The old house was quiet but for the few creaks and groans it made as it settled, like an ancient woman lowering herself into a chair.

"It *is* good to see you," Sam said.

"You, too. We never should have let it go so long. I've missed you guys."

"Me, too." Sam picked at the damp label on the beer bottle. His cousins had once been the best part of his life. Losing all of them had cost him more than he wanted to think about.

Silence stretched out until all they heard was the ticking of the clock, like a heartbeat, measuring time. Then finally setting his unfinished beer on the table, Connor stood up and said, "I'd better get going."

"You sure you don't want to stay here?"

"I'm sure. I mean, I'm glad to see you. And

Jeremiah. But the memories are a little thick in this old house."

Sam couldn't argue with that one.

"Besides," he said, picking up his long black coat off the back of a kitchen chair, "I've got to work while I'm here, and with all of us staying here, that'll never happen."

Sam nodded and followed his cousin as he walked out of the kitchen. "Can't believe you rented the Hollis place," he said. "People still say it's haunted."

Cooper stopped, one hand on the car door, and grinned at his cousin. "Why the hell do you think I picked that place? What better house for a horror writer to live in for the summer?"

"Right."

"I'll see you tomorrow."

Sam nodded and lifted one hand as Cooper steered his rental car out of the yard and headed for the main road.

When the grumble of the car's engine had died away and the only sound was that of leaves being pushed along the dirt by the wind, Sam turned to look at Maggie's house. One light was burning—in her bedroom.

He wanted to go to her. Hold her and feel her warmth wrap itself around him. But he doubted she felt like seeing him at the moment. Sam shoved his hands into his back pockets and kept his gaze fixed on that slice of golden light framed in her bedroom window.

He pictured her there, in her bed, under the flowered quilt, and he wondered what she was thinking. Feeling.

Did she feel as empty as he did?

Was she lonely?

Or was the child growing within her enough to keep the shadows at bay?

# Twelve

Over the next few days Jeremiah seemed to get ten years younger. His smile was broader, his eyes brighter and his laugh just a little louder.

Sam watched the older man and felt the sharp teeth of guilt take another bite out of him. He'd stayed away for his own selfish reasons but had never considered that he was punishing his family, too.

He hadn't only avoided the Lonergan ranch and his grandfather, he'd also managed to ignore his parents in his own need to keep moving. To keep running from the shadows chasing him.

And now it was too late to make it up to them. Both of his parents had died five years ago in a small-plane crash. The old man's other three sons were also gone now. Accidents, mostly. As if the Lonergan family were cursed. The only family he had left now were his cousins and grandfather.

He was only just realizing how important they were to him. How important *living* was to him.

All because of Maggie.

Shaking his head, he pulled the worn brown leather work gloves off his hands, tucked them in the waistband of his jeans, then pulled off his T-shirt. The morning sun was already heating up, and sweat streamed down his chest and back.

It felt good.

Good to be standing still rather than running.

Good to be working on a place that still held such a large part of his heart.

His gaze swept the yard and the surrounding fields as he tossed his damp shirt across the closest fence post. In the last few weeks this place had gotten to him again, as it had when he was a kid. And the thought of leaving was more painful than he'd expected.

But that probably had more to do with *who* he'd be leaving this time. Slowly he shifted his gaze to the small house where Maggie lived. She wasn't home. He knew that. And yet…something of her remained even when she was gone.

For a few weeks he'd found peace in her arms.

He'd found solace and comfort and a sense of *homecoming* that he'd never known before. Yet even while he enjoyed those feelings, they terrified him. Because he couldn't stay. Couldn't be what she wanted—*needed*.

Could he?

"How can one man have so many questions and so few answers?" he muttered, pushing his hair back from his face and tipping his head back. He stared up at the brilliant blue sky shimmering with the heat of the sun. He felt the sunlight on his face, the heat slipping into him as his skin baked.

And still he felt cold.

Right down to his bones.

The worst of it was he had the distinct feeling that it was all his own damn fault.

A car's engine grumbled into the silence, and Sam turned, hoping that Jeremiah and Cooper were back from the homecoming tour of Coleville the old man had insisted on. God knew, Sam was tired of his own company. Too much time to think gave a man way too much room for self-reflection.

But it wasn't Cooper's rented SUV roaring into the yard. It was the ranch truck, with Maggie at the wheel.

Instantly Sam's heartbeat quickened and his mouth went dry. Sunlight glanced off the windshield, throwing a wide enough glare that he couldn't see her. Strangely enough, though, that didn't seem to matter. Just knowing she was close had his body tightening and his long-suppressed emotions racing.

She opened the truck door and climbed down, tossing her hair back over her shoulder as she glanced at him. "Hello, Sam."

Her smile was soft and sad and tugged at the corners of his heart. God, he missed her. Missed being with her. Missed laughing with her, talking with her.

And when he left her, he didn't know how he'd make it without her.

"Is Jeremiah back yet?" she asked, closing the door and reaching over the side of the truck for the sacks of groceries in the flatbed.

"No," Sam said ,already heading for her.

"I thought I'd make a chocolate cake—a *celebration* since the two of you are here." She went up on her toes, grabbed two plastic sacks and started to lift them.

"Don't," Sam said, stepping up to brush her hands away and grab the bags himself. Shooting her a quick warning look, he said, "You shouldn't be lifting heavy things. Not now."

She smiled up at him. "I'm fine, Sam. The baby's fine. And I can carry groceries myself."

Stung, he paid no attention and gathered up the bags anyway, lifting them over the edge of the truck's side before looking at her again. "You're not going to. Not while I'm here."

Something flickered in her eyes and her smile faded. "I'll have to do it when you leave."

A cold fist tightened around his heart and gave it a squeeze that sent pain shooting through him. "I'm not gone yet," he reminded her.

"Okay, then. Just set them on the kitchen counter." She waved a hand at the main house and then led the way. She opened the back door and held it so he could go in first, and as he set the bags down, she started unloading them.

"I can do that, too," he said, suddenly needing to help. To do what he could, *while* he could.

She set a box of cake mix onto the counter and looked up at him. "Sam, I know you're only trying to be nice, but—"

"Maggie, it's important to me to…*help*." Damn, that sounded pretty lame, even to him. Help? He was going to help the mother of his child unload groceries now and then leave her completely in another couple of months? Yeah. Great plan.

She sighed and reached up to him, touching him for the first time in days. Her fingertips against his cheek felt cool and soft and more wonderful than anything else he'd ever experienced. God, he'd missed her touch.

And just when he was giving himself up to the sweet rush of sensation, she let her hand drop again. He tried not to notice just how empty he felt.

"Sam, I can't do this," she said softly, her eyes glimmering with a sheen of tears she determinedly refused to allow to fall. "I can't…be *close* to you and not love you."

"Maggie—"

She lifted one hand to quiet him. "And I can't love you and think about you leaving. I'm sorry. I really am. But if you want to help me, then please… just give me some space."

A flush of remorse and shame swept through him and Sam took a step back from her, though that one small action cost him. It felt as though dozens of knives were slicing off tiny sections of his heart, whittling it down to a cold, hard stone that would be with him for the rest of his life.

But this wasn't about him. "You're right. I'll, uh, go back out and finish fixing the fence." He turned for the back door and stopped, one hand on the knob. "Just…do me a favor and don't lift anything heavy."

She forced a smile that looked as empty as he felt. "I won't."

"Thanks. I'll be out—" He broke off when the phone rang and Maggie stepped to one side to snatch the receiver off the wall hook.

"Lonergan ranch," she said, fingering the old phone's twisted yellow cord. "Hi, Susan. What's—oh. Okay, I'll tell him. Yes," she said, glancing at Sam, "he's right here. Okay, tell Katie not to worry."

When she hung up, Sam asked, "What's wrong?"

"That was Susan Bateman. Their dog's in labor and little Katie's terrified that something 'bad' will happen. She wants *you* to come and help."

"Me?" Sam laughed shortly and then frowned. "Katie knows I'm a people doctor, right?"

"Yes," Maggie said, "but she's a little girl who loves her dog. She's scared. And she trusts you."

Trust.

A heavy burden.

Especially to a man who kept trying to step back from people and all of their expectations.

Maggie sensed his withdrawal and wanted to cry. But then, since finding out she was pregnant, she'd done a lot of crying. It shouldn't be this hard, she thought. Being in love, having a child…she should be *happy*. Celebrating the wonder of it all.

Instead she was already in mourning for the loss of the man who couldn't—or *wouldn't*—see what was right in front of him.

"You said you wanted to help me," she said softly, watching his eyes, seeing the wariness and sighing for it. "If you really mean that, then go help Katie."

His jaw worked as if he were chewing on words that tasted bitter. Finally, though, he nodded. "All right. I'll be back later."

Then he was gone, and Maggie leaned against

the kitchen counter wishing she could change things. Wishing he could see that they belonged together. The three of them.

The dog wasn't interested in his help.

A pale yellow golden retriever, she gave Sam a look that clearly said, *If you'll just keep out of my way, I'll be done in a bit.*

So he did. Sitting with Katie, Sam watched as the fifth puppy pushed itself into the world, then wriggled blindly until it found its way to its mother's side.

"Does it hurt?" Katie asked, keeping a viselike grip on his index finger.

"A little," he said, but added quickly, pointing at the dog lying on a bed of blankets, "but Duchess doesn't seem to mind, does she?"

"No." Katie scooted around to sit on Sam's lap. "Look, another one!"

Sure enough, a sixth puppy was born, and after a few minutes numbers seven and eight made their appearance. Soon all of the puppies were cleaned up to their mother's satisfaction and happily nursing while Duchess took a well-deserved nap.

"Mommy, they're all here," Katie called out.

Susan Bateman poked her head into the service-porch area and gave Sam a smile. "Thanks for coming over. She was so worried."

"It's not a problem," he said.

"You can have a puppy if you want," Katie said, tipping her head back so she could look at him. "Jeremiah wants one, and you could have one, too."

"Oh, honey," Susan said quickly, giving Sam an apologetic smile. "Dr. Sam's not going to be staying here. And he doesn't really have a home, so he couldn't have a dog with him."

He frowned a little, not much liking the explanation, but what could he say? She was right.

"You don't have a house?"

"No," he started to say.

"He's a busy man," Susan said for him. "He works all over the world."

"But you don't hafta," Katie said, leaning back into him and giving his hand a pat. "You could stay 'n' have a dog 'n' a house 'n' a little girl for me to play wif 'n'—"

"Katie…" Her mother sounded tired but amused. "Why don't you go upstairs, wash your hands for lunch."

"Ooookaaaaayyy…" Clearly disgusted, Katie did as she was told.

Once she was gone, Susan shrugged and said, "Thanks for coming over. It meant a lot to Katie."

"No problem," he said, standing up and brushing his palms together. "Happy to help."

She didn't look as if she believed him, but she

smiled anyway. "Some people think I spoil Katie, I know, but it's hard not to."

"She's an only child?"

"Actually, no," she said softly. "We had two children. But our son, Jacob, died two years ago."

Her quiet voice, the simple words, shook him hard.

"I don't know what to say," he said helplessly.

"It's okay. No reason why you should. Come with me, I want to show you something." She gave him a smile and led the way into the living room. Sunlight slashed through a wide bay window to lay across over-stuffed furniture and a faded braided rug on the gleaming wood floor. It was a big room, cozily crowded with kids' toys, magazines spread across a wide coffee table and several books stacked on an end table.

Susan walked to the far wall, where dozens of framed snapshots and collages of family pictures cluttered the wall with smiling faces. There, she showed him a studio portrait of a laughing boy about three years old with pale blond hair and shining blue eyes just like his sister's. "That's Jacob."

"He's beautiful." Sam slanted her a look and felt his heart break a little to know that child had died. Looking back at the child who would forever be three years old. "What happened?"

She sighed, folded her arms across her chest and said simply, "When we moved in here, we'd planned to put in a fence out front. But we hadn't gotten around to it yet." Her voice went faint, distant. "We got *busy*." She shook herself and added, "Jacob chased a ball into the street. The driver of the car never saw him."

*God.* "I'm so sorry."

"So were we," she said quietly and turned to look at him as she took a long, deep breath to steady herself. "It took a long time, but life finally goes on anyway. We still have our memories of Jacob. And we have Katie and—" she patted her flat abdomen, "number three is on his way."

Even after experiencing something no parent should have to live through, she'd found a way to go on. To try again. Touched by her courage, Sam asked, "How do you get past the pain?"

"You don't," she said. "You just learn to live with it. But you know that already. Jeremiah's told me about your cousin Mac."

Some of us live with it, Sam thought, as Susan left to check on Katie, and some of us run from it. It shamed him to admit that this woman showed more quiet courage every day of her life than he'd been able to find in the last fifteen years.

And in the next instant his world suddenly came into focus. Heart pounding, eyes stinging, throat tight, he finally *got it*. Finally understood that running wasn't healing. That hiding from pain didn't protect you. That unless he found a way to *really* live again, he was just as dead as Mac.

* * *

"I'm sorry, Mac," Sam said, staring out over the dark, still water of the lake. Strange as it seemed, he could have sworn that he *felt* Mac's presence. And he was grateful for it. "Sorry I let you down that day. Sorry it took me so long to come back here."

The wind kicked up and ripples spun across the surface of the lake, spreading out from edge to edge in a silent, inexorable march.

"I still miss you. Every damn day." He bent down, picked up a rock and tossed it high and far, watching it until it splashed down in the center of the water and quickly sank beneath the surface. "But I think I'm finally going to be okay. I just…wanted you to know that."

Then he stood in the silence, and for the first time since that summer day so long ago, he felt…*alive*.


A knock on her door startled Maggie enough that she spilled her hot tea down the front of her pale green shirt. Glancing at the door, she fought down a surge of excitement and told herself to get a grip.

Sam hadn't come to her since the day she'd told him about the baby. And that was the way she wanted it.

Right?

Muttering under her breath, she set her mug down on the coffee table and stood up. She crossed the room, opened the door and stared up at Sam.

But this was a *different* Sam than the man she'd seen a few hours ago. This man's eyes were alive with joy, with hope, and she felt a quick jolt of something like hope herself.

"Sam?"

"Can I come in, Maggie?" Both of his hands were braced on the doorjamb as if he were actually holding himself back from charging into the room.

"I don't know—" Hope was there, but she couldn't let herself believe. Couldn't set herself up for disappointment.

"Please, Maggie. There's so much I want to tell you—*ask* you."

Chills swept up and down her spine and she swallowed hard as she followed her instincts. Stepping back, she waved him inside. He strode in with a few long steps that carried him to the center of the room. Then he turned to look at her.

"Maggie, I'm an idiot."

"Okay…" She closed the door quietly and waited, afraid to believe. Afraid to wish.

He pushed both hands through his hair, then let his hands drop to his sides. "Something clicked for me today."

"What?"

"You. Us. The baby." He laughed and threw his hands wide. "*Life*."

Frowning, she stepped away from the door and walked a few steps closer to him. "What're you talking about, Sam?"

"I love you."

She staggered and slapped one hand to her chest as if she could hold her foolishly thumping heart in place. "What?"

"I *love* you, Maggie," he repeated and came toward her. "I think I have from the first time I saw you. I was just too stupid—or too *scared*—to realize it. To let myself believe in it."

"Sam, I don't know what to say…." *Oh, God,* she prayed silently, *please let him mean this.*

"Don't say anything. Let me talk. Let me tell you what you mean to me." He came to her, cupped her face between his palms and stared down into her eyes. "You reminded me what it was like to live again, Maggie. You laughed with me, argued with me. You showed me that life without love isn't life at all."

"Sam…" Her voice broke and she blinked away tears that were blinding her. She didn't want to miss this. Didn't want to be blinded to the emotions flashing in his eyes.

"I've spent fifteen years running," he said, his fingers spearing through her hair as his gaze moved over her features slowly, like a lover's touch. "I've hidden away from everything and everyone I loved. I lost time with people who were important to me. Time I can *never* get back. I clung to guilt because I thought I wasn't allowed to be happy. I buried my feelings because to care about someone meant risking that horrific pain again."

She reached up and touched his cheek, felt the scrape of his whiskers against her palm and smiled when he turned his face into her touch and kissed the heart of her hand.

"But, Maggie, today I realized that *not* risking love brings its own kind of pain." He pulled her closer and watched her eyes. "I've been alone and empty. I don't want to be alone anymore, Maggie. I want to love you. I want to *be* loved by you. I want to raise our baby—and all the other babies we'll have together."

"All?" she managed to squeak.

"*All*," he said with a wild laugh. "Let's have a dozen."

"Sam…"

"I'm ready to risk it all again, Maggie. I'm ready to have faith. To believe. And what I believe in is *you*."

Everything in her went warm and gooey. She felt as though if he let go of her, she might just ooze into a puddle on the floor. It was more. So much more than she'd hoped for—prayed for. "Oh, Sam, I—"

He talked right over her, his excitement coloring his voice. "I already talked to Doc Evans. I'm going to take over his practice in town—"

"You are?" Eyes wide, she grinned, overwhelmed by him, by the knowledge of the future they were going to share after all.

"But if it's okay with you, I'd like to live *here*. At the ranch. Jeremiah's getting up there and he could use the help, and damn it, I want my family back. I want my roots. This place."

Maggie laughed through her tears. "Of *course* it's okay with me. This is my home. I love it here. I love Jeremiah."

"And me?" he asked breathlessly. "Please tell me you still love me, Maggie. Please tell me I haven't waited too long."

"I love you, Sam," she said, her heart in her voice, her tears blinding her completely. But it didn't matter now. Because she knew she'd be able to see him every day. She'd always be able to see the light of love in his eyes. "I'll *always* love you."

"Then you'll marry me?" he asked and sounded a little nervous about it.

"Yes, I'll marry you," she whispered and felt her heart fill to bursting. "And I swear I will love you forever."

As he pulled her in for a kiss, he whispered, "That may not be long enough, Maggie. Not nearly long enough."

\* \* \* \* \*

# THE SINS OF HIS PAST

by
Roxanne St Claire

This book is dedicated to the gang who gathers at our field of dreams every weekend. From my side of the chain-link fence, I'm often reminded that it's not whether you win or lose, but how incredibly cute you look playing the game. Special love to the coach I married, the shortstop who takes my breath away and the littlest cheerleader by my side.

## ROXANNE ST CLAIRE

is an award-winning, national bestselling author who began writing romance in 1999 after nearly two decades as a public relations and marketing executive. Walking away from the corporate world to write fiction is one of the most rewarding accomplishments in her life. The others are her marriage to a real-life alpha hero and the joys of raising two young children. In addition to contemporary romance, Roxanne writes romantic suspense and women's fiction. Her work has been critically acclaimed and nominated for multiple national awards, including the prestigious RITA® Award from the Romance Writers of America, the National Readers' Choice Award, the Award of Excellence and the Bookseller's Best Award. She loves to hear from readers through e-mail at roxannestc@aol.com and snail mail, care of the Space Coast Authors of Romance, PO Box 410787, Melbourne, Florida 32941, USA. Visit her website at www.roxannestclaire.com to win books and prizes!

Dear Reader,

When I'm not writing about dynamic women and the alpha heroes who torment and delight them, you can find me on the wrong side of a chain-link fence. I'm a "baseball mum" and I've spent the better part of my nights and weekends observing a sport many think is a metaphor for life. Certainly, few things are as compelling as the face of a young boy rounding third base and heading straight for home. Although, sometimes, the umpire calls him out and then there's heartbreak all around.

That's exactly what inspired me to write a book with a baseball hero. Not just because those athletes are so big and cute and cool. (Well, partly.) But there's something inspiring and vulnerable about those boys of summer, and Deuce Monroe is no different. When he heads for home, he expects to be the game-winning hero. Instead, he runs smack into the sins of his past…in the form of a smart and sassy woman who's standing directly in the way of the one thing he wants most.

I had a blast writing *The Sins of His Past* – like any close game, it's full of hope, heartache and, of course, a grand-slam love affair. I hope it keeps you enthralled.

Roxanne St Claire
aka "Dante's Mum"

# One

Only once before could Deuce Monroe remember being speechless. When he'd met Yaz. He'd shaken the great man's hand and tried to utter a word, but he'd been rendered mute in the presence of his hero, Carl Yastrzemski.

But standing in the warm April sunshine on the main drag in Rockingham, Massachusetts, staring at a building that had once been as familiar to him as his home field pitcher's mound, he was damn near dumbstruck.

*Where was Monroe's?*

He peered at the sign over the door. Well, it *said* Monroe's. With no capital *M* and a sketch of a laptop computer and a coffee mug next to it. But the whole place just seemed like Monroe's on steroids. In addition to taking up way more space than he remembered, the clapboard had been replaced by a layer of exposed brick covered in ivy, and three bay windows now jutted into the sidewalk.

At least the old mahogany door hadn't changed. He gripped the familiar brass handle, yanked it toward him and stepped inside.

Where he froze and swallowed a curse. Instead of the familiar comfort of a neighborhood bar, there was a wide-open area full of sofas and sunlight and…*computers?*

Where the hell was Monroe's?

The real Monroe's—not this…this *cyber salon.*

He scanned the space, aching for something familiar, some memory, some scent that would embrace him like his long-lost best friend.

But all he could smell was…*coffee.*

They didn't serve coffee at his parents' bar. Ice-cold Bud on tap, sure. Plenty of whiskey, rum and even tequila, but not coffee. Not here, where the locals gathered after the Rock High games to replay every one of Deuce's unpredictable but deadly knuckleballs. Not here, where all available wall space was filled with action shots from big games, framed team jerseys and newspaper clippings touting his accomplishments and talent. Not here, where—

"Can I help you, sir?"

Deuce blinked, still adjusting to the streaming sunlight where there shouldn't be any, and focused on a young woman standing in front of him.

"Would you like a computer station?" she asked.

What he'd like is a Stoli on the rocks. He glanced at the bar. At least that was still there. But the only person sitting at it was drinking something out of a cup. With a saucer.

"Is Seamus Monroe here?" Not that he expected his father to be anywhere near the bar on a Tuesday morning, but he'd already tried the house and it was empty. Deserted-looking, actually. A little wave of guilt threatened, but he shook it off.

"Mr. Monroe isn't here today," the young lady beamed at him. "Are you the new software vendor?"

*As if.*

He sneaked a glimpse at the wall where Mom had hung his first autographed Nevada Snake Eyes jersey at the end of his rookie season. Instead of the familiar red number two, a black and white photograph of a snow-covered mountain hung in a silver frame.

"Do you have a phone number where I can reach him?"

She shook her head. "I couldn't give you that, I'm sorry. Our manager is in the back. Would you like me to get her?"

Her? Dad had hired a female manager?

Then a little of the tension he'd felt for the past few weeks subsided. This was the right thing to do. It took a career-ending injury caused by monumental stupidity, but coming home to take over the bar was definitely the right thing to do.

Obviously, someone had already exploited his father's loss of interest in the place and made one too many changes. Deuce would set it all straight in no time.

"Yeah, I'll talk to her," he agreed.

She indicated the near-empty bar with a sweep of her hand. "Feel free to have a cup of coffee while I get Ms. Locke."

*Locke?*

That was the first familiar sound since he'd arrived in Rockingham. He knew every Locke who had ever lived in this town.

In fact, Deuce had just had an e-mail from Jackson Locke, his old high-school buddy. A typical what-a-jerk-you-are missive laced with just enough sympathy to know Jack felt Deuce's pain for ending a stellar baseball career at only thirty-three years old. Jack's parents had moved to Florida years ago...so that left Jack's sister, Kendra.

Deuce swallowed hard. The last time he'd seen Kendra was the week he'd come home for his mother's funeral, about nine years ago. Jack's baby sister had been…well, she'd been no *baby* then.

And Deuce had been a total chicken scumbag and never called her, not once, afterwards. Even though he'd wanted to. Really wanted to.

But it couldn't be Kendra, he decided as the hostess scooted away. Back then Kendra was weeks away from starting her junior year at Harvard. Surely the *Hahvahd* girl with a titanium-trap brain and a slightly smartass mouth hadn't ended up managing Monroe's. She'd been on fire with ambition.

And on fire with a few other things, too. His whole body tightened at the memory, oddly vivid for having taken place a long time and a lot of women ago.

This Locke must be a cousin, or a coincidence.

He leaned against the hostess stand—another unwelcome addition to Monroe's—and studied the semi-circle of computers residing precisely where the pool table used to be.

Someone had sure as hell messed with this place.

"Excuse me, I understand you need to speak with me?"

Turning, the first thing he saw was a pair of almond-shaped eyes exactly the color of his favorite Levi's, and just as inviting.

"Deuce?" The eyes flashed with shock and recognition.

He had to make an effort to keep from registering the same reaction.

Was it possible he'd slept with this gorgeous woman, kissed that sexy mouth that now opened into a perfect O and raked his fingers through that cornsilk-blond hair—and then *left* without ever calling her again?

*Idiot* took on a whole new meaning.

"Kendra." He had absolutely no willpower over his gaze, which took a long, slow trip over alabaster skin, straight down to the scoop neck of a tight white T-shirt and the rolling letters of *Monroe's* across her chest. All lower-case.

The letters, that was. The chest was definitely upper-case.

A rosy tone deepened her pale complexion. Her chin tilted upward, and those blue eyes turned icy with distrust. "What are you doing here?"

"I came home," he said. The words must have sounded unbelievable to her, too, based on the slanted eyebrow of incredulity he got in response. He took another quick trip over the logo, and this time let his gaze continue down to a tiny waist and skin-tight jeans hugging some seriously sweet hips.

He gave her his most dazzling smile. Maybe she'd forgiven him for not calling. Maybe she'd stay on and work for him after he took over the bar. Maybe she'd...

But, first things first. "I'm looking for my dad."

She tucked a strand of sunny blond hair behind her ear. "Why don't you try Diana Lynn's house?"

Diana Lynn's house? What the hell was that? Had he gone to assisted living or something? "Is she taking care of Dad?"

That earned him a caustic laugh. "I'll say. Diana Lynn Turner is your father's fiancée."

"His what?" Men who'd had pacemakers put in a year ago didn't have fiancées. Widowed men with pacemakers, especially.

"His fiancée. It's French for bride-to-be, Deuce." She put a hand on her hip like a little punctuation mark to underscore her sarcasm. "Your dad spends most of his days—and all of his nights—at her house. But they're leaving tomorrow morning for a trip, so if you want to see him, you better hustle over there."

Deuce had been scarce for a lot of years, no doubt about it. But would his father really get engaged and not tell him?

Of course he would. He'd think Deuce would hate the idea of Seamus Monroe remarrying. And he'd be right.

"So, where does this Diana Lynn live?"

She waved her hand to the left. "At the old Swain mansion."

He frowned. "That run-down dump on the beach?"

"Not so run-down since Diana Lynn worked her magic." She reached into the hostess stand and pulled out some plastic menus, tapping them on the wood to line them up. "She has a way of livening everything up."

Oh, so that's what was going down; some kind of gold digger had got her teeth into the old man. Deuce hadn't gotten home a moment too soon.

"Don't tell me," he said with a quick glance toward the pit of computers to his right. "She's the mastermind behind the extreme makeover of the bar."

"The bar?" Kendra slid the menus back into their slot and looked in the opposite direction—toward the bar that lined one whole wall. "Well, we haven't been able to close long enough to rip the bar out yet."

He didn't know what word to seize. *We* or *rip* or *yet*.

"Why would you do that?"

She shrugged and appeared to study the bank of cherrywood that had been in Deuce's life as long as he'd lived. He'd bet any amount of money that the notches that marked his height as a toddler were still carved into the wood under the keg station. "The bar's not really a money-maker for us."

Us, was it? "That's funny," he said, purposely giving her the stare he saved for scared rookies at the plate. "Most times the *bar* is the most profitable part of a *bar*."

His intimidating glare didn't seem to work. In fact, he could have sworn he saw that spark of true grit he'd come to recognize right before some jerk slammed his curve ball into another county.

"I'm sure that's true in other business models," she said slowly, a bemused frown somehow just making her prettier. "But the fact is, the bar's not the most profitable part of an Internet café."

He choked a laugh of disbelief. "Since when is Monroe's an Internet café?"

"Since I bought it."

He could practically hear the ball zing straight over the left-field fence, followed by a way-too familiar sinking sensation in his gut.

"Since you *what?*"

He didn't know. Kendra realized by the genuine shock in those espresso-colored eyes that Deuce had no idea that she and his father shared a two-year-old business arrangement. She'd never had the nerve to ask Seamus if he'd told his son. In fact, she and Seamus Senior had politely danced around the subject of Seamus Junior for a long, long time.

But it looked like the dance was about to end.

"I bought Monroe's a while ago. Well, half of it. And I run it, although your dad still owns fifty percent." All right, fifty-one. Did Deuce need to know that little detail?

"Really," he said, thoughtfully rubbing a cheek that hadn't seen a razor in, oh, maybe twenty-nine hours. Giving him the ideal amount of Hollywood stubble on his chiseled, handsome features. It even formed the most alluring little shadow in the cleft on his chin.

She'd dipped her tongue into that shadow. Once.

"Yes, really." She pulled the menus out again just to keep her hands busy. Otherwise, they might betray her and reach out for a quick feel of that nice Hollywood stubble.

"And you turned it into—" He sent a disdainful glare toward the main floor "—the Twilight Zone."

She couldn't help laughing. He'd always made her laugh. Even when she was eleven and he'd teased her. He'd made her giggle, and then she'd run upstairs and throw herself on her bed and cry for the sheer love of him. "We call it the twenty-first century, Deuce, and you're welcome to log on anytime."

"No, thanks." He took a step backward, sweeping her with one of those appraising looks that made her feel as if she'd just licked her finger and stuck it in the nearest electrical outlet.

When his gaze finally meandered back up to her face, she forced herself to look into his dark-brown eyes. They were still surrounded by long, black lashes and topped with those seriously brash eyebrows. The cynicism, the daring, the I-don't-give-a-rat's-ass-what-anyone-thinks look still burned in his eyes. It was that look, along with a well-known penchant for fun and games, and the occasional out-of-control pitch, that had earned him the most memorable yearbook caption in Rockingham High School history: Deuce Is Wild. And her brother was on the page to the left with his own epigram: Jacks Are Better.

Their gaze stayed locked a little too long and she felt a wave of heat singe her cheeks. How much did he remember? That she'd admitted a lifelong crush on her big brother's best friend and biggest rival?

Did he remember that she'd never once used the word *no* during their passionate night together? That she'd whispered "I love you" when her body had melted into his and a childhood of fantasizing about one boy finally came true?

Sophie hustled toward the hostess stand, holding out a manila envelope, and blessedly breaking the silence.

"The kid from Kinko's dropped this off," she said, giving Deuce a quick glance as though to apologize for the interruption. Or to steal another look.

Kendra took the envelope. "Are you sure they sent over everything, Soph?"

The young woman nodded. "And the disk is in there, too. For backup."

Kendra gripped the package a little tighter. This was it. Seamus and Diana Lynn were on their way to Boston, New York and San Francisco to nail down the financing that would allow her to finish the transformation of Monroe's into the premier Internet café and artists' space in all of Cape Cod. Two years of research and planning—and what seemed like a lifetime of agonizingly slow higher education—all came down to this presentation.

"Seamus just called," Sophie added. "He's anxious to see it today, so he has time to go over any fine points with you before they leave."

She glanced at Deuce, who managed to take up too much space and breathe too much air just by being there. He'd always be larger than life in her wretched, idolizing eyes, regardless of the fact that he was responsible for putting an end to all of her dreams.

Then a sickening thought seized her. Everyone knew that Deuce's baseball career was over. Was he back for good? If so, then he had the ability to wreck her plans once again. Not because she would fall into his bed like a lovesick schoolgirl—she'd never make *that* mistake again—but because he had the power to change his father's mind.

If he wanted Monroe's, Seamus would give it to him. If

Deuce wanted the moon and stars and a couple of meteors for good measure, Seamus would surely book a seat on the next rocket launch to go get them.

The prodigal son had returned, and the surrogate daughter might just be left out in the cold.

Kendra squared her shoulders and studied the face she'd once loved so much it hurt her heart just to look at him. Deuce Monroe could not waltz back into Rockingham and wreck her life…again.

But she'd never give him the satisfaction of knowing he had any power—then or now.

"You can follow me over there," she said with such believable indifference that she had to mentally pat herself on the back.

"You can ride with me," he replied.

"No thanks." How far could she push indifference? Didn't he remember what had happened the last time they'd been in a car together?

"You can trust me." He winked at her. "I've only been banned from race tracks, not the street."

Of course, he was referring to his well-publicized car crash, not their past.

"I just meant that I saw your father yesterday. You haven't seen him in years. No doubt you'll want to stay longer than I do."

"Depends on how I'm received." He turned toward the door, but shot her a cocky grin. "It's been a while."

"No kidding."

The grin widened as he added another one of those endless full-body eye exams that tested her ability to stand without sinking into the knees that had turned to water. "Is that your way of saying you missed me, Kendra?"

If any cells in her body had remained at rest, they woke up now and went to work making her flush and ache and tingle.

She managed to clear her throat. "I'm sure this is impossible for you to comprehend, Deuce, but somehow, some way, without formal therapy or controlled substances, every single resident in the town of Rockingham, Massachusetts, has managed to survive your long absence. Every. Single. One."

He just laughed softly and gave her a non-verbal touché with those delicious brown eyes. "Come on, Ken-doll. I'll drive. Do you have everything you need?"

No. She needed blinders to keep from staring at him, and a box of tissue to wipe the drool. Throw in some steel armor for her heart and a fail-safe chastity belt, and then she'd be good to go.

But he didn't need to know that. Any more than he needed to know why she'd dropped out of Harvard in the middle of her junior year.

"I have everything I need." She held the envelope in front of her chest and gave him her brightest smile. "This is all that matters."

She couldn't forget that.


"So what the hell happened to this place?" Deuce threw a glance to his right, ostensibly at the cutesy antique stores and art galleries that lined High Castle Boulevard, but he couldn't resist a quick glimpse at the passenger in his rented Mustang.

Because she looked a lot better than the changes in his hometown. Her jeans-clad legs were crossed and she leaned her elbow out the open window, her head casually tipped against her knuckles as the spring breeze lifted strands of her shoulder-length blond hair.

"What happened? Diana Lynn Turner happened," she answered.

The famous Diana Lynn again. "Don't tell me she erected the long pink walls and endless acres of housing developments I saw on the way into town. Everything's got a name. Rocky Shores. Point Place. Shoreline Estates. Since when did we have *estates* in Rockingham?"

"Since Diana Lynn arrived," she said, with a note of impatience at the fact that he didn't quite get the Power Of Diana thing.

"What is she? A one-man construction company?"

Kendra laughed softly, a sound so damn *girly* that it caused an unexpected twist in his gut. "She didn't build the walls or houses, but she brought in the builders, convinced the Board of Selectmen to influence the Planning Commission, then started her own real estate company and marketed the daylights out of Rockingham, Mass."

"Why?"

"For a number of reasons." She held up her index finger. "One, because Cape Cod is booming as a Hamptons-type destination and we want Rockingham to get a piece of the action instead of just being a stop en route to more interesting places." She raised a second finger. "Two, because the town coffers were almost empty and the schools were using outdated books and the stoplights needed to be computerized and the one policeman in town was about to retire and we had no money to attract a new force." Before point number three, he closed his fist around her fingers and gently pushed her hand down.

"I get the idea. Progress." He reluctantly let go of her silky-smooth skin. "So Diana Lynn isn't a gold digger."

She let out a quick laugh. "She's a gold digger all right.

She's dug the gold right out of Rockingham and put it back in those empty coffers."

He was silent for a minute as he turned onto Beachline Road and caught the reflection of April sunshine on the deep, blue waters of Nantucket Sound. Instead of the unbroken vista he remembered, the waterfront now featured an enclave of shops, which had to be brand-new even though they sported that salt-weathered look of New England. *Fake* salt-weathered, he realized. Like when they banged nicks into perfectly good furniture and called it "distressed."

He didn't like Diana Lynn Turner. Period. "So, just how far into him *are* her claws?"

"Her claws?" Kendra's voice rose in an amused question. "She doesn't have claws, Deuce. And if you'd bothered to come home once in a while to see your father in the past few years, you'd know that."

He tapped the brakes at a light he could have sworn was not on the road when he was learning to drive. "That didn't take long."

"What?"

"The guilt trip."

She blew out a little breath. "You'll get no guilt from me, Deuce."

Not even for not calling after a marathon of unforgettable sex? He didn't believe her. "No guilt? What would you call that last comment?"

As she shifted in her seat, he noticed her back had straightened and the body language of detachment she was trying so hard to project was rapidly disappearing. "Just a fact, Deuce. You haven't seen your dad for a long, long—"

"Correction. I haven't been *in Rockingham* for a long, long time. Dad came to every game the Snakes played in Boston. And he came out to Vegas a few times, too."

"And you barely had time to have dinner with him."

This time he exhaled, long and slow. He didn't expect her to understand. He didn't expect anyone to understand. Especially the man he was about to go see. Dinner with Dad was about all the motivational speaking he could stand. The endless coaching, the pushing, the drive. Deuce liked to do things his way. And that was rarely the way his father wanted them done.

Staying away was just easier.

"I talk to your brother Jack every once in a while," he said, as though that connection to Rockingham showed he wasn't quite the Missing Person she was making him out to be.

"Really?" She seemed surprised. "He never mentions that."

"He seems to like his job." It was the first thing he could think of to prove he really *did* talk to Jack.

She nodded. "He was born to be in advertising, that's for sure. He's married to that company, I swear."

How could he resist that opening? Besides, he was dying to know. "What about you?" He remembered the hostess calling her Ms. Locke. But these days, that didn't mean anything. "Got a husband, house and two-point-five kids yet, Ken-doll?"

Her silence was just a beat too long. Did she still hate the nickname he'd bestowed on her when she was a skinny little ten-year-old spying on the big boys in the basement?

"No, I don't, *Seamus*."

He grinned at the comeback. "So why aren't you in New York or Boston? Don't tell me that *Hahvahd* education landed you right back in the old Rockeroo."

He saw her swallow. "Actually, I never graduated from Harvard."

He glanced at her, noticing the firm set of her jaw. "No kidding? You were halfway through last time…" He let his voice drift a little. "When my mother passed away."

A whisper of color darkened her cheeks as she was no doubt wondering what else he recalled about his last visit to Rockingham. Surprisingly, everything. Every little detail remained sharp in his memory.

"I got very involved in business here," she said curtly.

Something in her voice said "don't go there" so he sucked in the salty air through the open windows of his rental car, immediately punched with memories.

"Smells like baseball," he said, almost to himself.

"Excuse me?"

"April in New England. It smells like spring, and spring means baseball." At least, it had for the past twenty-seven years of his life. Since he'd first picked up a bat and his father had started Rockingham's Little League just so Deuce could play T-ball, spring had meant "hit the field."

"You miss it?" she asked, her gentle tone actually more painful than the question.

"Nah," he said quickly. "I was about to retire anyway." A total lie. He was thirty-three and threw knuckleballs half the time. His elbow might be aching, but he could still pitch. But his taste for fast cars had lured him to a race track just for fun.

Fun that was most definitely not welcomed by the owners of the Nevada Snake Eyes, or the lawyers who wrote the fine print in his contract. He rubbed his right elbow, a move that he'd made so many times in his life, it was like breathing.

"You had a good year last year," she noted.

He couldn't help smiling, thinking of her little speech back at the bar. "You think anybody in Rockingham slowed down from all that *surviving* long enough to notice?"

Her return smile revealed a hint of dimples against creamy skin. "Yeah. We noticed."

The Swain mansion was around the corner. Instinctively, he slowed the car, unwilling to face his father, and wanting to extend the encounter with Kendra a little longer.

"I see my great season didn't stop someone from redecorating the walls of Monroe's." With mountains, instead of…memories.

Her smile grew wistful. "Things change, Deuce."

Evidently, they did. But if he had his way, he could change things right back again. Maybe not the pink houses and antique shops. But he sure as hell could make Monroe's a happening bar and recapture some of his celebrated youth in the meantime.

And while he was at it, maybe he could recapture some of those vivid memories of one night with Kendra. "Then I'll need someone to help me get reacquainted with the new Rockingham," he said, his voice rich with invitation.

She folded her hands on top of the envelope she'd been clinging to and stared straight ahead. "I'm sure you'll find someone."

His gaze drifted over her again. He'd *found* someone. "I'm sure I will."

# Two

**D**euce did a classic double take as they rounded the last corner to where a rambling, dilapidated mansion built by the heir to a sausage-casing fortune once stood.

"Whoa." He blew out a surprised breath. "I bet old Elizabeth Swain would roll over in her grave."

Kendra tried to see the place through his eyes. Instead of the missing shingles, broken windows and overgrown foliage he must remember, there stood a rambling three-story New England cape home with gray shake siding and a black roof, trimmed with decks and columns and walls of glass that overlooked Nantucket Sound. The driveway was lined with stately maples sprouting spring-green leaves. The carpet of grass in the front looked ready for one of Diana's lively games of croquet.

"Dad lives *here?*" Before she could, he corrected himself. "I mean, his...his friend does?"

Kendra laughed softly. "He almost lives here. But he's old-fashioned, you know. He won't officially move in until they get married."

Deuce tore his gaze from the house to give her a look of horror. "Which will be…?"

As soon as the expansion of Monroe's was financed and finalized. "They're not in a hurry, really. They're both busy with their careers and—"

"Careers?" He sounded as though he didn't think owning Monroe's was a career. Well too bad for that misconception. It was *her* career. "Not that I think they should rush into anything," he added.

He pulled into the driveway that no longer kicked up gravel since Diana had repaved it in gray-and-white brick. As he stopped the car, he rubbed his elbow again and peered up at the impressive structure.

"I can't believe this is the old Swain place. We used to break in and have keg parties in there."

Oh, yes. She remembered hearing about those. At three years younger than Jack and his Rock High friends, Kendra had never participated in a "Swain Brain Drain," but she'd certainly heard the details the next day.

Her information had come courtesy of the heating duct between her bedroom and the basement in the Locke home. When the heat was off, Kendra could lie on her bedroom floor, her ear pressed against the metal grate, and listen to boy talk, punctuated by much laughter and the crack of billiard balls.

It was her special secret. She knew more about Deuce than all the girls who adored him at Rock High. Jackson Locke's little sister knew *everything*. At least, as long as the heat wasn't turned on.

"You won't recognize the inside of this house," she told him. "Diana's got a magical touch with decor. And she's an amazing photographer. All the art in Monroe's is her work. And look at this place. She's never met a fixer-upper she couldn't—"

He jerked the car door open. "Let's go."

She sat still for a moment, the rest of her sentence still in her mouth. What did he have against this woman he'd never even bothered to meet? It was almost ten years since his mother had died. Didn't he think Seamus deserved some happiness?

She hustled out of the car to catch up with him as he walked toward the front door. "We can just go in through the kitchen," she told him.

He paused in mid step, then redirected himself to where she pointed. "You're a regular here, huh?"

A regular? She lived in the unattached guest house a hundred yards away on the beach. "I come over with the sales reports every day." She jiggled the handle of a sliding glass door and opened it. "Diana! Seamus? Anybody home?"

In the distance a dog barked.

"I have a surprise for you," she called. Did she ever.

"We're upstairs, Kennie!" A woman's voice called. "Get some coffee, hon. We'll be down as soon as we get dressed."

She felt Deuce stiffen next to her.

A smile tugged at the corners of her lips. "They're always…well, they're in love." She didn't have to look at him to get his reaction. She could feel the distaste rolling off him. As if he'd never spent the night at a woman's house.

"Have a seat." She touched one of the high-back chairs at the table under a bay window. "Want a cup of coffee?"

"No, thanks." He folded his long frame into a chair, his

gaze moving around the large country kitchen, to the cozy Wedgewood-blue family room on the other side of a long granite counter, and the formal dining room across the hall. "You're right. I can't believe this is the same old wreck."

She decided not to sing Diana's praises again. Taking a seat across from him, she set a mug of steaming coffee on the table, and carefully placed the envelope in front of her.

With one long look at Deuce, she took a deep breath. Before Diana swooped in here and charmed him, before Seamus barreled in and coached him, before the rest of Rockingham *discovered* him, she had to know. She just had to know for herself.

"Why did you come back?"

He leaned the chair on two legs and folded his arms across the breadth of his powerful chest, the sleeves of his polo shirt tightening over his muscular arms. She willed her gaze to stay on his face and not devour every heart-stopping ripple and cut.

"Well, I'm retired now, as you know."

The whole world knew he wasn't *retired*. His contract had been terminated after he blatantly disregarded the fine print and took to a race track—and wrecked a car—with a couple of famous NASCAR drivers. But, she let it go.

"Are you planning to…" Oh, God. *Ask it.* "…live here?" Please say no. *Please say no.* Could her heart and head take it if he said yes?

"Yes."

She sipped her coffee with remarkable nonchalance.

"I'm sick of living in Vegas," he added, coming down hard on the front two legs of the delicate chair.

"I thought you lived outside of Las Vegas."

He lifted one shoulder. "Same difference. I have no reason to stay there if I'm not playing ball for the Snake Eyes."

"What about coaching? Don't a lot of major leaguers do that after they…after they quit?"

He massaged his right arm again, a gesture she knew so well she could close her eyes and see it. But this time, his features tightened with a grimace.

"I don't know. We'll see. I'll need to find a good PT. You know any?"

A physical therapist who worked on professional athletes? On Cape Cod? "You'll have to go to Boston."

"That's over an hour from here."

Then go live *there.* "Two, now, with traffic." She sipped the coffee again and tried for the most noncommittal voice she could find. "So, what are you going to do here?"

Instead of answering, he snagged the envelope. She lunged for it, but he was too fast. "What is this?"

She wasn't ready to reveal her plans to Deuce. His dad would probably tell him all about their grandiose scheme, but she didn't want to. She'd shared her dreams with him a long time ago, and here she was, nine years later, and she still hadn't realized them. And he was the reason why.

"Just some paperwork on the café."

"It's a bar," he corrected, dropping the packet back on the table. "Not a café."

"Not anymore."

"Oh my God." Diana Lynn's gravelly tone seized their attention.

They both turned to where she stood in the kitchen doorway, a vision in white from head to toe, her precious Newman in her arms. "I recognize you from your pictures, Deuce." At the sight of a stranger, Newman yelped and squiggled for freedom.

Deuce stared at Diana for a moment, then stood. "That's what they call me," he said.

Diana breezed in, releasing the jittery little spaniel who leaped on Kendra's lap and barked at Deuce.

"I'm Diana Lynn Turner." She held out her hand to him. "And thank God for that pacemaker, because otherwise your father would have a heart attack when he comes downstairs."

Diana beamed at him as they shook hands, sweeping him up and down with the look of keen appraisal she was known to give a smart investment property. Her mouth widened into an appreciative smile that she directed to Kendra.

"No wonder you've had a crush on him your whole life. He is simply *delicious.*"

Diana was nothing if not blunt. Kendra willed her color not to rise as she conjured up a look of utter disinterest and a shrug. "Guess that depends on how you define delicious."

Deuce filed the lifelong crush comment for later, and turned his attention back to the most unlikely maternal replacement he could imagine.

Her smile was as blinding as the sun in his eyes when he squinted for a pop fly. Jet-black hair pulled straight back off-set wide, copper-brown eyes, and she had so few wrinkles she'd either been born with magnificent genes or had her own personal plastic surgeon. While she was certainly not his father's age of seventy-one, something about her bearing told him she'd passed through her fifties already. And enjoyed every minute of the journey.

He released her power grip. "You've done quite a number on this house."

She arched one shapely eyebrow and toyed with a strand of pearls that hung around her neck. "That's what I do. Numbers. What on earth made you decide to finally come home?"

No bush-beating for this one, he noted. "I retired."

She choked out a quick laugh. "Hardly. But your father will be over the moon to see you. How long are you staying?"

He casually scratched his face. He'd already admitted his plans. "A while."

"How long is a while?" Diana asked.

"For good."

"Good?" Her bronze eyes widened. "You're staying here in Rockingham for good?"

"Who is staying for good?" The booming voice of Seamus Monroe accompanied his heavy footsteps on a staircase. He came around the corner and stopped dead in his tracks.

"Good God in Heaven," he muttered, putting one of his mighty hands over his chest. For a moment Deuce's gut tightened, thinking he *had* given his father a heart attack. He barely had time to take in the fact that Dad's classic black-Irish dark hair had now fully transformed to a distinguished gray, but his eyebrows hadn't seemed to catch up yet. Then the older man lunged toward him with both arms open and squeezed until neither man could breathe.

Deuce thought his own chest would explode with relief as they embraced. Although his father had been the most demanding human who ever raised a son, he'd also loved that son to distraction. Deuce was counting on that. That and the fact that age might have mellowed the old man.

They slapped each other's backs and Dad pulled back and took Deuce's face in his hands, shaking it with only slightly more force than the hug. "What the hell were you thinking getting in that race car, son?"

Maybe *mellowed* would be pushing it.

Deuce laughed as he pulled away. "I was thinking I wouldn't get caught."

"You could have been killed!" his father said, his eyes

glinting with a fury Deuce had seen a million times. And those words. How many times had Seamus Monroe uttered "you could have been killed" after Deuce had "gotten caught"?

There was only one answer. Deuce had used it a few times, too. "I wasn't killed, Dad."

"But your career was."

Deuce extended his right arm and shook it out. "Hey, I'm thirty-three. Time to let the young dudes take the mound."

Seamus made a harumphing noise that usually translated into "baloney" or something harder if ladies weren't present. Then he brightened and reached out for one of the ladies who was present. "And you've met the love of—Diana."

*His life.*

Mom couldn't be the love of his life forever, and the mature man in Deuce knew that. It was that temperamental little boy in him who wanted to punch a wall at the thought.

"Sure did. And I'm impressed with this house. Doesn't look anything like the old Swain place."

"Have you seen Monroe's?" Dad said, throwing a proud look at Kendra.

She still sat at the kitchen table, the brown-and-white dog sizing him up from her lap. The almost-blush that Diana had caused had faded, but Kendra's eyes were still unnaturally bright.

"Yep," Deuce said, his gaze still on her. "I saw the bar. Big changes there, too." He dug his hands into his pockets and leaned against one of the high-gloss countertops. "In fact this whole town looks completely different."

Dad squeezed Diana a little closer to his side. "This is the reason, Deuce. This lady right here has done it all. She's a one-woman growth curve." He slid his hand over her waist and patted her hip, then glanced back at Kendra. "And so's our little firestorm, Kennie."

"So what's going on down there, Dad? Kendra tells me you're sticking your toes into the Internet waters."

"We've been testing the waters for over a year and we haven't drowned yet." Dad laughed softly. "And if everything goes like we think it might, we're going in deeper. Right, Kennie?"

She leaned forward and slid her mysterious envelope across the table. "And here's the boat we're taking out."

"Oh!" Diana squealed and grabbed the envelope hungrily. "Let me see! How wonderful that Deuce is here for the final unveiling. Have some coffee, everyone. We'll go into the family room and have a look at Kennie's masterpiece."

Kennie's masterpiece? Not exactly *just some paperwork*. Deuce gave her another hard look, but she gathered up the dog and her mug and turned her back to him.

As the women moved to the other room, Deuce sidled up to his dad. "So, how you feeling? That, uh, thing working okay?"

The older man gave him a sly smile. "My thing works fine. I don't even take that little blue pill."

Deuce closed his eyes for a moment. "I meant the pacemaker."

Dad laughed. "I know what you meant. It's fine. I've never been healthier in my life." He looked to the family room at Diana, his classic Irish eyes softening to a clear blue. "And I haven't been happier in a long time, either."

Things had changed, all right. And some things weren't meant to change back.

"I can tell," Deuce responded. He purposely kept the note of resignation out of his voice.

He couldn't argue. Dad looked as vibrant as Deuce could remember him in the past nine years. Not that he'd seen him very often.

In the family room, Kendra had spread computer printouts of bar charts and graphs over a large coffee table. Alongside were architectural blueprints, and hand-drawn sketches of tables and computers. He took a deep breath and let his attention fall on an architect's drawing of some kind of stage and auditorium. What the hell was a stage doing in Monroe's?

He could try to deal with Dad's romance, but messing with the bar he grew up in might be too much.

"So what's this all about?" he asked.

"This, son, is the future of Monroe's." Dad squeezed into a loveseat next to Diana and curled his arm around her shoulder, beaming as he continued. "We've tested the concept, made it work profitably and now we're ready to expand it."

Deuce dropped onto the sofa across from them, close to where Kendra knelt on the floor organizing the papers. "It already looked pretty expanded to me," he said.

"Well, we did buy out the card shop next door and added some space," Diana said. "But Kennie's plans are much, much bigger than that."

"Is that so?" He looked at her and waited for an explanation. "How big?"

She met his gaze, and held it, a challenge in her wide blue eyes. "We're hoping to buy the rest of the block, so we can eventually add a small theater for performance art, a gallery for local artists and a full DVD rental business."

He worked to keep his jaw from hitting his chest.

"Tell him about the learning center," his father coaxed.

"Well," she said, shifting on her hips, "We're going to add an area just for people who are not technically savvy. They can make appointments with our employees for hands-on Internet training."

He just stared at her. All he wanted to do was run a sports

bar with TVs playing ESPN and beer flowing freely. It sure as hell didn't take place on the *information highway* and karaoke night was as close to *performance art* as he wanted his customers to get.

But Deuce stayed quiet. He'd figure out a strategy. As soon as Dad found out that Deuce planned to buy the place, surely he'd change his mind. And Deuce would buy out Kendra's fifty percent if he had to. She could open her theater and gallery and learning center somewhere else in Rockingham.

He'd make his father understand that he had a plan for the future and it made sense. It didn't include baseball for the first time in his life, but that was okay.

His only option was coaching and with his track record for breaking rules, he doubted too many teams would be lined up to have him as a role model for younger players. He had no interest in television, or working an insurance company, or being the spokesperson for allergy medicine, like the rest of the has-been ballplayers of the world.

He just wanted to be home. Maybe he couldn't be the King of the Rock anymore, but this is where he grew up. And where he wanted to grow old.

But not in a flippin' Internet café.

That was one compromise he couldn't make.

It was impossible to concentrate with Deuce's long, hard, masculine body taking up half the sofa, his unspoken distaste for her plans hanging in the air. Not to mention the fact that his father now sought his opinion on everything.

Kendra hadn't counted on this kind of distraction.

"This chart emphasizes the growth of the Internet café business," she said, but for a moment, she lost her place.

The bar graphs and colored circles swam in front of her.

And Deuce's long, khaki-clad legs were just inches away from her. Her gaze slid to the muscle of his thigh. Newman, the little brat, had actually taken up residence next to him and was staring at him like some kind of star-struck baseball fan. Even dogs were in awe of Deuce.

"You showed us that one, honey," Diana said quietly, leaning forward to pull another chart. "I think you wanted the research about how Internet cafés are the social centers of this century. How people don't want to be isolated while they are in cyber-space. Remember? The findings are here."

Oh, cripes. Of course she remembered. She'd written the analysis of the research. She'd used it to convince Seamus to launch the overhaul of Monroe's. She'd based her whole future on that trend.

And all she could think about was…thigh muscles.

"What do you think, Deuce?" Seamus asked for the twentieth time. "You see these cafés out in Vegas?"

"Never saw one in my life."

Kendra gave him an incredulous look, then remembered what his life was like. On the road, in hotels. "But surely you have a computer, a laptop or a PDA, and an e-mail address."

He nodded. "I told you I got an e-mail from Jack. And some of my friends' kids taught me a cool game called Backyard Baseball." He ignored her eye-roll and looked at his father. "Frankly, I don't know what's going on here in Cape Cod, but the rest of the world still expects to go into a bar and *drink*. They can't smoke, thank God, but I haven't been in a bar where keyboards replaced cocktails. At least not until today."

Seamus leaned back and regarded his son. "Well, our bar profits were sinking fast, son. Two years ago, we were as close to the red as I've been in many years. Big-name chains have come into this place in droves, squeezing our business with national advertising."

"Monroe's has been through tough times before, Dad," Deuce argued. "It always survives."

"The demographics of Rockingham have changed," Diana interjected. "This isn't the sleepy vacation town it used to be. Our population has skyrocketed, and the town is full of young, savvy, hip residents."

"And young, hip residents don't go to bars anymore?" Deuce asked. "They do in every other city I've ever been in."

An uncomfortable silence was his only answer.

Finally, Seamus asked, "What don't you like about this, Deuce?"

Deuce leaned forward, flexing the thigh muscle Kendra shouldn't have been watching. "I came home so I could take over Monroe's and run it as a first-rate sports bar."

Kendra closed her eyes and took the punch in her stomach. She *knew* it. She'd known this the minute he'd walked in the door.

Was Deuce Monroe put on this earth for the sole reason of ruining her life? He didn't know what he'd done last time—the result of their recklessness was her burden, and, ultimately, her loss. But this time, he could see what it meant to her.

And so could Seamus. She looked up at the man who'd been like a father to her ever since her own parents had distanced themselves physically and emotionally. But Seamus's gaze remained locked on his son, an expression of astonishment, joy and worry mixed in the lines on his face.

How could she let herself forget for one moment that Seamus loved Deuce above all and everything? No matter how many times Deuce had gone against his wishes, his love for his only child was constant.

"I had no idea, son."

Kendra just *knew* what was coming next. There was no way to avoid what was about to be said.

"Dad, the bar's been in the family for more than seventy years."

Bingo. There was the bomb she'd been waiting for him to drop. Monroe's belonged to *Monroes*. Always had…always will.

Diana leaned forward and snagged Deuce with one of those riveting stares that withered opponents at the negotiating table. "When, exactly, were you planning to tell your father that you intended to carry on that tradition?"

"Today," he replied without missing a beat. "I wanted to talk in person, not over the phone. My house in Vegas is on the market. I'm planning to move here as soon as we…settle things."

Seamus took a long, slow breath and pulled Diana back into his side with a gentle tug. "I wish you had told me sooner," he said to Deuce.

*Why? Would that have changed things?* Kendra had to bite her lip from shouting out her question. If Seamus had known Deuce wanted to take over the bar, would he have stopped her expansion plans from the beginning? Even when profits were so low they almost had to sell?

"I think Kendra has a say on all this," Diana finally commented. "She owns forty-nine percent of the business."

She felt Deuce's gaze and had no doubt he remembered she'd told him "fifty" percent. Lies. They always come back to bite you.

Kendra shifted again, wishing she weren't the only one sitting on the floor. "I'm sure you all know how I feel. The expansion is the business I've always dreamed of owning."

"But Monroe's," Seamus said quietly, "is my blood."

And so was Deuce.

Deuce, who hadn't come home from a road trip when his father had a pacemaker put in. Deuce, who'd refused to go to college on a baseball scholarship as his father had begged him, instead going straight into the minor leagues. Deuce, who had never called her after they'd made love, so therefore had never even found out that she'd gotten pregnant…and lost that child.

"Are you serious about this?" Seamus asked his son. "Are you absolutely committed or are you just screwing around here until some better job offer comes along?"

"I'm dead serious, Dad."

Well. There went that dream.

"And you aren't serious very often," Seamus said with a soft laugh of understatement. "I guess this is something for me to consider."

"I came home to run the bar," Deuce said, his baritone voice oddly soft. "I can't play ball. I don't want to coach. I'm not interested in TV or business or anything else I can think of. I want to be home, Dad. I want to run Monroe's. I want to buy it outright, to free you from the day-to-day operations." He looked at Kendra. "Of course, I didn't know you'd already had such great help. I'm sure we can work something out. That is," he looked back at his father, his face sincere, "if you'll consider me."

Without a word, Kendra started to scoop up graphs and presentation pages. She'd have to take her idea elsewhere. It was still viable. She'd figure something out.

She'd spent every dime to buy out half of Seamus's business, but she'd been in worse places before. Worse financial, emotional and physical places. She would survive. She always did.

"What are you doing, Kennie?" Seamus's sharp tone stopped her cold.

"We don't need to go through this presentation. Not now, anyway," she said, wishing like mad that she'd driven her own car so she could escape.

She looked up to see a pained expression in the older man's eyes. They'd never discussed it, but in that moment, that look in his eyes confirmed what she'd always suspected. He knew who'd put an end to Harvard for her. He knew.

"Not so fast," Seamus said.

Could that mean he wasn't sure yet?

"Well, until you decide what to do…" She continued to gather papers, and Deuce reached forward to help, his arm brushing hers. She jerked away from him and cursed the reaction to the most casual touch.

Her mouth went bone-dry, and she realized with a sickening horror that a huge lump had formed in her throat. She would not give him the satisfaction of seeing her cry. Taking a deep breath, she forced herself to stand.

"I'm going to get something at home," she managed to say. "I'll be back in a few minutes."

"Where's home?" Deuce asked.

"Kendra lives in the guest house on the beach," Diana Lynn said. "Go ahead, dear. We'll be here."

Kendra shot her a grateful look. No doubt she'd picked up the near-tears vibe.

"Why don't you walk over there with her, Deuce?" Seamus asked. Clearly he had *not* picked up that same vibe. "I need a few minutes alone with Diana."

Kendra resisted the urge to spear Seamus with a dirty look. Couldn't she get a break today? But Deuce stood and gestured toward the door. "Show me the way," he said.

Kendra stole one more pleading look at Diana, who gave a nearly imperceptible nod. *Go,* her eyes said. *Let me talk to him.*

"All right," Kendra said. "We'll be back in a few minutes."

"Take your time," Seamus responded. "We have some serious thinking to do here."

But Kendra knew that, for Seamus, there was no *thinking* where Deuce was involved. The old Irishman ran on pure heart, and nothing filled his heart more than the love for his son. No matter how many errors—on the field or in judgment—Deuce made. He was Seamus's weakness.

And how could she blame him? He'd been her weakness, too.

Without another word, she headed toward the sliding door, with Deuce behind her, and Newman at his heels.

She'd barely stepped into the sunshine when Deuce leaned over and whispered into her ear, "Your whole life, huh? That's some wicked crush."

# Three

Kendra never missed a beat. At his comment, she reached down for the little brown-and-white dog, who leaped into her arms.

"Do you hear anything, Newman? I don't hear anything."

Newman barked and nuzzled into her neck. And licked her. Lucky puppy.

"Oh, you're ignoring me?" Deuce asked with a laugh as he trotted down a set of wooden steps to catch up with her. "That's really mature."

"This from the poster boy of maturity." She set the dog down when they reached a stone path that paralleled the beach. "Or have you stopped setting firecrackers inside basketballs in the teachers' parking lot?"

He chuckled. "That was your brother's idea. Anyway, I've grown up."

"Oh, yes. I noticed in all the coverage about that racing stunt just how much you've grown up."

He considered a few comebacks, but there was nothing to combat the truth.

"Well, you certainly have," he said. At her confused look, he added, "Grown up, that is."

Her face softened momentarily, but then she squared her shoulders and she strode toward the house. He couldn't help smiling. Torturing Jack's little sister had always been fun. Even when she was ten and scrawny and folded into giggles, and tears. But it was even more fun now, when she was *not* ten and scrawny, but older and *curvy.*

"I live right here," she announced as they neared a gray shake-covered beach cottage at the end of the path. "You can come in, or, if you prefer, go down to the water and gaze at your reflection for a while."

He snorted at the comment. "I'll come in. Cute place. How long have you lived here?"

"About a year and a half. After Diana finished renovating the property, I was her first renter." She gave him a smug smile. "I introduced her to Seamus."

"I can't believe he's never even told me he was involved with someone."

"It's not like you actually *talked* to him a whole lot in the past year."

Past decade, is what she meant, and he knew it. "Not that I owe you an explanation, but I have been pretty busy playing ball."

"From October to March?"

"I played in Japan."

"The season you were out injured for four weeks?"

She knew that? "I was in physical therapy every day."

"During All Star breaks?" She moved ahead of him as they reached the back door, tugging a set of keys from her pocket. "Every single minute, you were busy?"

"I'm here now, aren't I? And you don't seem too happy about it."

She spun around to face him and pointed a key toward his chest. "Do you really expect me to jump for joy because you imploded your own career and now you want to come and horn in on mine?"

"I didn't know about this Internet café stuff. Dad never mentioned it, he never mentioned a—a girlfriend, and he never mentioned you."

She stared at him for a minute, no doubt a thousand smart-aleck retorts spinning through her head. Instead she snapped her fingers to call the dog who'd meandered toward the beach, and pivoted back to the door.

Which gave him a really nice view of her hips and back-side in worn jeans.

A flash of those taut legs wrapped around him on a blanket in the sand danced through his mind. She'd worn jeans that night, too. He remembered sliding down her zipper, dipping his hand into her soft, feminine flesh, then peeling the denim down her legs.

A rush of blood through his body didn't surprise him. In the years that had passed, he'd never remembered that night without a natural, instinctive and powerful response. For some reason, that sandy, sexy encounter had never felt like a one-night stand. Probably because it involved a girl who he should have been able to resist—his best friend's little sister.

"Look," he said, stabbing his hands in his pants pockets, which really just helped him resist the urge to reach out and touch her. "I had no idea things had changed this much, or that you and Dad had plans for something entirely different."

"Well, we do." She entered the house and held the door for him.

He followed her, but his mind was whirring. Was he expected to back off the bar entirely? His family name was still on the door, damn it. The only name that ever had been on that particular door, with or without capital letters.

"Maybe there's a compromise somewhere," he suggested. "Maybe we could keep a few computers in one corner of the bar—you know, for the people who aren't watching games? And you could find some nearby property for your gallery or whatever."

Instead of brightening, her scowl deepened. She opened her mouth to say something, then slammed it shut again.

"What?" he asked. "What were you going to say?"

"Nothing."

He dug his hands deeper. "You won't even consider a compromise?"

Inhaling unevenly, she closed her eyes. "I've already compromised enough where you're concerned."

"What the hell does that mean?"

She held up both hands as though to stop everything. "Never mind." She turned away, toward a small hallway behind her. "Excuse me for a minute."

She turned to stalk down the hallway, but he seized her elbow in one quick grab. "What are you talking about?"

"Nothing," she spat the word, shaking him off. "Forget I said that."

He let her go.

What had she *compromised* for him?

In the tiny living room, he dropped onto a sofa and stared

at the serene water of the Sound through a sliding glass door, remembering again the incredible night they'd spent together.

He'd never forgotten that night. Maybe because he knew he shouldn't have seduced Jack's sister…but maybe because her response to him was so real and strong. So real, that he couldn't understand where "compromise" came into play. There were two very, *very* consenting adults during that beach-blanket bingo.

He'd come home after his mother had died of an aneurysm, too old at twenty-four to feel as though his mommy had left him, but brokenhearted anyway. Kendra had been about twenty, maybe twenty-one, and smack between her sophomore and junior years at Harvard. A business major, he recalled.

He remembered how impressed he'd been—she was smart, and quick-witted, and had grown up into a complete knockout. Even in the chaos and sadness of his mother's passing, he'd noticed that Kendra Locke had spent every minute at the bar, calmly taking care of things he and his father were not even thinking about.

His last night in town, he'd gone to the bar and ended up staying until it closed, drinking soda and watching Kendra work. That's when he officially stopped thinking of her as Ken-doll.

The name just wasn't feminine enough for a woman that attractive. They'd talked and flirted. She made him laugh for the first time that week.

When her shift ended, they'd gone for a ride. He still could remember pulling her toward him in his dad's car and their first, heated kiss.

He leaned forward and raked his fingers through his hair. He'd felt guilty, and a little remorseful at seducing a girl he'd always considered a little sister. But she'd been willing.

No, no. That was an understatement. She'd been more than willing. Sweet, tender and innocent, he remembered with a cringe. Certainly a virgin. Was that the compromise she'd made?

Probably. And he'd been a world-class jerk for not calling afterwards. It wasn't as if he'd forgotten her. He just…couldn't. He looked down the hallway expectantly. No wonder she still hated him. Especially now that she had what he wanted.

He muttered a curse. Wasn't it *unspoken* that he'd always be back? Sure it had happened a little sooner than they all thought, but Dad always knew it. Didn't she realize that when she bought forty-nine percent—not *fifty*—of the bar that she was essentially buying into his inheritance?

He heard her footsteps in the hall and looked up to see her walking toward him, looking as calm as the waters beyond the glass doors. Game face *on*.

"How much time do you think we should give them?" she asked.

"Not too much. Evidently, they get easily distracted by each other."

She laughed a little and put both hands on the backrest of a bentwood chair, her casual indifference back in place. "We can go back. I got what I needed."

"What was that?"

"My wits." She deepened those dimples with a disarming grin.

Was she offering a truce? He was game. "I'm sure we'll work something out." He gave her a friendly wink. "You never know. I bet we work well together."

Her eyes narrowed. "I bet we don't."

"How can you say that?" He stood slowly, his gaze locked on her as he moved closer. "Don't tell me you forgot—"

"Newman!" She snapped her fingers in the air, a warning look flashing in those sky-blue eyes. The message was silent...but clear.

There would be no discussing that night.

The dog came tripping down the hallway with a bark, surprising Deuce by sidling up to his leg instead of that of the woman snapping for him.

Kendra rolled her eyes as Newman rubbed Deuce's pantleg.

"He likes me," Deuce noted.

"He's easily impressed. Let's go back to Diana's."

Laughing, he held the door for her. "I don't know. Think the jury's back already, Ken-doll?"

"We're about to find out, Seamus."

Diana looked happier than usual. Kendra noticed the diamond-like sparkle in her eyes, which usually meant she'd gotten what she wanted. Please God, let it be so. Diana would back Kendra and push Seamus to move on with their plans. She was always in favor of progress and change.

As Diana puttered in the kitchen, straightening an already neat counter, Seamus sat on the sofa, elbows resting on his knees and knuckles supporting his chin. He only moved his eyes, looking up as Kendra and Deuce entered the family room. Unlike his fiancée, Seamus looked anything but pleased with the turn of events.

All of the papers and sketches had been neatly piled on the coffee table. Would those documents be making the trip into banks and venture-capital firms this week...or going home with Kendra?

Kendra stood to one side, but Deuce took a seat across from his father. "So, Dad. Whad'ya think?"

For a long moment, Seamus said nothing, staring first at

Deuce, then at the papers on the table. Kendra's throat tightened and she dared another look at Diana, who had paused in her counter-wiping and turned to watch the drama unfolding in her family room.

"I think I have quite a dilemma."

No one said a word in response. Kendra willed her heart to slow, certain that the thumping could be heard in the silence. Even Newman lifted his head from the floor, his classic King Charles spaniel face looking expectantly at the humans around him.

"Deuce, you need to understand something," Seamus began. "This Internet café and artist's gallery is something we've been working on for almost two years. I really like the idea of bringing Monroe's into the next century."

Deuce leaned forward and opened his mouth to speak, but Seamus silenced him with one look. Kendra wished she'd taken a seat when they walked in, because her legs felt shaky as she waited for Seamus's next words.

"And Kennie, you know that my father opened Monroe's in 1933, the year I was born. He ran it until he died, more than thirty years later, in 1965. Then I took over, at—" he looked at Deuce "—thirty-three years of age."

Kendra bit her lip as she listened. Did Seamus see this as poetic justice? As history repeating itself? As some etched-in-stone prediction from on high? *As the Monroe Man turneth thirty-three, so shall he inherit the bar.*

Sheez. Her gaze shifted to Deuce and she could have sworn his lip curled upward. Was he thinking the same thing? Or was he just so damn sure of himself that he could afford to be cocky?

Instead of a snide remark, though, Deuce leaned forward again. "Dad," he said, forcefully enough that he wouldn't be stopped by his father's glare. "Isn't there some way we can compromise? Some way to keep Monroe's in the family, as a bar, and find another property for this...other stuff."

"That's not feasible," Kendra argued before Seamus could respond. "These blueprints have been drawn up by an architect—an expensive one, by the way—expressly for that property and the other buildings on the block."

"So use one of the other buildings," Deuce countered.

"We are. As soon as we rip out the bar altogether and push that whole wall fifty feet in another direction for an art gallery."

"An art gallery? In that space?" Deuce looked as though she'd suggested turning it into a nursery school. "That's perfect for a pool hall and twenty TV screens, each tuned to a different football game on Sunday. They have these satellite dishes—"

"Sunday? That's one of our biggest days. We do so much Internet business—"

"Not from football fans."

"You two need to work this out," Seamus said.

"Precisely!" Diana slammed her hands hard on the kitchen counter. Kendra, like the men and the dog, turned to stare at her. "You need to work side by side, together."

"What?" Kendra and Deuce responded in unison.

"She's right," Seamus acknowledged. "I can't make a choice without hurting someone I care about. We'll go on our trip, and you two run the place together."

"What do you mean—together?" Deuce asked.

Diana came around the breakfast bar into the family room, her gaze on Seamus, a shared, secret arcing between them, but Kendra had no idea what it was. "Why doesn't Kendra run the Internet café in the day, and Deuce run the bar at night? Let the customers decide where and when they want to spend their money."

"Run a bar at night?" Kendra almost sputtered in shock. "And lose all my nighttime business?"

"That's been a tiny percentage of the profits," Seamus responded. "You've been shutting down by nine o'clock lately."

"But it's April now. The warm weather is starting, more tourists are coming." She worked to modulate her voice, refusing to whine. "Those are the people who need Internet access, who bring their laptops so they can work on vacation."

"People *drink* on vacation," Deuce corrected her. "At least at night." He slapped his hands on his thighs and slid them over his khaki pants, a smug smile in place. "I think it's a great idea."

They all looked at her expectantly. Was she going to back down? Let Deuce appear more willing to take the challenge than she was?

No one came in that bar looking for a drink anymore. What remained of the liquor bottles had to be regularly dusted. She'd been running Monroe's as though it were a coffee shop and Internet café for a long time; her customers were loyal online users. The people looking for a neighborhood bar went to the bigger chains that had come into town.

"Okay. Fine. Whatever you want, Seamus."

"I want you both to have a chance." He stood slowly, his gaze moving between them. "I'd like to see the decision be made by you, not me."

"We'll let the people of Rockingham decide," Deuce said, looking at Diana as he echoed her thoughts. Sure, now they were allies.

But Deuce had no idea what he was up against, getting between a woman and her dream. Twice.

Her Internet café was significantly more profitable than a bar, and Diana and Seamus's trip was only two weeks long.

There was no way Deuce could turn a profit in less than a month.

Seamus stepped toward Diana and slid his arm around her again. "Tomorrow, Diana and I are leaving for Boston, New York and San Francisco for meetings arranged with investors and banks." He paused and pulled Diana closer, sharing that secret smile again. "And we've decided to tack on an early honeymoon."

"What do you mean?" Kendra asked.

"We were going to tell you this morning, honey," Diana said, "but we were so surprised by Deuce's visit."

"Tell us what?" Deuce looked horrified. "Did you already get married?"

Diana laughed lightly. "No. But I found the most amazing timeshare in Hawaii. A gorgeous house in Kauai, on the water. We couldn't resist."

"How long will you be gone?" Kendra asked, a sinking sensation tugging at her stomach.

Seamus grinned. "A month in Hawaii, plus the two weeks of business trip."

"A month?" Kendra looked from one to the other. "You'll be gone for six weeks?"

"Great," Deuce said, standing up. "Diana, do you think you can find me a place to rent until I sell my house in Vegas?"

Kendra glared at him. "Why don't you wait to sell your place until we see who…what happens."

"You can stay here," Diana offered. "Newman seems to have taken a liking to you."

"I take care of Newman," Kendra said. Good Lord, she didn't want Deuce a hundred yards away from her for six weeks.

"You can handle him in the evenings," Deuce said, his gaze on her. "I'll be at the bar."

"There's no way you're going to be there, in charge and alone," she said quickly. "I'll do my paperwork at night."

"Then I'll do mine during the day."

Kendra hadn't noticed that Seamus and Diana had slipped into the kitchen, until she heard their soft laughter. They stood with their heads close to each other, slowly walking toward the hallway.

"I kind of hate to leave," Seamus whispered. "Just when it's getting interesting."

Deuce grinned at Kendra. She glared at him.

"This is *so* not interesting," she mumbled, turning to retrieve her papers and put them back in order.

"I disagree," he said, suddenly way too close to her back. "This could be very interesting. Remember the night we—"

She spun around and stuck her finger right in his face. "Don't go there, Deuce Monroe."

With a playful smile, he put both hands over his heart, feigning pain. "Was that night so horrible that you can't even think about it?"

If only he knew. If only. But he wouldn't, Kendra swore silently. He would never know.

She gave him a blank stare. "What night, Deuce? I have no idea what you're talking about."

"Is that right?" His voice was silky smooth, and the dark glimmer in his eyes sent firecrackers right down to her toes. "I bet I can make you remember."

"One bet's enough for me today," she said, seizing one of the sketches of the new Monroe's layout and holding it in front of her face. "And I bet I get *this*."

He slid the paper out of her hand, and leaned so close to

her mouth she could just about feel that Hollywood stubble as it threatened to graze her.

"Let's play ball," he whispered.

# Four

**W**ithout knocking, Deuce leaned against the solid wood door that separated a back office from the storage areas piled high with empty computer hardware boxes. He'd done as much as he could for the past two days from Diana's home. He'd stopped into Monroe's a few times, perused the small kitchen and made a few changes around the bar. But he hadn't yet entered what he still thought of as Dad's office. Which was always occupied by Kendra Locke.

He eased the door open without any hesitation over the latch. Because there was no latch. There'd never been a working latch as long as he could remember. But, were the employees of Monroe's still as trustworthy today as in the past? He might have to get that old lock fixed after all.

Despite the unfamiliar high-tech logos and the aroma of a Colombian countryside surrounding him, the solid mass of wood under his shoulder felt very much like *home*. As the door creaked open, he half expected his father to look up from the scarred oak desk, his broad shoulders dropping, his eyes softening at the sight of his son—right before he launched into a speech about how Deuce could do something *better.*

Instead of his father's Irish eyes, he met a blue gaze as chilly as the glycol cooling block he'd just assembled on the long-dormant beer tap behind the bar.

"It's five-thirty," he announced to Kendra. "Time for coffee drinking Internet surfers to pack up and go home. Monroe's is open for business."

She lowered the lid of her laptop an inch as she lifted her brows in surprise. "Today? Tonight? You've only been in town for two days. Don't you have to unpack, get settled and give me a week or two or three to prepare for these temporary changes in my business?"

"I'm ready for business. Tonight."

He stepped into the tiny space, noting that the old green walls were now...pinkish. The window that was really a two-way mirror over the bar was covered with wooden shutters that belonged on a Southern plantation. "And there's nothing temporary about..." He closed the door and peeked at the space behind it. Aw, *hell.* "What happened to the plaques commemorating Monroe's sponsorship of Rockingham's state champion Little League team?"

Her gaze followed his to yet another of those black-and-white nature still-life shots that he'd seen in about six places now. He could have sworn her lips fought a smile.

"Diana Lynn took that photograph," she said simply. "She was inside a sequoia in California. Pretty, huh?"

He didn't comment. He'd find the Little League plaques. Dad must have stored them somewhere. "There are two freaks left on the computers out there," he pointed over his shoulder with his thumb. "And they are both immersed not in the new millennium, but in the middle ages from what I can see."

"Runescape," she answered with a nod. "That's a very popular online medieval strategy game. And they are not freaks. That's Jerry and Larry Gibbons. Those brothers spend hours in here, every day."

"Do they drink beer?"

She shrugged. "It might impair their ability to trade jewels for farming equipment."

"They have to—"

"Stay," she interrupted, jerking her chin up to meet his gaze, even though he towered over her desk. "You can't kick out my customers at night. If they want to sit on those computers until 2:00 a.m., there's no reason for them not to."

"Suit yourself," he said affably. "But the TV monitors are about to be tuned into Sports Center, and the jukebox will be on all night. Loud."

She flipped the laptop open again and looked at the screen. "The jukebox hasn't worked for a year. My customers prefer quiet."

"It works now."

She gave him a sharp look. Did she have her head so deep in the books that she hadn't noticed him out there yesterday morning, installing a CD system in the box?

"No one is going to show up for a drink tonight," she said, turning her attention back to the computer.

"You don't know that." He resisted the urge to reach out and raise that sweet chin, just to see those mesmerizing eyes again. Regardless of how chilly they were. "With the front door open, anyone who passes by could stop in. Walk-in business is the heart of a bar." The fact that he'd worked the phone and called every familiar name in a fifty-mile radius wouldn't hurt either.

She shook her head slightly, her smile pure condescension. "Deuce, I hate to break it to you, but Monroe's pretty much shuts down around the dinner hour. We might have a few stragglers come in after seven or so, and Jerry and Larry usually stay until they realize they're hungry, but there's no business done here at night."

"And you just accept that? Don't you want to build nighttime revenue? I thought you were an entrepreneur. A capitalist." He almost made a Harvard joke, but something stopped him.

"I'm a realist," she said. "People pop into an Internet café during the day, when they need access to cyber space or a break in their schedule. At night, at home, they have computers."

"So change that," he countered.

"I'm working on it." She leaned back in the chair—not Dad's old squeaker, either, this one was sleek, modern and ergonomic. Crossing her arms over the rolling letters spelling Monroe's on her chest, she peered at him. "Were you paying any attention the other day or were you so wrapped up in resentment that you didn't even see my presentation? Remember the plans? The theater? The artists' gallery? The DVD-rental business?"

He'd gotten stuck on one word. "Resentment? Of what?"

"Of the fact that your father has found...love."

His elbow throbbed, but he ignored it. "I don't begrudge my dad happiness. You're imagining things."

One blond eyebrow arched in disbelief.

"I don't," he insisted. "His...lady friend seems..." Perfect. Attractive. Successful. Attentive. Why wouldn't he want all that for his dad? "Nice."

"She is that, and more." She shifted her focus to the keyboard again, and she began typing briskly. "Now, go run your bar, Deuce. I have work to do."

*You're dismissed.*

"I can't find any wineglasses."

She gave him a blank look, then resumed typing. "I have no idea where they are anymore. I may have given them away."

She wanted to play hardball? With him? "Fine. I'll just serve chardonnay to the ladies in coffee mugs."

That jerked her chain enough to drop her jaw. But she closed it fast enough. "You do that." Type, type, type.

"And you don't mind if I use those coffee stirrers for the cocktails?"

She narrowed her eyes and studied the screen as though she were writing *War and Peace.* "Whatever."

"And until I have time to place some orders for garnishes, I'll be dipping into your supply of fresh fruit for some cherries and orange slices. Will that be a problem?"

Her fingers paused, but then blasted over the keys at lightning speed. Unless she was the world's fastest typist, she couldn't possibly be writing anything comprehensible. "I do a tight inventory on every item in stock," she said over the tapping sound. "Please have anything you use replaced by tomorrow."

"Will you give me the names of your suppliers?"

She hit the spacebar four times. Hard. "I'm sure you can find your own."

"Can I borrow your Rolodex?"

Now her fingers stilled—as though she needed all her brain power to come up with a suitably smartass answer. "There's a Yellow Pages in the storage room."

She launched into another supersonic attack on the keyboard, her body language as dismissive as she could make it.

*Aw, honey. You don't want to do this. You'll lose when I start throwing curves.*

She typed. He waited. She typed more. He wound up.

"Kendra?"

"Hmmm?" She didn't look up.

"That window right there. You know it's a two-way mirror into the bar?"

"I'm aware of that," she said, still typing. "I don't need to monitor my patrons' activities. I have staff for that, and no one is in there getting drunk or stupid. At least not on my watch."

Low and inside. Strike one.

"That's true, but…" Slowly, he crept around the side of the desk toward the fancy white shutters. "Aren't you just a little bit curious about what I'll be up to out there?"

"Not in the least. I expect it'll be you and the empty bar for most of the night. Pretty dull stuff."

A slider. Strike two.

He opened the shutters with one flick, giving a direct shot through the mirror that hung over his newly assembled beer taps. "I'd think a girl who'd spent so many hours with her face pressed to the heat register just to hear the boys in the basement would be naturally voyeuristic."

He heard the slight intake of breath just as he turned to see a screen full of jibberish. She opened her mouth to speak. Then closed it with the same force with which she snapped down the lid of the laptop. A soft pink rush of color darkened her pretty cheeks.

"Come to think of it, I'll work at home tonight."

Steee-rike three.

"That's not necessary." He grinned at her, but she was already sliding a handbag over her shoulder.

As she opened the door, she tossed him one last look. There was something in her eyes. Some shadow, some secret. Some hurt. As quickly as it appeared, it was gone.

"Good luck tonight," she said, then her pretty lips lifted into a sweet, if totally phony, smile. "Call me if you get hammered with the big nine-o'clock rush."

When the door closed behind her, the room seemed utterly empty, with only a faint lingering smell of something fresh and floral mixed with the aroma of coffee.

Taking a deep breath, he turned to the California sequoia, ready to remove it for spite. But that would be childish.

Instead, he looked through the two-way mirror in time to see Kendra pause at the bar to check out the newly assembled beer taps. She touched one, yanked it forward, then flinched when it spurted.

She bent down, out of his view for a moment, then arose, a coffee mug in hand. Pulling on the tap again, she tilted the mug and let about six ounces of brew flow in, expertly letting the foam slide down the side.

She lifted the mug to the mirror, offering a silent, mock toast directly at him. Then she brought the rim to her mouth, closed her eyes, and took one long, slow chug. Her eyes closed. Her throat pulsed. Her chest rose and fell with each swallow.

And a couple of gallons of blood drained from his head and traveled to the lower half of his body.

When she finished the drink, she dabbed the foam at the corner of her mouth, looked right into the mirror and winked at him.

The taste of the bitter brew still remained in Kendra's mouth several hours later. She'd walked Newman, made dinner, reviewed her inventory numbers, puttered around her bungalow, and even sunk into a long, hot bath.

But no distraction took her mind off Deuce Monroe. Her

brain, normally chock-full of facts, figures and ideas, reeled with unanswered questions.

How could she get through six weeks of this? Where would she get the fortitude to keep up the cavalier, devil-may-care, I-don't-give-a-hoot acting job she was digging out of her depths? What could she do to make him go away? What if he discovered the truth about what happened nine years ago?

There were no answers, only more questions. The last one she asked out loud as she opened Diana's door for a third time to gather up Newman. "Why does that man still get to me after all these years?" The dog looked up, surprised.

"I'm lonely, Newman," she admitted. "Let's take another walk."

Newman never said no. He trotted over to the hook where Diana hung his leash.

Sighing, Kendra closed the slider and wrapped the strap around her wrist letting Newman scamper ahead while her gaze traveled over the wide beach. In the moonlight, the white froth sparkled against the sand, each rhythmic crest rising over the next in an unending tempo.

It had been a night much like this one, on a beach not three miles away, that Kendra Locke had given her love, loyalty and virginity to a boy she'd adored since first grade. And now, so many years later, that boy was at *her* café, driving away *her* customers, changing *her* plans and upsetting *her* peaceful existence.

"And he probably doesn't have a clue how to close the place," she told Newman, who barked in hearty agreement. "What if he screws up?" she asked, picking up her pace across the stone walkway to her beach house. "He doesn't know how to cash out or power down the computers."

Newman barked twice.

"I agree," she whispered, tugging his leash toward her beach house. "We better do what we can to save the place."

In ten minutes, she'd stripped off her sweats and slipped into khaki pants, an old T-shirt, sandals and, oh heck, just a dash of makeup. She rushed through the process, not wanting to change her mind, but definitely not wanting to arrive too late and find the café abandoned, the back door open, the computers still humming.

Kendra navigated the streets of Rockingham, mindful of the ever-growing population of tourists and locals. Something huge must be going on because even the tiny parking lot behind Monroe's was full. She finally nailed a parallel parking space a block away, and it was already ten-fifteen when she and Newman hustled down High Castle Boulevard toward Monroe's. He'd probably bailed by the time the Gibbons brothers left, around eight-thirty.

She expected the front door to be locked when she tugged at the brass handle. But the door whipped open from the other side, propelled by a laughing couple who almost mowed her down in their enthusiasm to get to their car. Kendra stood in the doorway, stunned as they brushed by her and mumbled excuses.

One step into Monroe's and she froze again. From speakers she didn't know she still had, Bruce Springsteen wailed. A stock-car race flashed on one TV monitor, a baseball game on another. Glasses and mugs clanged and loud voices of fifty or sixty people echoed with toasts and laughter, and somewhere, in the distance, she smelled...barbecued chicken.

Kendra ventured a few steps through the door. Had she fallen asleep in the bathtub and got stuck in a really vivid dream?

A total stranger tended the bar. A woman she'd never seen waltzed through a cluster of tables and chairs carrying an old brown drink tray laden with glasses. And, as though her eyes weren't playing enough tricks on her, Jerry and Larry Gibbons were over in the corner, flirting with some girls, sipping ice-cold brews from the brand-new tap.

Kendra tried to breathe, tried to think. How had he done this? How had he—

"Well look what the..." Deuce's chocolate gaze traveled over her, pausing at the floor. "...dog dragged in."

Newman skittered across the hardwood toward him, but Kendra tugged his leash. She opened her mouth, but before she could utter a sound, Deuce was next to her, sliding one solid, strong arm around her waist. His face dipped close enough for his lips to touch her hair.

"Don't tell me," he said, the musky scent of him mixed with beer and barbecue filling her head. "You were worried I couldn't handle the nine o'clock rush?"

The only rush she felt was a bolt of electricity charging from her head, down her body and leaving a thousand goose bumps in its wake. "I was worried you had no clue how to close up."

"We're not closing for hours, Ken-doll. And I hope you'll stay for the duration."

She looked up at him, her razor-sharp brain taking an unexpected vacation. Words, praise, criticism—anything intelligent—eluded her. Everything except the heart-stopping desire to kiss him. And that was not intelligent.

"How did you do this?" she managed to ask.

"Word spreads. It seems Rockingham is still a very small town," he said, his eyes glinting in a tease.

She glanced at the patrons, two deep at the bar. "And, apparently, a thirsty one."

She was enough of a professional to appreciate the revenue flow. And enough of a competitor to be more than a little bit jealous.

She sniffed. "What's that smell?"

"Profits," he whispered, that mighty arm squeezing her waist even tighter. "You smell revenue on the rise."

"I smell barbecue chicken."

"Oh that," he laughed, guiding her closer to the bar. "You know JC Myers owns The Wingman now?"

She assumed the ownership of Rockingham's favorite barbecue joint was a rhetorical question and didn't answer.

"He agreed to provide some emergency assistance."

"What emergency?"

"A munchie emergency. You can't serve gallons of alcohol and no food." He waved a hand toward the crowd. "We've got to keep these people happy."

"There's food in the back," she said defensively.

He rolled his eyes. "Granola bars and cupcakes."

"Muffins," she corrected.

"Not exactly sports-bar food."

Newman pattered around her and she scooped him up protectively, before she wandered farther into the fray. She saw some familiar faces from around town, and plenty of new ones. Who *were* all these people and why had they suddenly shown up?

"Who's tending bar?" she asked.

"You don't remember Dec Clifford? My old first baseman?"

As if she'd ever noticed anyone on any team he played on besides…the pitcher. "Vaguely. I didn't realize he was still in Rockingham."

"He's a lawyer in Boston now," Deuce told her, his hand

firmly planted on the small of her back, making sure those goose bumps had no chance of disappearing. "And over there is Eric Fleming, outfielder. But now he's in commercial real estate in New Hampshire. That's Ginger Alouette serving drinks. She was a track star in high school, if you don't remember. She lives in Provincetown. Most of these people still live on Cape Cod—I just had to dig them up."

A lawyer from Boston, a developer from New Hampshire and Ginger from P-town. They'd all come to see him—to work for him.

"I'll get real staff soon," he promised. "I just wanted to get open as soon as possible and so I had a little help from my friends."

He was still the draw, not Monroe's Bar & Grill & Wannabe Cyber Café. Deuce was the main attraction and, suddenly, with sickening clarity, she faced the truth. He could make this work. He could make a raging success out of the bar…and she'd be doing Seamus a disservice by trying to fight it.

"I can't believe you brought a dog in here," he said, reaching for a quick pet of Newman, who nuzzled into Kendra.

She'd never dreamed the place would be packed, or Newman would have stayed home. As she would have. "I thought you'd…" *Be all alone.* "Need some—"

"Company?" he asked with a grin.

"No, just help." But that had been ridiculous. He had all the assistance he needed. She looked pointedly at the black screens of her computers. "How did you figure out how to get all the systems down?"

"I just installed a glycolic cooling unit, a CD player and a satellite dish, Kendra. It didn't take a Harvard degree to turn off a bunch of computers."

The comment jabbed her right in the stomach. She swallowed a hundred retorts and looked away. He had no idea what he'd said, and she could hardly zing him anymore for incompetence. He had it all going on, and more.

"Would you like a drink?" he asked, as they reached one empty barstool. "Dec, remember Jack's little sister? Get the lady whatever she likes. It's on the house."

Jack's little sister. That's what she'd always be to him. Not the owner of this establishment. Not the woman he'd deflowered a decade ago. Not…anything. Just Jack's little sister.

"On the house?" She allowed him to ease her onto a barstool. "I *am* the house."

He just laughed, leaning so close to her ear she thought he was about to plant a kiss on her neck.

"I believe you've already had a sample of our new draft selection, right, Ken-doll?"

She just looked at the bartender, vaguely remembering a younger version of his face that had no doubt spent hours with the baseball boys in the basement. She'd been so blinded to anyone but Deuce. "I'll just have a soda, please," she told him.

And then Deuce was gone. A whisper of "Excuse me," and the warmth of his body disappeared from behind her. She fought the urge to turn and watch him work the crowd. Instead, she cuddled Newman in her lap and gratefully accepted the cold drink for her dry throat.

"He's absolutely adorable."

Kendra turned to see the familiar, friendly face of Sophie Swenson, her hostess and right hand at the café. Sophie held a glass of white wine—in a stem glass—and her deep-blue eyes glinted with excitement.

"Yeah, he's adorable," Kendra assured her, with a disdainful glance back at Deuce. "But he knows it."

Sophie let out a soft giggle. "I meant the dog."

"Oh." Kendra couldn't help laughing as she pulled New-man higher on her lap. "Well, Newman knows he's adorable, too." She narrowed her eyes at Sophie, noticing the flush on her pretty cheeks, the way her gaze darted around the crowd. Would her most senior employee want to slide over to the Dark Side now? "You want to switch to a new evening sched-ule, Soph?"

Sophie shrugged and settled into the barstool. "If the ac-tion stays like this, I might. I mean is Monroe's going back to being a bar? What about the expansion plans?"

Kendra let out a long, slow sigh. "I have no idea," she ad-mitted. "I just wish he'd go back to where he came from."

"He came from…here." Sophie's eyes were without humor. "I mean, his dad owns the bar."

Kendra's shoulders slumped slightly. "I own half of this bar."

Sophie raised a surprised eyebrow.

"Internet café," Kendra corrected, burying her fingers in Newman's soft fur and scratching him. "And I'm not going to walk away because the mighty Deuce has come home."

Sophie's gaze moved from Kendra to Deuce, then back to Kendra. "He's crazy about you."

Her heartbeat skidded up to triple time. "I doubt that."

"He hasn't taken his eyes off you since you walked in here."

Why did that fact send yet another shower of goose bumps over her? Kendra closed her eyes until it passed. "No, we're just in an oddly competitive situation right now."

Kendra stole one more glance over her shoulder. Ginger the track star-turned cocktail waitress gazed up at Deuce and gig-gled. Another athletic-looking man slapped him on the back. But Deuce's gaze moved over everyone and locked on

Kendra. There was that secret smile, that cocky tease in his eyes. And, as it had since before she knew how to write his name in cursive, the old zingy sensation washed over her.

Oh, Lord, not still. Not at thirty years old. That incapacitating girlhood crush had resulted in nothing but sleepless nights and pillows drenched in tears. A lost opportunity to graduate from the finest university in the country. And she wouldn't even think about the baby. She'd trained herself not to ever, ever do that.

Hadn't she paid enough for the honor of worshipping at Deuce's altar?

"Call it competition if you like," Sophie said, yanking Kendra back to the present. "But that man's got you front and center on his radar screen."

"Well then I'll just have to disappear."

"That's kind of difficult since you're both working in the same place," Sophie said.

"Not at all," Kendra said, gathering up Newman with determination. "I work days, he works nights. And never the twain shall meet."

Sophie tilted her head a centimeter to the right in a secret warning. "The twains are about to meet, honey. Hunky baseball player on your six."

Clutching Newman, Kendra slid off the stool and took a speed course through the crowd around the bar. The back door was closest, so she focused on it like a beacon for a lost ship. If she could just get into the kitchen before he got to her, she could slip into the back parking lot.

She breezed through the storage area, ignored the surprised looks from the borrowed employees of The Wingman who were plating up chicken in the little kitchen, and flung the back door open into the night.

"That wasn't so hard, was it?" she whispered to Newman, setting him gently on the concrete.

Newman sniffed at the corner of the Dumpster.

"No time for trash, Newman." She tugged on his leash and led him along a brick wall through the side alley and to the main road.

Where she walked smack into one six-foot-two-inch former baseball player wearing that triumphant grin that used to melt her in the stands of Rockingham Field.

"The party just started, Ken-doll," he said softly, placing those incredible hands on her shoulders and pulling her just an inch too close to that solid wall of chest. "You can't run away yet."

The definition of stupid, she thought desperately, is making the same mistake twice. And Kendra Locke, who'd scored a coveted scholarship to Harvard and masterminded the makeover of Rockingham's version of Silicon Valley was not *stupid*. Was she?

"I'm not running away," she insisted. "It's too crowded in there for a dog. And I—" she cleared her throat. "I have to go home."

"I'd like you to stay." He dipped his face close to hers. She didn't move. Couldn't breathe. Couldn't possibly think.

Deuce was going to kiss her. She opened her mouth to say something, something like "This is a bad idea," but before she could manage a word, he covered her mouth with his.

She stood stone-still as his fingers tightened his grip and his lips moved imperceptibly over hers. He closed a little bit of space between them, his chest touched hers, his legs touched hers, his tongue touched hers.

Was she really going to do this? She, the former Mensa candidate and Rockingham High valedictorian? Could she be that foolish and wild? Could she dare let history repeat itself?

Opening her mouth, she did the only thing she could possibly think to do.

She kissed him back.

# Five

$K$endra slid her arms around Deuce's shoulders, which was all the body language he needed to completely close the space between them.

A soft moan rumbled in her throat as he tested the waters by grazing her teeth with his tongue. In that instant, it all came back. The magical kisses of an eager, sweet girl. The memory of that extraordinary night hit him as hard as the surf that they'd let pound them as they'd lain naked on the sand.

He touched the dip of her waist and skimmed his hands over the curve of her backside, hardening instantly against her stomach, moving automatically against her hips.

"Deuce." He could feel his name tumble from her lips as she reluctantly broke the kiss. "Newman."

*Newman?*

Then he realized the dog was parting them by pulling on

his leash. He gave the leather strap a good tug. "Hey bud. Gimme a break."

That was enough to kill the moment. Even though her blue eyes were darkened by the same arousal that twisted through him, Kendra backed up.

"Listen to me," she said softly, but with a whispered vehemence that made him look hard at her. "I'm not the same girl I was back then."

"No, you're not," he agreed, pulling her just enough into him so there was no doubt of the effect she had on him. "Now you're a woman." He traced his thumb along her jaw. "Smart, willful and…beautiful."

She dipped away from his touch, the darkness in her eyes shifting from arousal to wariness.

"I'm smart all right," she insisted, and he sensed she was telling this to herself as much as to him. "Too smart to…" Her voice drifted as she managed to untangle herself from his arm. "I'm going home now."

He smiled at her. "I like you, Kendra."

She backed up farther and gave him a dubious look. "What are you up to, Deuce Monroe?"

"You don't trust me at all, do you?"

Her eyes suddenly widened. "Do you think seducing me is going to win you the bar? You think I'll just back down from this fight because you swept me off my feet and into bed?"

The words punched him. "No." Truthfully, the thought hadn't even occurred to him. "I just…like you."

Nothing on her face said she believed him.

"Why don't you stay until I close up?" he suggested. "We can talk about the business, about how we can…figure this out."

"You don't want to talk."

No, he didn't. But he would. "Come on, Kendra. Stay. I can take you home later."

Newman skittered toward the street, suddenly impatient with the conversation, and Kendra went with him as though she felt exactly the same. "Just lock all the doors when you leave. And put the cash in the green zipper case in the bottom drawer of the office."

"Oh, yeah, I'll put the cash in the office that doesn't lock."

"The desk does," she said, reaching into her pocket. "Here." She held up a key chain. "The little gold one locks the cash drawer. Leave it on Diana's kitchen table and I'll stop in and walk Newman in the morning."

Maybe he'd leave them on his dresser so she'd have to come in his bedroom to get them. Maybe, if he hadn't lost his touch, she'd be right there in the bed next to him in the morning.

He reached for her hand. "I'd really like if you'd stay."

She shook her head in warning. "My car's right there," she said. "Bye."

Before he could get a grip on her arm, she'd taken off with the dog in tow, hustling down the street. Guess he *had* lost his touch.

He let his arousal subside as he waited in the street to see her get into a car and drive away. Pocketing the keys, he watched until the taillights disappeared at the bend away from the beach.

He touched his mouth, the feel of her lips still fresh. He was not done with her. Not by a long shot.

The front door of the bar flung open and two of his old teammates came bounding out, their laughter loud, their guts showing that beer consumption had replaced batting practice as their favorite pastime.

"Man, Deuce, it's good to have you back." Charlie Lotane pounded Deuce's back. "This is going to be an awesome bar. You got the touch, man."

"Ya think, C-Lo?" The old nicknames came back easily. "I was just wondering if I'd lost it."

"Deuce, you are the man!" Charlie assured him over his shoulder. "We really needed a place like this in the Rock. Way to go, bro."

"Thank God you came back, Deuce."

Deuce watched them disappear down High Castle and suddenly wondered just what the hell he'd come back to prove. That he was still "the man" who could pack Monroe's? That he was still the main event in town? That he could still see adoration in Jack's little sister's eyes?

Was he that shallow and insecure?

The door burst open again and he welcomed the distraction.

Newman curled into the corner of Kendra's living room, as at home in this beach bungalow as he was in Diana's mansion. He was sound asleep by the time Kendra realized exactly what she needed to do in order get her head back on straight.

She needed to read her notebook.

She'd never been one to buy a diary, with a pretty filigree lock, or an embroidered design on the cover. It seemed so planned and pathetic, as though a formal diary somehow legitimized her longings. Plus, she'd known at a very young age that such a girlish item would be too tempting to Jack...and the thought of him sharing her diary with the boys in the basement still sent a rush of heat to her cheeks.

So she'd kept a simple spiral notebook, college-ruled and ragged at the edges. It never drew anyone's attention; instead it blended in with her many schoolbooks, another tool of a brainiac child bound and determined to get to the Ivy League.

But this was no ordinary notebook. The dates of the entries were far apart, but over the course of about a dozen years, it was just about full. Written on both sides of every page, in a script that had started out awkward, moved to a girlish flourish, and ended up as scratchy as a doctor's prescription.

She hadn't looked at the book in at least four years. But tonight, her body still humming from the electrical charge of that kiss, she'd gone to the bottom of a box of rarely worn sweaters to find a piece of her heart that had never quite healed. Sliding her nail into one of the curled corners, she wet her lips, still warm from the taste of Deuce.

The man could kiss and that was a fact.

In truth, it had been right in the middle of that heart-tripping lip-lock that the notebook had flashed in her mind like a big red flag. Warning. *Warning.* Serious, severe discontentment and disappointment ahead.

She lifted the cover. "Perhaps we need a little history lesson," she whispered to herself.

She opened it randomly, to about the fifth or sixth page.

The words "Mrs. Deuce Monroe" decorated the margins. The *O*'s in Monroe were hearts. Kendra laughed softly. She had to. Otherwise, she'd cry. The penmanship was classic third-grade, early cursive.

Tomorrow, my family is driving all the way to Fall River for my brother's baseball tournament. And guess what???? Deuce is coming too!!! In our car!!! His parents said he could drive with Jack!!! I will be in the car with him for hours and hours!!! I'm excited and happy tonight.

Kendra smiled, shaking her head. She remembered the trip vividly. Jack and Deuce had traded baseball cards and listened to the Red Sox game the entire time and never once said a word to her. Except when they rolled in laughter because she had to stop and go to the bathroom so often. And they'd lost the tournament on one of Deuce's classic out-of-control pitches, so the trip home was real quiet.

She flipped to the middle. Her handwriting had matured, and the date told her the entry was made when she was fourteen years old.

I hate Anne Keppler. I just hate her and her black hair and her perfect cheerleader's body. He calls her "Annie"—I heard him. She's down there right now, playing pool and giggling like a hyena along with that completely *dumb* Dawn Hallet(osis) who runs after Jack like a puppy-dog. Oh, God. He likes her. Deuce likes Anne Keppler. I heard him tell Jack last night after everyone left their noisy party. He *kissed* her! I heard him tell Jack he got *tongue*. How gross is that?

Her limbs grew heavy at the memory of Deuce's tongue. Not gross at all, as a matter of fact.

A series of broken-heart sketches followed that entry, but many months passed before she wrote again. A few words about entering high school, taking difficult courses, then...

Oh, lovely little piece of paper...I'm holding my driver's license. Yes! The State of Massachusetts and some really obnoxious old lady with orange hair agreed that I could drive (they were mercifully understanding about the parallel parking problem—the parallel parking that Jack *swore* I wouldn't have to do). Mom said I could go to Star Market this afternoon for some groceries. Guess I'll have to take a quick spin past Rock Field…there's baseball practice tonight….

She'd taken that drive about a million times. And she'd made up another million excuses to wander over to the stands, to give something to Jack, to watch Deuce out in the field, throwing pitches, getting chewed out by Coach Delacorte. Rarely, if ever, did Deuce notice her. Still, she was certain that if she just waited, if she just grew up a little more, if she just got rid of the braces, if she just could fill a C-cup, he would realize that he'd loved her all along.

By the time she grew up and the braces came off and the bra size increased, Deuce had ditched Rockingham for the major leagues. She tried to forget him and, for the most part, with her focus on getting into Harvard, and staying there, she succeeded. It was even possible to work at Monroe's in the summers and not think too much about him.

Until Leah Monroe died, and Deuce came home, in need of comfort and love.

She didn't bother to look for a passage in the journal that described the night she lost her virginity on the beach. She'd never written about it, trusting her memory to keep every single detail crystal-clear in her memory.

But as time passed, she did turn to her red notebook to write about the pain. The first entry was made when it began to dawn on her that she'd never hear from him again.

Deuce has been gone for nine days. Like a fool, I check my messages every hour. I pick up the phone to see if it's working. I run to the mailbox for a card, a note, a letter.

The closest I can get to him is the box scores in the paper. He pitched last night. Lost. Does he think about me when he goes back to his hotel? Does he think it's too late to call? Or does he have a girl in Chicago, in Detroit, in Baltimore…wherever he is right now.

Oh, God, why doesn't he call? How could he have been so sweet, so loving, so tender? Was it all an act?

There was one more entry, but Kendra shut the notebook and tossed it on the table. The walk down memory lane was no pleasant stroll; the exercise had worked. She'd never meant any more to Deuce than Annie Keppler or any other girl in his past. Of course, since their paths were crossing again, being the professional player that he was, he hit on her tonight. One kiss in the dark. Another meaningless display of affection. He was just high on his packed house and she was the available female of the moment.

He had no idea how their one night of pleasure had ruined her entire life. Evidently, Jack had never told Deuce his sister got pregnant and had to drop out of Harvard. Even though her brother had stuck by her and was still close to her, Jack had been as embarrassed by her stupidity as her parents. And the father of her baby remained the closest-guarded secret in her life. She'd never told anyone. Not even Seamus, who had never, ever passed judgment on her. He'd just given her a job when she needed one.

Newman's sudden bark yanked her back to reality, followed by a soft knock on her door. "Kendra? Are you still up?"

Oh God. Deuce.

She grabbed the red notebook and stuffed it into the first available hiding place, the softsided bag she took to and from work.

"What's the matter?" She asked as she approached the door. Her voice sounded thick. How long had she been lying there, dreaming of Deuce?

"Nothing," he called. "I wanted to give you back your key."

Slowly, she opened the door a crack and reached her hand out, palm up.

He closed his fingers over hers, and pulled her hand to his mouth. The soft kiss made her knees weak.

"We made over a thousand dollars tonight," he whispered.

She jerked her hand away and let the door open wider. "Get outta town!"

He grinned in the moonlight, holding up her set of keys. "I did that already. And now I'm back." Stepping closer to the door, he whispered, "Can I come in and tell you about what a great night it was?"

*How could he have been so sweet, so loving, so tender? Was it all an act?*

She swiped the keys dangling from his hand. "No. Just leave these on Diana's kitchen table in the future. I'll be sure you can find them on my desk at the end of the day."

Then she dug deep for every ounce of willpower she'd ever had and closed the door in his face.

Something she should have done a long time ago.

Deuce laced his fingers through the chain-link fence that surrounded Rock Field and sucked in a chest full of his favorite smell. Freshly turned clay and recently mowed spring grass. A groundskeeper worked the dirt around the mound, raking it to the perfect height for a six-foot pitcher to slide some fire in the hole.

He didn't have to be at the bar for another hour or so for his second full night of operation. All day long he'd fought the urge to go to Monroe's and find Kendra to see what she really thought of his success the previous night. At the same time, he fought the urge to make a trip to his old stomping grounds.

Eventually, he lost one of the fights, and drove the short distance to Rockingham High, knowing that he'd probably arrive on a practice afternoon. In April, every afternoon was practice.

His elbow throbbed as he tightened his grip on the metal, pushing his face into the fence as though he could walk right through it. Come to think of it, he *could* walk right through it. All he'd have to do is whistle to the groundskeeper, who'd amble over and ask what he needed, assuming he was a parent or even a scout. Deuce would introduce himself, and watch the man's face light up in recognition.

Deuce Monroe? Rockingham High's most famous graduate? *Well, get on the field, Deuce!*

He heard a burst of laughter and turned to see half a dozen lanky high-schoolers dressed in mismatched practice clothes, dragging bat bags. One balanced three helmets on his head, another circled his arm over his shoulder to warm it up.

Somebody swore and more laughter ensued; one boy spat as they started unloading their gear.

After a few minutes of stretching out, some of the players took off for windsprints and laps. A guy who looked to be about forty, wearing sweats and a whistle, jogged onto the field. He eyed Deuce for a minute, then started calling out to the players.

Rick Delacorte, the only coach who'd ever known how to handle him, had retired last year after twenty years at Rock High. Deuce had stayed in touch with Rick, knew he and his wife had headed out to Arizona to spend their golden years in a condo strategically located within driving distance of the Diamondbacks' stadium.

He couldn't remember the name of this new guy, somebody Rick said had moved up from Maryland or D.C. to take the job. Deuce watched him needle a few players, sending some more for laps. A couple of catchers started blocking drills, and the infielders lined up for hit-downs and cut-offs.

An easy sense of familiarity settled over Deuce as he watched a few pitchers warm up for a long toss. In less than three throws, Deuce could see one of the kids limiting his range of motion. The new coach didn't notice, and Deuce bit back the urge to call out a correction. Instead, he sat down on the aluminum stands. Just for a minute. Just to see how they played.

He only realized what time it was when batting practice ended, and the coach called for the last run. He was seriously late for the bar, but hell, this had been too relaxing. As he stood, the groundskeeper emerged from the afternoon shadows behind the visitor's dugout.

"Excuse me?" the man called out.

Deuce acknowledged him with a nod.

"You lookin' for someone in particular, son?"

"Just watching the practice," he said, squinting into the sun that now sat just above the horizon.

The older man approached slowly, an odd smile tugging at his lips. "What do you think of the new coach, Deuce?"

Deuce started in surprise. "Do we know each other?"

The man laughed. "I know you, but you probably don't

remember me. The name's Martin Hatcher and I used to be—"

"The Hatchet Man," Deuce finished for him, taking the hand that was offered to shake. "I'm sorry I didn't recognize you, sir."

The former principal of Rockingham High laughed easily. "Well, I'm not as imposing with a rake in my hand as I was waving your pink slips."

Deuce shook his head and chuckled. "What are you doing out here?" The juxtaposition of the feared and revered principal now in the position of field caretaker seemed preposterous.

"I'm retired, Deuce," he said, stuffing his hands in the pockets of his pants. "But I volunteer here just like a lot of ex-Rock High teachers and staff. I still love the school, so I do what needs to be done. Last week, I worked in the cafeteria for a few days. That's always a bit of an education in human behavior."

Deuce took in the network of wrinkles over the familiar face, and the shock of gray hair. He'd done his share to add to the whitening of that head, he was sure.

"Don't feel bad that you didn't recognize me, Deuce. I'm not sure I would have known you, either. But I heard rumors that your own retirement brought you back to town."

"Wasn't exactly retirement," he said with a grin. "More like lifelong detention."

That earned him another hearty laugh and a pat on the shoulder. "You always could charm your way out of anything, Mr. Monroe."

"I couldn't charm the contract lawyer for the Nevada Snake Eyes."

"Their loss, our gain. It's just too bad it didn't happen a season earlier."

"Why? I had my best year last year."

"Indeed you did. I thought you could have been a Cy Young contender."

Deuce snorted. "Not that good."

"But if you'd have pulled your little race-car exploit before Rock High hired him…" He jutted his chin toward the dugout where the new coach stood, surrounded by ballplayers, some of whom listened to his lectures, while others looked anxious to leave.

"What's his name?" Deuce asked.

"George Ellis. He's teaching science, too, which I think he's much better at than coaching."

Deuce's gaze moved to the field, then back to Martin. "He's not bad. Lots of energy. Seems to know how to get them to hit."

"You'd have been better."

"Me?" Deuce coughed back a laugh. "No, thanks. I have no interest in going out there and motivating guys who think they know everything." Guys like *him*.

They fell into pace together toward the parking lot. "So you'd rather run a bar."

Deuce heard the skepticism in his tone. "It's called Monroe's, Mr. Hatcher. And, since I am called that, too, it feels like the right thing to do."

"I'm not your principal anymore, Deuce. You don't have to call me Mr. Hatcher, and you don't have to give me your load of BS."

Deuce slowed his step and peered at the man who once had spent hours threatening, cajoling and teasing Deuce. "That was no load of BS."

"Monroe's isn't even a bar anymore."

"We're working on that."

Martin chewed his lip for a moment, then lowered his voice. "Seems to me Kendra Locke has some pretty big plans for the place."

The Hatchet Man, Deuce remembered from numerous trips to his office, always had a subtle way of making his point.

"I have plans, too." But then, subtle had never worked that well on Deuce.

Martin paused at the edge of the parking lot, crossing him arms and nodding. "Kendra was a favorite student of mine. Of course, she was a few years behind you."

"Her brother Jack was my best friend."

"Oh, yes. I remember Jackson Locke. A rebel, but very artistic. And he liked those basketball bombs over in the teacher's lot." He chuckled again. "Let you take the heat for the big one that dented Rose Cavendish's old Dodge Dart, as I recall."

Deuce just smiled. "Ancient history."

"We got a lot of that around here," Martin mused, his gaze traveling toward the red brick two-story building of the Rockingham High that sat up on an impressive hill. "Kendra has quite a history, too."

Kendra? Where was he going with this? Deuce waited for him to continue, as he would have if he'd been sitting across Principal Hatcher's imposing desk, discussing his latest infraction.

"She went to Harvard, did you know that?" Martin asked.

"Yes."

"Didn't finish, though."

"That seems a shame," Deuce said. "She was real smart." And kissed like a goddess, too.

"I only had a few Harvard-bound seniors in my twenty-five years at Rock High. So I remember every one."

"Why didn't she finish?"

"You'll have to ask her," he said, unlocking the door of an older model SUV. "And by the way, she's *still* real smart."

"I know."

"And you still love baseball."

Deuce grinned. "I'm not going to coach."

The other man just laughed and climbed into the driver's seat. "You spent a lot of time watching practice."

That Hatchet Man. He was always an observant dude. "Nice to see you again, Mr…Martin."

"I'll stop in the bar sometime, Deuce. I heard you packed them in last night."

"News travels fast around Rockingham."

Martin nodded. "It sure does."

Deuce closed the driver's-side door and said goodbye, watching his old friend and nemesis drive away. Then he turned to the field and took one more deep breath of baseball.

But suddenly he really wanted to know why Kendra Locke had given up her dream, and why that one piece of news didn't seem to travel like everything else around Rockingham.

# Six

Flat on his back, the cold dampness of the tile floor seeping through an old Yomuri Giants sweatshirt, Deuce swore softly as the broken nozzle of the soda spritzer slipped from his fingers and bounced on his chest. He'd been under the bar for half an hour and still didn't have the damn thing working right.

Five days into his latest endeavor, and he was fixing his own equipment. At eight in the morning, no less. A decision he made the night before when the sprayer had malfunctioned. As much as he'd like to sleep after a late night running Monroe's, he wanted to get in before any of the Internet café customers showed up.

Yeah. *Right.* He shook off a dribble of club soda that trickled onto his cheek and clamped his teeth tighter over the flashlight that shone on the unit.

Who the hell was he kidding? Cybersurfers didn't care if

the bar was being worked on while they shopped online and played medieval trading games.

He'd come in before the place opened because Kendra had made a science out of avoiding him. And Deuce didn't want to be avoided any more.

But when he'd slipped in the back that morning, he'd heard voices raised in confrontation from behind the partially closed door to the office. He picked up Sophie's complaints about an employee who was supposed to have done something regarding a software update, and Kendra's calmly spoken instructions that Sophie take care of the problem.

Instead of interrupting, he'd gone straight to the bar and slid underneath to inspect the faulty spritzer. As he worked, he heard the sounds of the café opening up, and the ubiquitous smell of coffee being brewed.

He just about had the nozzle reinstalled when the coffee aroma was superseded by something light and spicy and pretty. Turning his head, his penlight lit a pair of high-heeled sandals a few feet from his face. His gaze slid up, up, up a long set of bare legs to a short skirt with a flippy hemline.

Man, there was something to be said for a view from the floor.

One of the cream-colored shoes tapped.

"Come on, Deuce," Kendra whispered to herself. "Where did you hide the soda thingy?"

She shoved a few of the stainless-steel cocktail shakers to the side, and yanked at the hose that was connected to the nozzle in his hand. "What the heck's the matter with this?"

She pulled harder, hand over hand toward the end of the hose…where she gasped as they came face to face.

"Oh my God! You scared me. What are you doing down there?"

The flashlight beam made another slow journey up her legs, stopping on a particularly sweet mid-thigh muscle. It flexed under his scrutiny.

"Adjusting my equipment," he managed to say without unlocking his teeth. "And enjoying the show."

She backed out of the beam. "I should step on you."

That made him laugh and the flashlight fell out of his mouth. Slowly, he slid out from under the lower shelf and stood to his full height. She tried not to look at him, but failed.

He wiped at some grime on his jeans and held the sprayer toward her. "Soda, water or diet? They were getting all mixed into one messy flow last night."

"Certainly didn't affect the *cash* flow."

He grinned. "Oh, so you counted it already?"

Over the past week, they'd started an unspoken exchange. He locked the pouch in the drawer each night, and left the keys on Diana's kitchen table. She picked up the keys early the next morning when she walked Newman, while Deuce was still asleep. When her day was over—always a few minutes after he arrived—she took the pouch to the bank and left the keys on the desk for him. All the while, she managed to avoid spending any significant amount of time with him.

"As a matter of fact, I have a meeting with the architect in a few minutes," she told him. "I was planning to make a cash drop at the bank on my way."

"Oh, that's why you're dressed up?" He took another leisurely gaze over a silk blouse buttoned just high enough to make him want to…unbutton it. "I thought it was to impress me."

"I don't imagine a skirt and blouse are too impressive to you."

He shrugged. "You look nice. But I'm kind of partial to leather."

She rolled her eyes and opened her right palm to reveal two pills. "You're not helping my headache."

He retrieved a clean glass, filled it with water and handed it to her. As she put the pills in her mouth, he said, "Don't blame me. I heard you fighting with Sophie."

Her eyes popped open, but she managed to get the aspirin down. "I wasn't fighting with her," she denied hotly after she'd swallowed. "We were just working out some issues."

"Sounded like she wasn't happy."

She sighed softly and spilled the remaining water in the sink, her gaze moving across to the computer area where Sophie worked at a terminal. "She's not."

"What's the matter?"

"Just some coworker issues." She settled a sincere blue gaze on him. "Nothing I can't handle."

"Well, maybe I can help," he offered. "I know a little about teamwork."

She regarded him for a minute, an internal battle whether or not to confide in him waged over her expression. "She just has some problems with newer employees," she finally said. "Not everyone is quite as competent as she is and, well, she tends to let them know it."

"Like the veteran and the rookies."

She looked questioningly at him, then smiled. "Not all of life can be equated to baseball."

"Yes it can," he answered matter-of-factly. "Why don't you put her in charge of training?"

"Training?"

"Give her responsibility for their success. Coaches do that all the time in the spring when they're trying to build cohesion between the old, seasoned guys who know everything and the hotshots up from the minors who *think* they know everything."

She glanced at Sophie, then back at him. "What do they do, exactly?"

"If you give her the job of training them, and tie their success to hers, she might be more prone to want them to succeed."

"She does want them to succeed," she countered. "She also wants everyone to be as good as she is. With the computers, with the customers, with everything. And some of these kids are just out of college."

"Precisely." He glided the sprayer hose back into place and twisted a faucet to wash his hands. "But make her feel like their accomplishments reflect her skills. Trust me. It'll work."

She said nothing as he soaped and rinsed his hands, then gave him that gut-tightening smile. The real one. The one where she let down her guard. "Thanks for the advice. Now what are you doing here at this hour?"

"I wanted to talk to you."

"Oh?"

"I can't seem to get you alone for five minutes."

"I'm busy." She lifted a shoulder of indifference, but the cavalier act wasn't working. She was avoiding him and they both knew it. "I'm busy. You work nights. I work days. And, by the way, you're making my life complicated."

He managed not to smile. "I am?"

"All this money, Deuce. How can I make a compelling argument to your father that we shouldn't have a bar in here?"

"You can't. That's the idea. And look at this place." He gestured toward the computer stations, many that were taken with busy patrons. "You're not exactly losing money while I'm making it."

She nodded. "As a matter of fact, café and Internet access revenues are up, too."

"Good, then you won't mind investing in a pizza oven."

"A pizza oven?" She backed up to stare at him. "Now you want to turn this place into a pizzeria?"

He swept a hand toward the wall of booze behind him. "They drink, they have to eat. I did some research and pizza is a very high-profit item. Especially per slice."

She looked dubious. "I don't know."

"You might be able to serve it in the afternoon, too."

"With coffee?"

He winked. "It's best with beer."

"Deuce." Her shoulders sank. "I'm on my way to meet with the architect and you are changing my business plan by the minute."

"To the tune of a grand a night."

"I know. I can count." She put her fingertips to her temples and rubbed gently. His fingers itched to help alleviate the headache. "Let me think about the pizza oven and—"

"I'm just going to order it. I wanted to know if you have a particular supplier you use."

"I do. Buddy McCrosson, over in Fall River. But I have to deal with him because he's an old bag of wind and wouldn't give you the best price."

"Then you can come with me to pick it out."

"I can't, I have a new employee starting tomorrow—"

"Put Sophie in charge of your new employee." He gave her a victorious smile. "And we'll take a drive out to Fall River tomorrow."

She shook her head, a flash of terror in her eyes. Was she afraid of the spontaneous change to her plans…or of being alone with him?

"Kendra," he leaned lower. "We're partners here." He almost closed the space between her temple and his lips. Would a kiss on that aching spot make her feel better?

"We're not partners," she said stiffly, her eyes locked on his.

"But you can't avoid me for the next four weeks."

She closed her eyes as though his very proximity made her dizzy, sending a splash of satisfaction through him. He set his lips on the soft skin of her hairline and forehead and kissed. "I hope your headache goes away."

"You are my headache," she said softly. "You make my head *throb*."

He laughed softly. "Great. We can work down from there."

There was no doubt Sophie loved the idea of creating a training manual and implementing it. She fairly danced out of Kendra's office the next morning, and even held the door for Deuce who had been waiting outside. For how long, Kendra had no idea.

"So that went well, huh?" he asked, his dark eyes glimmering.

She hated to admit it, but he'd been right, and one good turn probably deserved another. "Thank you for your advice," she told him. "I owe you one."

"Great. I figure we can be in Fall River by noon, pick out the pizza oven of our dreams and kiss off the rest of the afternoon with an intimate beachside lunch."

Intimate? Kiss? *Dreams?* She ignored the rush of anticipation that meandered from her heart through her stomach and settled way, way too low. "I owe you one, Deuce, not a day and lunch. Anyway, it won't take two hours to get there. We can be home and back to work by one o'clock."

"I need a pizza oven, sweetheart." He waved a dismissive hand toward the disarray of papers and files on her desk. "And you need a break."

That much was true. Seamus had called from San Francisco to tell her that a few of the meetings had gone so well that the investors needed some more data. She'd pulled that together, which was no mean feat considering she wasn't working evenings. Blowing off the day with Deuce seemed both insane and inspired.

He leaned one impressive shoulder against the doorjamb and her gaze flickered over the taut fit of his navy-blue polo shirt, tucked into the narrow hips of a pair of khaki pants. He'd dressed nicely for their day trip. She'd worn jeans and a sweater—not fully believing he'd follow up on his threats to take her to Fall River. But here he was…looking…

"You going to stare at me for an hour or are we leaving?"

*Stare.* She blinked. "You're imagining things. I'm just wondering what my restaurant supplier will think of you." She made a showing of hunting for her bag. "I guess if he likes baseball, we're in good shape."

"No," he said, his serious tone forcing her to look up. "Let's just leave my former career out of it."

She regarded him for a moment, the weight of her tote bag seeming as heavy as his voice. "Really?" She dropped the handle of the tote bag and just grabbed her purse. "That's not like you."

"I'm full of surprises," he said with a laugh, levity back in place. "I even have one in the parking lot."

In the kitchen she stopped to talk to Sophie and explain where they were going. Ignoring Sophie's subtle raised eyebrow implying "isn't this an interesting development?" she followed Deuce into the back lot, where his rented car had been replaced with a bright-red Mercedes two-seater…top down.

"Surprise," he said. "I decided to upgrade."

Her breath caught in her throat and all she could think about was the last time he took her out in a convertible. It was Seamus's car and she didn't remember the make, only that when he'd pushed the driver's seat all the way back, she'd fit perfectly between his body and the steering wheel.

Heat lightning flashed through her veins at the memory.

"I thought it would be nice since we'll take Highway 28 over to the south shore," Deuce said.

It took her a moment to erase the memory of his rock-hard body and soul-melting kisses to process what he'd just said. "The beach road? That'll take forever. Route 6 is much faster."

"What's your rush?" He opened the passenger door and indicated for her to climb in. "I thought it would be fun to see the beaches. I haven't been to some of those places in…years."

Oh, this was a bad idea. A joyride along the beach—*that* beach—in a convertible with Deuce. How did this happen? She had been so adept at avoiding him and now she was walking right into hell on four wheels.

Or was it heaven?

In the side-view mirror, she saw him study her backside as she slipped into the deep-red leather, already warmed from the sun. His gaze lingered just long enough for her to glance over her shoulder and burn him with a warning glare.

He made no attempt to look away. Instead, his scrutiny burned hotter than the leather against her body. "You always did do justice to a pair of jeans, Kendra."

Oh, hell. It *was* heaven.

Did Deuce deliberately slow down as they passed the dunes of West Rock Beach? Did he even remember that this was the beach…their beach? Or was Kendra the only one who nurtured those memories?

In nine years, she'd never returned to West Rock Beach.

She battled the urge to look to her left, to look at the sandy backdrop and the few reeds of tall grass, and at the man who sat next to her.

"Tell me something, Ken-doll." The serious tone made her stomach drop. "Do you think of me when you pass this spot?"

She leaned her head back and let the sun stream over her face. "Why would I do that?"

Laughing, he accelerated and pulled the gearshift into fourth, his knuckles just grazing the worn denim of her jeans. "You are bound and determined not to talk about it, aren't you?"

Oh, God. "Correct."

"You think if we just act like it never happened, then we can pretend it didn't, don't you?"

"Correct again."

She opened her eyes to find his gaze locked on her. "It did happen, Kendra. And I want to talk about it."

"Watch the road," she warned. "And I don't."

A truck rumbled by in the other direction, forcing blessed silence. Did he really want to do this? To what end?

"You're mad because I never called."

She snorted softly. "Ya think?"

His hand slid from the gearshift to her leg, his powerful palm and fingers covering half of her thigh and sending a wicked shot of excitement straight through her. She eased right out of his touch, earning a look from him.

"I'm sorry," he said softly.

She brushed her leg as though she could erase the impact of his fingertips. Yeah, right. "It's okay."

The wind off the waters of Nantucket Sound whipped her hair across her face, and she left it there, letting it hide the expressions that might give away her real feelings.

Wanting Deuce was so fundamental to her. It was like breathing.

Damn it all, nothing had changed. It was as if nearly a decade hadn't past. As if he'd come home a month after they'd shared every intimacy, and picked up without missing a beat. And her stupid, foolish girl's heart was ready to just open up again.

"Are you sure it's okay?" he asked, breaking the quiet of her thoughts.

"You're forgiven for not calling," she said quietly. Maybe if she let him off the hook, he'd back away.

"You're not lying?"

She shook her head. "I would never lie." But she didn't exactly want the whole truth out there for discussion, either.

For what seemed like an eternity, he didn't speak. Eventually, she flipped the lock of hair off her face, using it as an excuse to glance his way. His jaw was locked tight, his eyes, behind his own sunglasses, were narrowed in deep thought.

"Then I'll tell you the truth," he said.

She waited while he collected his thoughts, and passed a pickup truck.

"I had to cut off everything that was Rockingham," he finally said, so softly she almost didn't hear him over the wind and the engine of the Ford F-150 he'd just blown around.

"Why?"

"Because…" he shook his head and ran his tongue over his lips. No act of nature could get her to look away as she studied his serious expression. Serious…and beautiful. It still hurt to look at him.

He barreled the car forward right up to the rear bumper of a minivan, then ripped into the other lane, floored it, and whizzed by the poor young woman in the driver's seat. He lowered his speed back to the limit and sucked in a breath.

"Without my mother to run interference…" He spoke slowly, candor softening his voice. "I couldn't handle my dad. Without my mother… I just missed her too much. I couldn't come back."

Seamus could be overbearing. Way beyond overbearing where Deuce was concerned. "I understand that." *But why the hell didn't you call to tell me?* Years of training herself not to reveal her true feelings to Deuce kept her from asking the question. Maybe that was foolish, maybe that was just chicken. But that was the only way she knew how to handle him.

The one time she had admitted her feelings…

"And if I couldn't come back…" he continued, "what was the use of calling you?"

She shrugged. "Oh, I don't know. Common decency? A lifelong acquaintance? Acknowledgement of…" *The baby I carried.* "…my feelings?"

"I'm really sorry, Kendra." He swallowed hard enough for his voice to crack. Her heart did the same. "It was a shitty thing to do."

This time she patted his leg. "Forget about it, Deuce. I forgot about it a long time ago." Liar, liar, liar.

"So why'd you leave Harvard?"

The question was so unexpected it practically took her breath away. "I lost my scholarship and couldn't afford to finish." That was the God's truth.

He shot her a look of pure disbelief. "You had almost a full ride. How'd you lose it?"

"My grades went in the toilet." Along with most breakfasts those few months.

Traffic forced his gaze back to the road. "What happened? You were an A student. A genius. I remember that."

Yeah, a genius who didn't use birth control. She repositioned herself in the bucket seat. "I screwed up, Deuce. It happens all the time. Or did you forget about the racing incident that landed you here?"

He gave her a wry smile. "Not that you'd let me."

She'd have to keep the conversation on him. Otherwise, he'd probe too deeply. "So, what was your thought right before you hit the wall in that car?"

"My dad's gonna kill me."

"He was furious," she acknowledged. "The language was colorful, I can tell you."

He glanced at her. "How did you screw up?"

"Let it go, Deuce." *Please.*

"Was there a guy involved?"

"Yes." The truth.

"Did you love him?"

"Yes." More truth.

"Do you still?"

Oh Lord. "Once in a while, I think about him," she managed to say, despite the real estate her heart was taking up in her throat.

"Did he...hurt you?"

She thought of the blood and the pain and the insane trip to the hospital. All the guilt and disappointment, and, the worst part, the relief. "They were dark days." She'd lost the baby, Harvard and Deuce. "But I survived."

She pulled the seatbelt away from her chest, sucked in a breath of sea-salted air and smiled at him, aware that for the whole conversation, his hand had stayed firmly planted on her leg. "So what kind of pizza oven did you want to get?"

He shot her another disbelieving look at her sudden segue.

"You know, the more I think about it," she added before he could answer, "the more I think pizza would be a big hit at the café. I did a little research and Baker's Pride, Blodgett and Lincoln seem to be the best options." They stopped at a light, but she let the words roll out and fill the air. "The best price would be Blodgett, which is truly commercial grade, and I think we might even be able to get a refurbished—"

His fingers squeezed her thigh. "We were talking about your love life."

She put her hand over his, instantly loving the power she felt in those fingers, the hint of masculine hair tickling her skin, the sinewy muscles that baseball had formed. "Now we're talking about pizza ovens. Isn't that why we're here?"

"One of the reasons," he said, turning his hand so they were palm to palm and threading his fingers through hers. "The other reason is because I've been trying to get you alone for a week and it's impossible."

"I'm busy." She congratulated herself on yet another half truth that could not technically be called a lie. Why didn't she extricate her hand from his?

Because she couldn't. Any more than she could look away as he leaned closer to her face. His mouth was a breath away. His eyes locked on hers and his lips parted as he closed the remaining space between them.

The kiss was hotter than the sun that burned leather seats, and sweeter than anything Kendra could remember. At least, since the last time he'd kissed her.

A horn honked and startled them apart.

He held up his hand in apology to the car behind them, but didn't take his gaze from hers. "I'm not even close to done with talking about your love life." He shoved the gearshift into first. "Or kissing you."

# Seven

**D**euce saw the look of shock on Kendra's face when he'd introduced himself as Seamus Monroe to Buddy McCrosson, owner of Fall River Restaurant Supplies. Either Buddy didn't put two and two together with the names, or he wasn't a baseball fan. Either way, Deuce and Kendra spent nearly two hours with the man and no one mentioned the Snake Eyes or their former pitcher.

Watching Kendra in action was definitely the best part of the meeting. Although she never lost that feminine, sexy aura that surrounded her, she pounded out a tough deal, negotiated for way more than he'd have even thought of, and managed to let poor Buddy think it was all his idea.

All the while, Deuce studied her long, capable fingers as she examined a refurbished oven and imagined them on him. He listened to her soft laugh and fantasized about hearing it as he slowly undressed her. And, of course, he took

any excuse to brush her silky skin or touch her slender
shoulder.

He hadn't been kidding when he told her he wasn't done
kissing her. He wasn't.

While she'd gotten Buddy to knock off two percentage
points of interest on a short-term loan and throw in an $800
fryer—surprising him completely with her willingness to
add more unhealthy food to her café menu—Deuce had
started planning where and how and when he'd get back to
kissing her.

The minute they said goodbye to Buddy, he launched his
plan into action.

"I'm starved," he told her as they climbed back into the
450 SL.

"Anything but pizza," she agreed, buckling her seatbelt.
"There are tons of places between here and home."

"I know exactly where we're going." But he had no intention of telling her. "It'll be a little while before we eat, but I
promise, it's worth the wait."

She gave him a curious look, but didn't argue. She slid the
paperwork from their meeting into the side pocket of her door,
then dropped her head back and closed her eyes, letting the
sun light her face. As he turned to back out of the parking spot,
his gaze lingered on her face, her long throat, her sweet lips.

He wanted to kiss her right then. Why wait? Because, as
any good pitcher knew, timing was the key to success.

They listened to jazz and barely spoke as he drove toward
Rockingham. When they finally stopped at a deli in West
Dennis, she looked surprised.

"Barnstable Bagel?" She half laughed. "You in the mood
for a Reuben?"

"Great deli sandwiches here, if I recall correctly." If he told her he was going for atmosphere instead of cuisine, she'd fight him. "Wait here. I'll be right back."

When he returned, she took the bag of food and drinks that he handed her and tucked it into the space behind their seats. "We're eating in the car?"

"I believe it's called a picnic."

She lowered her sunglasses enough to look hard at him. "A picnic?"

"Chill out, Ken-doll. You'll like it." He hoped.

When he pulled up to the dunes at West Rock Beach, he practically felt her whole body tense. He shut off the engine and turned for the bag in the back. "I've always liked this beach."

She backed away to avoid contact. "Is this your idea of a joke?"

"No," he said slowly, pulling up the deli bag. "This is my idea of a picnic."

"This is… We don't have a blanket," she said quickly.

"We can sit on the benches."

Barely disguising a long, slow sigh, she climbed out of the car and they walked toward a low rise of the dunes, then stopped to take in the panorama of the Atlantic Ocean. A cool, salty breeze lifted his hair and filled his nostrils.

"Why are you doing this, Deuce?" she asked quietly.

"This has always been my favorite beach."

Without responding, she reached down and slid out of her loafers, then bounded toward the weather-worn bench that faced the ocean. He followed her, lumps of sand sliding into his own shoes.

"And because I want to make up for not calling you," he said as he sat next to her.

"By coming here?" She crossed her arms and faced the

water. "I told you, I've forgotten about it and I think you should, too."

"Turkey or roast beef?" He held out the two wrapped sandwiches and she took the one marked with the *T*.

"I'll take this one."

"You're lying, Kendra."

She looked up at him. "I like turkey."

"You haven't completely forgotten."

Wordlessly, she unwrapped the sandwich and made a little tray on her lap with the white deli paper. As he did the same, she nibbled at the crust of the whole grain bread, gazing at the blue-black waters of the Atlantic.

"Okay," she finally said, setting her sandwich in her lap, "I haven't forgotten. But I forgive. I mean, I forgive you for never calling. I don't see any reason to hold a grudge. Can we move on now?"

"But you remember everything else?"

She nodded, but didn't look at him.

"So do I," he admitted. Every kiss, every touch, even that long, shuddering sigh as he entered her.

He thought he saw her close her eyes behind her sunglasses, but then they ate in silence, only the rhythmic crashing of the waves and the occasional squawk of a gull breaking the mood. Two young mothers with three kids between them wandered by looking for shells, and a retired couple walked hand-in-hand by the water's edge. He stole a sideways glance to see which vignette held her attention.

Her focus was on the children. Funny, he'd thought she'd like the old people who still held hands. He regarded her as she took a bite of a potato chip, watching the children with rapt attention.

"You want kids, Kendra?"

Her jaw stopped moving and her whole being froze. Slowly, she wiped the corners of her mouth with a paper napkin and swallowed. "What brought that question on?"

He shrugged. "I don't know. You're about thirty, right?"

"As of last November."

"Well, don't most women your age want kids? Tick-tock and all that?"

She didn't answer, but that little vein jumped in her neck. She took a drink of water and he watched her throat rise and fall.

"I'm so involved with the café, I don't really think about it," she finally said.

He opened another water bottle for himself. "I want kids," he announced, surprising himself with the sudden candor. By the look on her face, he'd surprised her, too. "I do," he continued. "Nine boys so I could have my own little team."

She leaned back and let out that pretty laugh that sounded like music. "I pity the poor woman who has to give you nine children."

"Adoption." He could have sworn she sucked in a tiny breath at the word. "Seriously. Adopt a couple of sets of twins and bam, you got an infield."

"You're nuts." She folded up the white paper carefully, her fingers quivering a little.

"Are you cold?" he asked, reaching over to touch her hands. "We can go back to the car."

She shook her head. "No, I'm fine."

God, he loved holding her hand, touching her skin. He squeezed her fingers.

"Listen to me," he said softly. "It wasn't as if that night didn't leave an impression," he said slowly. "Because it did."

She whipped her hand out from his grip. "What part of I

don't want to talk about it anymore don't you understand, Deuce?"

"Why don't you want to talk about it?"

She blew out a disgusted breath. "Maybe because it embarrasses me."

"Why are you embarrassed? It was..." Incredible. Amazing. Mind-boggling. He got hard just thinking about it. "Great."

"I doubt you remember the details."

Oh but he did. "You're wrong."

She folded the deli paper into a tiny square and held a pickle to him. "Want this?"

"Don't change the subject again."

"I'm not changing the subject. I'm offering you a pickle."

"I'm offering you an apology."

"You did that already. Apology accepted. But you're going to owe me another one if you don't drop the subject."

He took the pickle and her deli wrap, stuffed them into the bag, and carried it all to a trash can about twenty feet away. She stayed on the bench, sipping her water.

When he returned, he held out his hand. "Let's take a walk."

She just looked up at him, a half smile tipping her lips, deepening her dimples. "Aren't you a little overdressed for a walk on the beach?"

He reached down and slid off his Docksiders and socks and tucked them under the bench next to her loafers. "Let's go."

For a moment, he thought she was about to refuse, but then she slipped her hand in his and stayed by his side as they walked down to the sand still packed solid by the morning tide.

"I wisely carried a blanket around in those days," he said. "Came in handy that night, didn't it?"

She playfully punched his arm with her free hand. "You won't let go, will you?" Before he could answer, she slowed her step, shaking her head. "Actually, as I recall, I grabbed the blanket from the bar before we left because it was chilly and you had your dad's car."

He frowned. "I thought I had a blanket in the trunk."

"See?" she said, her voice rich with both humor and accusation. "You don't remember a thing."

"Not true. I remember kissing you outside Monroe's, by that side wall." She'd tasted like oranges and cherries, as if she'd been sampling the bar garnishes.

"We were in the car the first time we kissed."

He closed his eyes for a minute. He could remember the taste of her, the need to pull her closer, but he didn't remember if they were standing or sitting. "Maybe. But I remember the kiss."

"Me too." She whispered the words into the wind, but he caught them.

Deuce let go of her hand and put his arm around her shoulders. "You were wearing a little pink top."

"Blue."

"Your hair was shorter."

"In a ponytail."

He tightened his grip and lowered his voice. "You had a snap-in-front bra."

"Finally, he gets something right."

"I bet I remember more details than you do," he insisted.

"You'd lose that bet."

"I would not."

"Cocky and arrogant as always." She dipped out of his touch and slowed her step. Deliberately, she pushed her sunglasses over her forehead and the look in her eyes hit him like a ninety-mile-an-hour fastball to the chest. "There is nothing, no detail, no minor, incidental facet of that night I have forgotten. Don't bet me, Deuce Monroe, because you'll lose."

He never lost. Didn't she know that? He took his own sunglasses off so she could see the seriousness in his eyes. "I'll bet you a reenactment."

She stopped dead in the sand. "Excuse me?"

"If I can remember more details about the night than you can, I get a reenactment. On the beach. Tonight. Maybe again the next night."

She shook her head, the only sound she could make was a disbelieving laugh. "And what if I win? What do I get?"

"A reenactment. That way we both win."

Just as her jaw dropped, he reached down and sealed the deal with that kiss he'd been wanting all day long.

Blood rushed through Kendra's head, deafening her and drowning out the sound of the waves. For stability, she reached up and grabbed Deuce's rock-hard shoulders just as he opened his mouth and deepened the kiss. Wide warm lips covered hers and the tip of his tongue slid against her teeth with unbelievable familiarity, a welcome invasion that made her whole body clutch.

He wrapped his arms around her and eased her against his body with a low, slow, nearly inaudible groan.

"For example, I remember that you like," he whispered huskily against her mouth as he broke the kiss, but not the body contact, "very deep, very long French kisses."

Arousal, quick and sharp, twisted inside her, forming a knot in her tummy and between her legs.

She dug deep for sanity and a clear head, but he ran his hands down to the small of her back and pressed her hips against his. Her throat felt as if she'd swallowed a mouthful of sand.

"And I remember," he said, making a tiny left-right motion with his hips, "that you can have an orgasm fully clothed and in the car."

Her hips responded with a mind of their own, driving against him with some uncontrollable need to prove him right. She couldn't argue with his memory. She couldn't argue with his body, kisses or silky voice either.

Lifting her face to his, she kissed him again for the sheer overwhelming joy of it, stalling the inevitable with one more dance of their tongues, one more minute of heaven.

With a long, deep breath she managed to ease him back and end the kiss.

"All lucky guesses," she told him. "You could be talking about any of the dozens of girls you seduced on this beach."

"No," he denied. "No one on this beach but you."

Wouldn't she like to believe that?

"I already told you two things you forgot," he teased. "And I bet you don't even remember what I wore that night."

She frowned and scoured her well-visited memory bank. Surely she knew every thread of clothing he had on that night. But all she could see was his face. His bare chest. His... Oh, of all the things to forget. What was he wearing that night? She had to blame the memory loss on the blood draining from her head to that achy spot between her legs. "Are you asking me if I remember what you wore?"

"You're stalling for time, Ken-doll. You heard me. What did I have on that night?" He raised a suggestive eyebrow. "That is until you undressed me."

Oh, yes, they'd undressed each other. She could still remember the feel of his flesh as she pushed his clothes away. As she closed her fingers around his shaft.

Another bolt of that heat lightning singed her at the thought.

She bit her lip and narrowed her eyes, infusing her tone with confidence. "A baseball shirt and jeans."

"Nice guess, but wrong."

"You don't remember what you were wearing," she countered. "You probably don't remember what you wore yesterday." But she did.

"Funny thing is, I do remember." He tunneled his fingers into the hair at the nape of her neck, his large hands engulfing the back of her head. Her stomach braced for another dizzying kiss. "I'd gone to the bar that night after having dinner with some relatives who were still in town for the funeral." He *did* remember that night. The realization that it was important to him made her almost as lightheaded as the way he was holding her. "So I had dress pants on, something like these. I wouldn't wear those with a baseball jersey." His smile was victorious.

"Okay, so you remember some things. But if we had a contest, I'd win." Why she'd admit that the night meant so much to her, she wasn't sure. Probably because the game was fun. His hands were fun. That last kiss was way more than fun.

"Care to exchange more memories, sweetheart? I'm really looking forward to the historic reenactment of…" He paused for a moment.

Bingo. She had him. "You don't remember the date."

"I do. Of course I do. It was June. Before the All-Star break." He dragged his hands up and down her spine, closing his eyes as though he was memorizing the feel of her, and for a moment she thought she might melt right into the sand. "June twelfth," he said. "A Friday night."

"I'm in trouble," she said with a laugh. "You're starting to scare me."

"I told you, I remember everything."

"The date and the style of my bra. Hardly everything."

He pulled her close again, putting his mouth up against her ear. "I remember what you said afterwards."

*I love you, Deuce Monroe. I've always loved you and I always will.*

Her heart really did stop, then it thundered in double-time against her chest. She waited for him to repeat her declaration and knew she couldn't deny it.

"You said…" His breath tickled her ear. "'I can't wait for the next time.'"

Yes, she'd said that, too. Maybe he didn't remember the whole I-love-you-forever-and-always part. She could hope.

"Guess what, Miss Locke?"

She backed away from his treacherous lips and looked at him. "What?"

"I think I out-remember you."

"Not a chance." Was there?

"What did I say to you when you left?"

She regarded him, looking for clues in those eyes. How could she forget? But she had? She had no memory of his last words to her. "You said, 'See ya later, Ken-doll.'"

He shook his head. "I win. I'll pick you up tonight after the bar closes. Say, midnight?"

"What did you say?" she asked, trying to ignore the voice in her head that was screaming *yes, I'll be ready at midnight!* "When we said goodbye, Deuce. What did you say to me?"

"I'll tell you tonight. Or better yet…" he grinned at her the way he did right after he left some poor kid at the plate not knowing what had hit him. "I'll tell you tomorrow morning when you wake up."

# Eight

Every time the front door of Monroe's opened, Deuce glanced up from the almost empty bar, expecting to see Kendra. Not that he really thought she'd come down to the bar to speed up the closing process so they could get to the beach…but he hoped. His blood simmered at the thought. She wouldn't back out, would she?

After all, a bet was a bet.

At eleven o'clock, only two stragglers sipped beers and watched the end of a Celtics game at one end of the bar. The medieval game-playing twins had abandoned their jousting to work a couple of girls at a table, but they'd already closed their tab. A few other tables were ready to call it a night.

Very soon, he could close up and collect on his bet. At the sound of the great door creaking open, he turned to see Martin Hatcher pulling off a bright-green trucker cap as he entered.

His eyes lit up at the sight of Deuce. "There's my favorite knuckleball man," he said, ambling over to the bar.

"Kind of late for you, isn't it, sir?" Would the Hatchet Man settle in for a few hours? Not that Deuce wouldn't enjoy the conversation, but tonight he wanted to close as early as possible.

Martin slipped onto a barstool and crossed his arms. "I'm retired, son. So it's no longer a school night for me. How about a draft?"

"Coming right up." Deuce poured the golden liquid, tilting the glass to create the perfect head. "Here you go, sir."

Martin raised the glass in salute. "Lose the *sir*, Deuce."

Deuce laughed and leaned on the bar. "You'll always be the voice of authority to me, Martin."

The glass halted halfway to his mouth as his lips twitched. "I've never been the voice of authority to you, Deuce. You always marched to your own…authority."

Then he drank. One of the bar patrons held up a twenty and Deuce cashed them out and said good night. Two down, a few to go. He moved back down to where the ex-principal sat.

"Been to any more practices?" Martin asked.

Deuce shook his head, but Martin's look stopped him. He could never fudge the truth with the Hatchet Man. "All right. One. Well, two."

Martin released a soft, knowing chuckle. "How's the elbow doing?"

"Not bad, actually." He rubbed the tender spot, and blessed the workouts he'd been secretly doing every day. "I can actually throw a knuckleball again. But man cannot live by knuckleballs alone."

"Keep working out and you can play again."

"I can play now," Deuce said defensively. "It's the lawyers

who blackballed me from baseball, not the doctors. I'd need more P.T., but…" his voice drifted away. "Anyway, I'm a barkeep now."

"You can't stay away from a ball field," Martin said with a wry smile. "I remember that was the only way I could really get to you. Detention, suspension, parental call-ins, nothing worked but keeping you off the field."

"That was where I wanted to be," Deuce agreed. "Although detention had its side benefits. That's where you find the cute bad girls."

Martin laughed at that and sipped some more draft, then glanced around. "But not your business partner," he mused. "She never did anything bad."

But she would. In an hour or two.

"Where is Kendra?" Martin asked.

Hopefully, slipping into something…easy to slip out of. "She only works days. I cover the nights."

"Interesting arrangement," Martin mused. "How's that going?"

"We're working on some changes." Deuce flipped on the water to wash the last of the glasses as a burst of laughter erupted from the Gibbons's table. Maybe they were getting ready to take the ladies home for a wild night of medieval sportsmanship.

"As I understand it, Kendra was already working on some changes for Monroe's. Did she tell you about them?"

Deuce looked up from the sink. "Of course. I've seen all the plans."

"What do you think?"

The truth was, he thought that her plans were great. But he also could make a sports bar profitable. Deep inside, he hoped for a compromise, but couldn't imagine her agreeing to it. "Jury's out."

Martin sipped. "She's been working on the whole cyber café and artists' space for a long time."

"Two years," Deuce noted. "That's how long she's been part-owner of this place."

"Oh, no, Deuce. She's really been at Monroe's for nearly ten or more." Martin's gray eyes looked particularly sharp. "Since she was first in college."

Why did Deuce get the idea he was being worked by the principal? "I remember," he said, turning to stack the clean glasses.

"But then she dropped out."

Deuce froze at the odd tone in Martin's voice. Was he accusing him of something...or was that just residual fear of the principal teasing Deuce. He reached for more glasses, clearing his throat. "She said she had a bad break-up."

When Martin didn't respond, Deuce looked up. The man wore the oddest expression.

"You know women," Deuce said, the old awkwardness of sitting in the principal's office sluicing through him. "They get...weird."

Martin just nodded, then slid his glass to make room for his elbows as he leaned toward Deuce. "I'd hate to see her unhappy again."

What was he saying? "Do you think my being here is making her unhappy?"

Martin frowned. "Did I say that?"

"Well, what are you saying?" Deuce demanded.

"I'm saying that she has—or had—big plans for this place and I happen to know they don't include a sports bar."

Staring at the man, Deuce searched his mind for a reasonable explanation for Martin's strange message. Then the truth dawned on him. He started laughing, which made the old Hatchet Man's eyes spark like cinders.

"Martin, I'm not going to coach the high-school baseball team. You can't psyche me into it with guilt over Kendra's café plans, sir."

"You call me sir again and I'll write you up, son." He winked and pushed his empty glass forward. "What do I owe you?"

Deuce shook his head. "Truth is, I owe you, Martin. That one's on the house."

"Maybe I'll see you at practice this week. I'm working the grounds."

They both knew he would.

When the last glass was clean, the register was cashed out and the night's draw was tucked into the pouch, Deuce locked the drawer in Kendra's office and pocketed the keys. As he pushed the chair back from the desk, his foot bumped into something soft.

Bending over, he spied the nylon tote bag Kendra carried between work and home. She must have left it when they went to Fall River and forgotten to pick it up before she'd gone home.

Well, she had been distracted. He grinned at the thought, reaching for the bag. Did she really need it tonight? With one finger, he inched the zippered opening to see what it contained. A laptop, a calculator, some folders, a red spiral notebook.

Nothing earth-shattering.

Deuce took the bag with him to his car, sliding it behind the passenger seat and made a mental note to leave it with the keys on Diana's table for her to find when she came over to walk Newman.

*Correction.* Tomorrow morning, Kendra would wake up in his bed. Then he could give her the bag in person.

He gunned the Mercedes's engine and pulled onto

High Castle with a sense of anticipation he hadn't felt since his last opening day.

From behind the two-foot protection of a sand dune, in the nearly moonless night, Kendra heard the rumble of the Mercedes's engine. Blue halogen headlights sliced into the night.

A trickle of guilt wound its way through her chest. Hiding out on the beach was a chicken thing to do, but if Deuce knocked on her door and melted her with that smile and annihilated her with that mouth...she'd be dead. She'd had all night to think about the "reenactment" he proposed, knowing full well he was basically asking her to sleep with him.

And, Lord have mercy, she wanted to say yes. Her skin practically ignited at the thought of giving in to the full-body ache he caused. She'd never say no if he had her out on West Rock Beach. Or in a bedroom. Or a car. Or the kitchen. Or...

The lights faded and she heard a car door. Kendra sank deeper into the sand.

She just had to keep avoiding him, and when Seamus and Diana returned, she'd tell them...*what?* She wasn't sure yet. The bar was profitable, no doubt. But the cyber café revenues were up as well. She was no closer to "working it out" with Deuce—as Seamus had instructed—than the day this all started.

She was, however, closer to giving in to that toe-curling attraction that had blinded and stupefied her for, oh, twenty-odd years now.

She imagined Deuce rounding the side of the house, peering at her darkened, quiet beach bungalow. Would he give up then, or would he knock?

He'd assume she was dead asleep...or out for the night. Then he'd surely go back to Diana's and slide the kitchen door open.

Newman would bark, so she'd know the coast was clear. After fifteen minutes, she'd sneak back into her house. Alone. Hungry. Achy.

Wrapping the blanket tighter around her shoulders, Kendra studied the C-shaped moon slice, surrounded by blackness and the smattering of stars that were always visible on Cape Cod.

Too bad she was a coward. They could have had one killer of a reenactment.

She closed her eyes and imagined his kiss, his hands, his breath in her mouth. A shudder quivered through her and she forced herself to listen for the noises to assure her he'd given up the idea and gone to bed. Alone. Hungry. Achy.

Why hadn't Newman barked yet? She wanted to rise up on her knees and peer over the sandbank, but with her luck that would be the very second Deuce chose to scope the beach.

Behind her, the grass rustled. She clamped her mouth closed to keep from even breathing, assessing how close the sound of that footfall really was.

She sensed him—felt his presence, sniffed his scent—before she actually saw him. Then he was there, not ten feet from where she sat, standing on the crest of the mound. Her eyes had long ago adjusted to the dark and she could make out every detail of him. His powerful chest rose and fell with a deep sigh. He stabbed his hair with one hand, leaving a lock loose on his brow, then he shoved both hands deep into the pockets of his jeans, his gaze out to the sea.

Surely the hammering staccato of her heart would give her away.

But he didn't seem to hear. He inhaled again, and closed his eyes as he let out the breath, shaking his head softly as though some thought amused or amazed him.

"Well this is just too damn sad," he said quietly. "I want her."

The admission drew a soft gasp from her throat, and he spun toward her, his surprise palpable even in the darkness. "Kendra?" In two long strides, he loomed above her. "What are you doing out here?" he asked.

She dropped part of the blanket on the sand and patted it for him to sit down. "Trying to avoid you."

He blew out a laugh and settled next to her, then reached over and brushed a strand of hair she hadn't realized fell on her cheek. His fingertips sent heat through her. "You're awfully damn good at that."

"Evidently I can run, but…well, you know."

He laughed again. "You don't have to hide, sweetheart. All you have to say is you'd rather not see me and I'll understand." He somehow managed to get closer, his body warmth far more effective than the blanket. "I won't hold you to the reenactment."

She nibbled on her lower lip, regarding him. "Anyway, we're at the wrong beach."

He smiled at her. "Let's not get hung up with the particulars."

She had no chance against this man. And, really, why fight it? The dark lock of hair still grazed his eyebrow, and under it, his eyes had the smoky, soulful darkness of arousal and desire. She could just smell the waves of his sexual appetite. Well, that might be a little of the Wing Man's chicken, but for some reason, that smelled sexy, too.

"I'm pathetic," she admitted, giving in to the urge to drop her head on his shoulder. "I even like the smell of barbecue on you."

He responded by pulling her into a hug. "Yeah? Bet it's nice mixed with the beer."

Oh, Lord, she had no chance.

He let out a small, low sound of masculine approval, sliding his hand under her hair to pull her closer. "We had a good night," he said softly. "About eight hundred dollars."

"We had a good day," she countered. "About six fifty."

"What a team," he chuckled. "Too bad we can't figure out a way to work the same hours."

She looked at him, knowing the kiss was inevitable. As he covered her mouth with his, she closed her eyes and let the sensations of warmth and want roll over her with the same force with which the ocean hit the sand.

"Oh, Deuce," she whispered into the kiss. "You're really messing with my plans."

"Forget your plans, sweetheart." His palm pressed the side of her breast and she ached for him to touch her.

"Is this the reenactment?"

"Mmmm." Slowly, easily, he leaned her back on the blanket. "Could be." He skimmed the rise of her breast, lingering on the pebbled nipple at the peak. "Remember that?"

A sharp, powerful bolt of desire stabbed through her, settling low between her hips and igniting the need to rock against him. "Yes, I do."

He eased on top of her, letting her feel the hardness of his erection as he spread his hand over her breast.

"Do you remember…" he kissed her hair, her eyelids, and slid his hand under the fabric of the cotton sweater she wore. "This?"

She gasped as the heat of his fingers seared her flesh, dropping her head back into the sand. She felt the grains crunch under her hair, and a sense of déjà vu flashed in her mind. "I do," she managed to say.

"And…" He grazed her stomach and found the clasp of her

bra. "This?" He laughed softly as he unclipped it effortlessly.
"I definitely remember this."

He kissed her again, parting her lips with his tongue, taking hers with authority. He tasted like mint, like soda,
like…Deuce.

With his other hand, he pushed the sweater higher as their
hips rolled against each other in perfect rhythm. Both hands
on her, he spread the silken fabric of her bra and cupped her
breasts, then lowered his head to suck her nipple.

Blood roared through her ears, deafening her to the sound
of the sea. All she could hear was his ragged breathing, his
whispered endearments, the sound of her own soft gasps with
each flick of his tongue.

He traveled back up to her mouth, his whole body now
covering hers.

She grasped the firm muscles of his backside, squeezing
through the denim and pushing harder against him, vaguely
aware of the sand that had somehow slipped between her fingertips.

Sand and Deuce. They belonged together.

With one hand, he unsnapped her jeans. She felt the fabric loosen, steeled herself in anticipation of his touch on her
stomach. Still she quaked as his hand slid into her panties and
a pleasure whipped through her.

"I remember this…" His tongue traced her mouth. "This
sweet place." He put his lips against her ear and his breath
fired through her. "I remember exactly what it felt like to be
inside of you."

He parted her delicate skin and grazed his fingertip over
her, mimicking the action of his finger with his tongue in her
ear. A moan of delight caught in her throat. Very, very slowly
he eased deeper into her.

"I want to make love to you again, Kendra." His voice was no more than hot, sweet air against her skin.

*I'll call you.*

The words suddenly reverberated in her head like a cannon shot into the night.

*I'll call you.*

"What?" Deuce lifted his head from her neck, his fingers suddenly still.

She didn't even realize she'd spoken. "You asked me what the last words you said were on…that night. You said 'I'll call you.' I just remembered."

He eased his hand away from her, and lifted himself just enough to look into her eyes. She half expected disgust, a look of "how can you hold me to that now?"

But that's not what she saw. Pain and remorse flashed in his eyes just before he closed them.

"I'm sorry I hurt you," he said gently. "It was a lousy thing to do."

Her heart twisted. "You had your reasons." Good heavens, was she rationalizing *for* him? She pushed him a little farther away. "But that doesn't make it right."

"No," he agreed. "It doesn't."

He removed his hand completely. Why had she remembered those words? Why had she said them out loud? Why couldn't he just be a normal, oversexed guy and keep going?

But he reached for one side of her bra, then the other. Disappointment spiraled through her and he covered her breasts, snapped the clasp and dropped a soft kiss on her cleavage.

"We're done," she said knowingly.

"Nowhere near." He tugged her sweater back over her chest and stomach. "I just also remember how uncomfortable the sand is." He eased her zipper up, his gaze on her face.

"This time, we're going to be warm and snug in my bed." He tucked his hands under her shoulders and gently lifted her. "And tomorrow, I will most definitely call you. About six times. Before noon."

Before she could respond, he kissed her again and pulled them both into a stand. The blanket fell off her shoulders, around her feet.

"Will you spend tonight with me, Kendra?" There was something so tender, so genuine about the question that her knees nearly buckled.

*How could he have been so sweet, so loving, so tender? Was it all an act?*

The words, in her own handwriting, danced before her eyes. She closed them to block out the mental image.

Could she be falling for him again?

This was it. Her moment to say no. Her senses had returned, she was on her feet and could use them to run right into her house and lock the door. Or straight into his bed and certain heartache. She took a deep breath, looked up at him and waited for "yes" or "no" to tumble out of her mouth.

"By the way," he whispered into her ear before she spoke, "You never heard the last words I said to you because you'd already closed the door."

She waited, her pulse jumping.

"I said that in my own way, I'd always loved you, too."

And then her decision was made.

Even in the moonlight, he could see the emotion spark in her silvery-blue eyes. A little fury, a lot of fear. Before he could decide what she was feeling, she jerked out of his grip, scooped up her blanket, and bolted up toward her house.

"Kendra," he called, taking long strides to easily catch up with her. "Where are you going?"

"Away from you."

He stopped for a moment, letting her get ahead, letting his blood settle and his brain work again. "Why?" It was the best he could manage, considering how far from his brain the blood actually was.

All he got was dismissive wave of her hand over her shoulder as she continued her march toward the beach house.

He caught up with her as she reached the door. "What's the matter?"

As she spun around, he realized there was no fear, just fury in those eyes. "How dare you make fun of me…of that."

"Of what? I did say that, Kendra, and I meant it."

She speared him with a disbelieving look and crossed her arms. "Liar."

"I am not lying." He practically sputtered. "You were always—"

She put her hand over his mouth. "Don't. Don't make it worse. You didn't need to make that up to get me to go to bed with you, Deuce. It was pretty obvious which way I was going on that one."

Circling her narrow wrist with his fingers, he moved her hand from his mouth. "I wasn't saying that to get you to go to bed with me," he said softly. "I was trying to tell you that all those years when you were young, all those years you…" He didn't know what to call her feelings for him. He knew they were there. He'd seen it in her eyes. Hero worship?

"Crush," she supplied. "I'd call what I had a crush."

He smiled. "I like that. Anyway, I was always aware of you."

"Deuce. I was *ten*."

"I know," he agreed. "I was aware of you like a sister, then you…" He shook his head. This wasn't coming out right. Closing his eyes, he took a deep breath. "The way you looked at me—like I was the only guy on earth—made me feel alive, Kendra. It made me feel great. I was just trying to say I loved you for it."

She searched his face, saying nothing. Wondering, no doubt, if he was even capable of the truth. He owed her the truth.

"That's why I never called," he finally said. "Because I kind of sensed I wasn't worthy of that level of…love."

She stared at him for a good thirty seconds before speaking. She shook her head, inched backwards. "You treated me like a baby for ten years, then a pariah for the next ten."

He couldn't argue with that. "Now I'd like to treat you like a woman." But that might be pushing it, and he knew it. He didn't wait for a response. "But that's probably not fair to you either."

She opened her mouth to speak, but he reached across the space between them and eased her jaw up.

"Shhh. You don't have to say anything." He kissed her forehead and ignored the hole in his gut. He had to turn around, walk away and let her be. He'd hurt her and he had no right to pick up where they'd left off as if…as if not calling her was acceptable.

It wasn't.

"Good night, Kendra." He turned and started across the stone path. He had his foot on the first of the wooden steps up to Diana's house when he felt her grip on his elbow.

"Wait a second."

He didn't move, giving her a chance to speak. When she didn't, he slowly turned around.

"It *is* fair." She took a deep breath and closed her eyes. "If you really see me as a grown woman, an equal, if you really can forget that little girl who worshipped you, and forget about the first time we…"

He grazed her cheek with his knuckle. "I'll never forget the first time, but I sure would like another chance. With this woman." He let his thumb caress her lower lip and felt it quiver under his touch. "This grown, beautiful, smart, sexy woman."

"If that's true, then…"

"Then…what?"

She reached up and pulled him to her, seizing his mouth in a hot, demanding kiss.

"Is that a yes?" he asked softly.

"I just can't fight this anymore."

Neither could he.

# Nine

**D**euce never let her say another word. It was as though he thought if they talked any more, she'd change her mind. Even if he hadn't pulled her into his chest, even if he hadn't possessively turned the kiss into his own, even if he hadn't flattened his hands against her bottom and pressed her stomach against his surging hard-on, Kendra wouldn't have changed her mind.

Life was too short and this magic was too dizzying to let him walk away. Tonight, she wouldn't think about the past, about mistakes or bad choices. All she wanted to think about was the cliff-dropping thrill of making love to Deuce.

He started to pull her toward Diana's.

"No," she whispered, tilting her head in the direction of her bungalow. "My house. My bed."

He groaned softly and lifted her to her toes, letting her stomach ride the ridge of his erection. "Any house, any bed," he said huskily. "But only this woman."

Her heart plummeted with a roller-coaster dip.

They kissed across the walkway, pausing at her door for him to slide his hands over her breasts and down her waist, dipping his fingertips into the top of her jeans.

She rocked her hips into him, her body so hot and wet that if he'd pushed her pants down, she could have made love on the porch, standing.

He fumbled with the door that she hadn't even locked, guided her inside, still kissing, still exploring, little desperate moans and surprised sighs escaping both of them.

The bungalow was pitch-black when the door closed behind them, and without turning on a light, Deuce yanked her sweater over her head and pushed her against the wall next to the door. His hands were everywhere, on her skin, under her bra, in her hair.

She ripped his shirttail out of his pants, silently cursing the buttons that she'd have to unfasten in the dark. Before she had the first one undone, he'd unsnapped her bra, easing the straps over her shoulders as he dipped his head to suckle her.

She almost screamed when his mouth closed over her breast.

Sliding his hands up the sides of her breasts, he caught her under her arms and pushed her up the wall, off her feet, never taking his mouth from the hardened nipple he sucked.

"Deuce," she half laughed, half moaned, still fighting one of his shirt buttons. "The bedroom?"

He licked the tip of her breast, his eyes closed with the pleasure. "I have to taste you."

The longing in his voice almost did her in. He wanted her as much as she wanted him and the thought nearly melted her.

Lowering her to her feet, he captured her mouth for another

kiss, caressing the breasts he'd just tasted, giving her the opportunity to finish the damn buttons.

Finally she could push his shirt open and press herself against the coarse hairs of his chest.

As she did, he thrust his erection against her.

Her whole lower half coiled with want. She skimmed her hands over his granite shoulders, clasped them behind his neck and raised herself up, just for the sheer bliss of riding the hardness between his legs. Denim against denim and it was almost enough to give her one mind-boggling vertical orgasm.

With his hands on her backside, he easily lifted her higher and she wrapped her legs around his hips, letting her head fall back, her eyes closed.

"We aren't going to the bedroom, are we?" she managed to ask.

"All right." He was already carrying her there. "But it better be really close."

"At the end of the hall. One room. One bed. No turns."

"Good." He growled the word into a kiss, just as he crossed the threshold of her bedroom, and laid her on top of the comforter.

Like a magician, he slid her out of her jeans and ripped off his. More hot kisses trailed from her throat down her breasts, over her ribs and navel. He licked at the lacy edge of her underwear, his hair tickling her skin.

Her heart hammered inside her chest, her throat tightened with a scream of desire and her hips seem to rise and fall without any effort on her part.

She dug her fingers deeper against his scalp.

He trapped the flimsy material between his front teeth and began to pull them off her, as though taking the time to use his hands would be too much.

Neither one could slow the need to eliminate anything that came between them—clothes, time or space. He shimmied her underwear over her backside and down her legs.

Blood rushed through her head as he looked at her, the darkness stealing her chance to really study his face.

He said her name, once and again. Lowering his head, he stroked her with his tongue, slowly at first, crazy slow, then faster, shooting fire straight up her body. She grasped his head, spread her legs and surrendered to his mouth. With wild, driving licks, he circled her sex, invaded her body and sucked the tender flesh until pleasure and pain knotted her. She bucked into his mouth. His fingers closed over her buttocks. Her flesh spasmed under his kisses, then, just before a climax rocked her, he feathered her stomach with kisses, drying his lips on her cleavage and stopping just long enough to suckle her hardened nipple.

His shaft found the heat between her legs. She was wet and warm and swollen with the need for him. Her throat too dry to speak, she tried to say his name, but her hips just rose and his erection inched into her.

"Kendra." His voice was as raw as her throat. In the dark, she could see the ache on his face, the need in his furrowed brow. "I don't have a…"

*Condom.*

Reality crashed down on her like a stinging shower of ice.

"Do you?" he asked hopefully.

She shook her head, as a million thoughts vied for space in her brain. Did she? Would she do without? Didn't he? And, oh, not again. Not *again.*

He let out a breath of pure frustration. "I have one. I have to go get it."

Diana's house might as well have been a million miles away.

"Not in your wallet?" She asked hopefully. Surely a guy like Deuce Monroe didn't leave the house unarmed.

He gave his head a vicious shake, and traced a line down her stomach. He slipped one finger into her moist flesh. "Just let me finish what I started."

For some reason, that struck her as terribly unselfish. Wasn't Deuce full of surprises today? She turned on her side, a move that eased his thick erection right into the space between her legs. "Not good enough, honey. I want you inside me."

He closed his eyes and slid along her, the velvet hardness of his erection torturing her flesh. "Right where I want to be." His breathing was still ragged and torn and under her hand she could feel his heart thudding as fast as hers.

"Go get one," she whispered. "Hurry. Don't stop to walk Newman."

He gave her a half smile. "Actually, it's in the car."

"They give you a box with every new Mercedes?"

He laughed. "I put it in the glove compartment this morning."

"You thought we'd have sex on the way to Fall River?"

"Hey," he chuckled, sliding in and out of the vortex of her legs. "A guy can hope."

He hoped? For her? She pressed her pelvis into him and sucked in a long, slow breath. "Go. No one is around. Grab those boxers, and get whatever you have in the car."

Reluctantly, he lifted himself from the bed.

"How many did you bring?" she asked.

"Just one…" He pulled on his boxers and grinned in the dark. "Box of twelve."

She giggled and watched him leave the room, an insane and wild and happy thrill dancing through her.

When she heard the front door open and close she scooted higher on the bed and slid between the cool sheets.

"I love him," she whispered and closed her eyes to let the joy of the realization rock her as thoroughly as his body just had. "I have always loved him and I always will." There was nothing, absolutely nothing, wrong with making love to someone you loved.

She glanced at the bedside clock. What was taking so long?

Dropping her head on the pillow, she ran her hands over her naked body, feeling her curves and flesh the way he did.

Maybe there could be a future. Maybe they could really and truly be together. Own Monroe's...together.

Was that so crazy?

The possibility sent wild sparks through her, curling her toes, making her heart tumble around as if it were no longer connected to her body.

Maybe Deuce could love her the way she loved him.

Finally, she heard the front door and she inched a little higher, purposely leaving the sheets low around her waist.

She heard his footsteps in the hall.

Suddenly the overhead light blinded her and she blinked, instinctively pulling up the sheet with one hand and shading her eyes with the other.

Deuce stood in the doorway, a look of horror and rage and confusion on his face.

"What's the matter?"

Something flew across the air and landed on the bed with a soft thump.

She blinked again.

All she could see was the tattered red cover.

"When the hell were you going to tell me there was a baby, Kendra?"

* * *

He could barely speak, rage pounding through him, fighting for space in his veins against all that hot-blooded lust.

A *baby*.

Kendra's face was as white as the sheet that barely covered her, her eyes and mouth wide with shock. "You…you *stole* my journal?"

He snorted and took a step toward the bed, unable to tear his gaze from her, no matter how much he wanted to pick up that notebook and throw it as far as his injured arm could. "Hardly a time to think about ethics, Kendra." One more step, and she pulled the sheet higher. "Since you obviously have *none*."

The fear on her face morphed instantly into something else. Her eyes narrowed to blue slivers as she leaned forward and pointed a finger at him, oblivious to the slip of the sheet when she let it go. "Don't you dare talk to me about ethics, Seamus Monroe. You had unprotected sex with the little sister of your best friend and never bothered to pick up the phone, ever, and say so much as thank you."

He opened his mouth to argue, then shut it again. There was no arguing with that. At least she didn't throw in the virgin part. Blowing out a pained breath he hadn't realized he'd been holding, he closed his eyes. "You should have called me."

"Maybe I should have." She slumped against the bed, but her gaze remained sharp. "But I kept waiting for you to do that."

Guilt punched him. "If I'd known…" His voice trailed off and his gaze landed on the worn notebook. He hadn't purposely read it, of course. "It fell out of your bag. I moved the bag to the front seat to remember to bring it in, and the whole thing spilled, then…I glanced down and saw the words on the page."

Lit by the inside car light. Damn. If he'd left the top down, he'd never have seen those unbelievable words.

Deuce's baby would have been a girl.

He'd frozen as the words slugged him. He'd read it twice. Felt the world slip sideways, then read on.

I wish I didn't know that, but the doctor told me. The hospital put her little body to rest today.

He'd read more, but the first few sentences had singed his memory, where they would no doubt remain for the rest of his life.

Stunned, he'd sat outside in the car and tried to process what those few sentences told him. She'd been pregnant, lost the child and had been far enough along to have a body to bury.

And he'd never even known about it.

He'd stumbled back in the house with the notebook, without a condom, but with more anger and shame and betrayal than he'd ever known.

She pointed toward the hall. "I want to get dressed. Can you leave?"

"No," he said simply. "I want to talk about this."

"I just meant leave the room. We'll talk." She pulled the sheet up. "Fully clothed."

The fact that he'd just seen her naked, kissed her senseless, and nearly shared the most intimate of personal relations with her seemed moot. He grabbed his jeans and shirt, then stepped out into the hall, dressing quickly in the bathroom. When he came out, her bedroom door was closed.

In the kitchen, he found coffee beans and a grinder. Questions, dozens of them, played in his head, as he went through the process of coffeemaking as he'd seen it done at Monroe's.

A baby.

The impact still kicked him in the head and heart.

And how had she handled that alone? How many people knew and didn't tell him? How far along had she been before... He sat at the table and stared at nothing while the coffee brewed.

God, why hadn't she told him?

He didn't actually focus until Kendra entered the room. She'd put on sweat pants and a T-shirt, and her little bit of makeup was smudged under her eyes as though she'd cried, or at least rubbed her eyes.

"I thought you hated coffee," she said, opening a cabinet and pulling out a mug.

"It seemed appropriate," he responded. "I think we're going to have a long night."

And not at all the kind of night he'd been envisioning an hour ago. The desire to climb *on* and *in* her still bubbled under the surface, pulling at him, making him feel guilty somehow. How could she have been willing to make love with that lie between them?

"How do you take it?" she asked, pouring a second mug.

"With whiskey." At her look, he offered up an apologetic gesture. "Hey, I'm Irish. But I'm also a wuss, so give me lots of milk and sugar."

Her movements were spare as she made both cups the same, her hands shaking just a tiny bit, her breath still a little uneven.

"You don't want to have this conversation any more than I do," he noted.

She turned from the counter, eyes blazing again. "Don't make this about you, Deuce."

"This is not about me," he countered. "This is about…" My *child*. Loss gripped him. "This is about what I did and didn't know."

As she settled into the chair across the table from him, she leaned her elbows on the table, and rested her chin on her knuckles. Her eyes looked sad, her complexion pale.

Not the fiery, sexy, hungry look he'd seen in the moonlight. Not the lover he'd had in bed. But a woman who'd experienced a great deal of pain.

He swore softly, fighting the urge to reach across the table and apologize for being the one to put her through that. Instead, he reached down for the anger he'd felt before. He needed answers. "Why didn't you tell me?"

She studied the coffee in her cup. "I just couldn't."

"Didn't you think I had a right to know?"

Her throat moved as she swallowed but didn't answer.

"Were you sure…I was…the…"

Slowly, she lifted her gaze and the expression "if looks could kill" reverberated in his head. "Don't you dare go there," she said, a cutting edge in her whisper.

Then where could he go? "How far along were you, Kendra? Why don't you tell me what happened?"

She inhaled and sighed. "I was just about seven months pregnant. Twenty-seven weeks, to be precise."

"And you had a miscarriage?"

"A stillbirth." She closed her eyes and took a deep swallow of coffee. When she looked at him, the pain in those blue eyes had turned to anguish. "I noticed that I hadn't felt…her…kicking or hiccupping."

When her voice cracked, he gave into the need to touch her.

Rubbing his thumb over the soft skin of her hand, he urged her to continue.

"I went to the doctor and…" she tried to shrug, but her shoulder shuddered instead. "Evidently, she got tangled in the umbilical cord."

He felt the air and life whoosh out of him. "I'm so sorry."

She nodded and blinked, but a tear fell anyway.

"And I'm sorry I wasn't there…for you."

"I handled it," she said stiffly and he had no doubt she did.

"Your parents? Jack?"

She shook her head and took a swipe at that tear. "My parents moved to Florida. They were not happy with me. Jack was in New York."

"Then who took care of you?"

With a tight smile, she said, "Seamus."

For a moment, he thought she meant him. Then the truth dawned on him. His father. His father had been there instead of him.

"Does he know? That it was mine?"

"Damn you, Deuce Monroe." She shoved back from the table with a jerk so forceful and sudden, coffee splashed over their cup rims. "Have you ever, ever thought about anyone but yourself in your entire life?"

He stood as she did. "I didn't ask because I was thinking of me, Kendra. I just—"

"You just wanted to know where you fit in. How this latest piece of news revolves around *you*." She turned from the table and took her cup to the sink, spilling the coffee out with one hand and leaning on the counter for support with the other.

"No." He was behind her in a moment, both hands on her shoulders to turn her toward him. "No, you're wrong. I can't believe you had to go through that alone. I can't believe I was such a stupid, selfish idiot to let you go. I can't believe—"

She put her hand over his mouth. "I get the general idea. Believe it. Now, go."

"Go? You want me to go?"

She leaned back. "You want to pick up where we left off, Deuce? With the arrival of the much-delayed condom?"

The words sliced him. "I want to try and catch up."

"On ten years?"

He nodded, undeterred by her bitterness. She had a right to be bitter. He'd listen, he'd understand, he'd try to make up for the very, very wrong thing he did. "Please."

"Okay, here's the Reader's Digest version. I had to give up my scholarship, work for your dad—and, no, we've never discussed the father of the child, but he's a very smart man—and, at a snail's pace, I got my degree in business and finally decided what I could do with my life and put together a brilliant plan for doing it. And then guess what happened?"

He just stared at her, the lingering acidic taste of coffee in his mouth. "I showed up."

"Bingo."

"To screw up your life again."

Her laugh was without any heart. "I'm lucky that way."

The impact of his arrival, of his cavalier expectations that Monroe's would be his, settled over his heart like the loss of the biggest game of his life.

How dare he? Who did he think he was?

He stepped away from her. Away from her warmth, her gaze, her sadness, all that femininity that he wanted to explore and have. "I'd better go."

"Back to Vegas?" she asked, a mix of hope and dread on her face.

"I was, uh, just thinking of next door."

"Okay," she whispered.

But he couldn't leave until he knew one thing. Why had she kept it from him? "Why didn't you pick up the phone and call me, and tell me. Why didn't you want support or advice or…demand something?" *Like marriage.*

"I guess you didn't read that whole journal."

He'd read enough. "Why?"

She looked up at him, the exquisite sweetness on her face squishing what was left of his heart. "Because I loved you. And I knew you'd do the right thing. And I didn't want to ruin your life or your career."

That kind of love, he suddenly realized, was a far cry from hero-worship. That was unselfish, noble and real.

That kind of love wouldn't have ruined his life at all. Hell, it might have saved his life. But it was too late to find out. All he could do now was somehow make it up to her.

He had to leave—he had to leave Rockingham. He had to let her have her dream, without the constant presence of the man who'd caused her nightmare.

Without another word, he pressed his lips to the top of her head, closed his eyes and inhaled that fresh, sweet scent of Kendra.

"See you later, Ken-doll."

# Ten

Kendra somehow made it through the motions of work the next day, regardless of the fact that her mind felt blank and her heart raw. Oddly enough, she had slept well, collapsing into deep, dreamless sleep after Deuce had left. When she woke, she decided that her sound sleep was a result of a clear conscience.

He finally knew the truth.

She could move on, the secret was out. She could finally let go of the one thing that forever tied her to Deuce. Except that she'd fallen back in love with him.

*Oh, get real, Kendra Locke.* She'd never fallen out of love with him.

When her office phone rang and she saw Diana Lynn's cell phone number on the caller ID, Kendra pulled together some focus. She opened her laptop so she could give Seamus some figures if he needed them, and hit the speaker phone.

"Kennie, we've made some progress," Seamus's voice filled the little office. "How about you and Deuce? Have you?"

Oh, yeah. Great progress last night. "We're working things out," she assured him. "The bar business has been…pretty good."

"I knew it," the older man said. "That boy has a golden touch."

Absently, she ran her hand down the front of her Monroe's T-shirt. *He sure did.* "How did it go in San Francisco, Seamus?"

"Well, I do have some news."

She held her breath and waited.

"There's one firm out here very interested in funding the project. Very."

There was something not entirely positive about his tone. "What's the 'but'?" she asked. There had to be one.

"They want to see better Internet café revenue numbers. Want to see that we're able to really pick those up by thirty percent for at least a month."

"They have improved," she said, clicking at the program of spreadsheets she'd been using that week. "But…" she peered at the screen. "Not quite thirty percent."

"All we need to do is close this month with a thirty percent increase, Kennie. Any chance we can do that?"

"He's not interested in the bar revenue?" That was up about eighty percent.

"Not if they're going to put the money in the cyber stuff. Think about it, Kennie. You might be able to come up with something."

"Maybe. How's Diana?" Kendra longed for the woman to return. She needed a friend. She needed to confide in another female who might understand the power of Deuce.

"She's great."

"You're leaving tomorrow for Hawaii, right?"

Seamus cleared his throat. "She's in charge of the schedule. We'll be in touch."

Kendra clicked out of the spreadsheet and stared at the blank screen. "I hope so."

"How are you and Deuce getting along?"

Hadn't he asked that already? "Fine."

"Just fine?"

Oh, well, there was this little incident last night. Almost sex that turned into a total freaking confession. "Yep. He's doing really well with the bar."

"Is he playing ball?"

Kendra frowned. "I think he wanders over to the Rock High field on occasion, but, Seamus, he's *retired.*"

She heard him blow out a breath. "Yeah, I know."

Guess Seamus didn't let go of his dreams so easily, either. "Have a blast in Hawaii."

"Get those numbers up by thirty percent."

*Fat chance.* "Really, don't give those investment people the idea that I can do that," she said. "Not without the actual funds we need. It's a Catch-22."

"It's worse than that," he said somberly. "There's really no one else but this firm. All the others are just not interested in investing in this competitive and soft market."

Kendra closed her eyes and let the disappointment spiral through her.

"So, if we meet these numbers, we can do the whole project with this firm," Seamus continued. "But if we don't, then Monroe's is going to stay just like it is."

She had to swallow the lump in her throat before she answered. "Then I guess we'll have to try and make that magical number."

"That's my girl," Seamus said with a laugh. "Now I better go find my other one."

"Give her a kiss for me."

"And you give Deuce...my best."

As she held down the speaker phone button to disconnect, she closed her eyes at the catch in his voice. They always had that in common, she and Seamus. They loved that boy.

"You look like he asked you for the witch's broomstick."

She started at the sound of Deuce's voice. "How long have you been out there?"

He strode into the office, all power and dark good looks, and Kendra cursed the way her body hummed at the sight and scent of him.

"Long enough," he said, dropping into the guest chair in front of the desk, "to remember my dad harbors the secret hope that I'm here playing baseball."

She smiled. "Some dreams die hard."

"They sure do," he said, more to himself than to her. "How'd you know I've been to Rock Field, by the way?"

She was done lying to Deuce. "Because I know you better than you know yourself."

He nodded, his eyes rich with warmth. "You know, Kendoll, it occurred to me this morning that we have quite a history."

She felt heat rise from her heart. "Yes, we do."

"We've known each other almost all our lives, and you spent a good bit of it listening to me grow up in your basement."

The heat blossomed into a full blush. "I did learn a lot through that heat register."

"And we've shared some, well, intimate moments." His gaze darkened and her body tensed. "And some losses."

She waited.

"You were there after my mother. And, well…" They both knew the other loss. It was an old scar for her, but a fresh wound for him.

"We do have a history," she agreed. And, oddly enough, a friendship. It was her problem that she still loved him. And not his fault.

For a long moment, he just looked at her. Then he shook his head a tiny bit, in amazement or confusion or something she couldn't name.

"I don't know, but—" he glanced at the calendar on the wall "—you have a little time before the month ends. And all you need to do is increase your Internet café business by thirty percent."

She almost wept at the change of subject. He'd almost said something…meaningful. Intimate. But the moment had passed. "A thirty-percent increase in profits, yes." She pulled herself back to the business problem at hand. "That would be the witch's broomstick you saw me pining for on the way in."

"Or you have to give up your dream."

*Some dreams die hard.* The echo of her words filled the room, but she didn't say them out loud again. "I'll find another," she said.

He glanced around her desk, his gaze on her Rolodex. "You have Jack's number at work in there?"

Jack? Why did he want to talk to her brother? A new worry trickled through her. Would he tell Jack the truth about the baby she'd lost? Jack never knew his unborn niece was fathered by Deuce Monroe, and Kendra wanted to keep it that way.

"Don't worry," he said gently, obviously seeing the horror on her face. "I just want to talk to him about something. About an idea I had."

"What is it?"

"I'm not telling." He grinned. "But you can press your face to the nearest heater and listen, if you like."

That made her laugh. "How do you know I did that anyway?"

"'Cause I know you almost as well as you know me."

Despite the hellacious traffic on the way to Logan Airport, Deuce was waiting at passenger arrival ten minutes before the flight he'd come to greet. As he glanced around the terminal and tracked the progress of the plane's arrival, his mind skimmed through all he'd done in the past week or so.

He'd made incredible progress and was only hours from making Kendra's dream come true, that's what he'd done.

And when he wasn't making arrangements, calling old acquaintances, e-mailing others and meeting on the sly with Principal Hatcher—he still couldn't think of him as Martin—he was hanging around Kendra to get the most of his last few days and weeks with her.

It took every ounce of willpower he could muster, but he hadn't so much as held her hand. He hadn't kissed her, or snuggled in for a good whiff of her sweet feminine perfume, he hadn't put his arm around her slender waist, or taken any number of opportunities at the bar to slide up behind her and let her know what she did to him.

He should have called after they'd made love; that was a stone-cold fact. He should have been there to help her through the pregnancy, and then...the tragedy. Hell, he could have easily paid for her to continue her education after she'd lost the baby.

And she'd never asked for help or pity. Not once. Now was the time to pay her back and that's what he'd spent the past week doing.

Then he'd have to go back to Vegas. Even though he liked being home, liked being at the bar, liked the idea that he might enjoy a mature and equal relationship with his father. But he'd be a constant reminder to Kendra of the past, and Seamus would want him around a lot. However, before he left, he had to help her get what she wanted.

And that's where Jack Locke came in.

When Jack sauntered across the wide-open terminal and flashed that audacious grin, Deuce knew he had the only man for the job. Kendra's brother was six-foot-two inches of irreverence and trouble who now, at thirty-three, held the position of one of the top art directors on Madison Avenue and was rewarded richly for his talent.

Except you'd never know it by the look of him, in a shirt that might have cost a fortune, but had been worn for a long time, and a pair of jeans that looked as old as their friendship. Burnished brown hair fell to his shoulders, a few locks almost covering that where's-the-party glint in his green eyes.

Jack had been a good-looking teenager, able to charm the panties off half the cheerleaders in Rock High, but as a man he'd grown into someone who looked completely comfortable in his own skin. And still charming those panties off, no doubt.

"Hey, man," Jack dropped his duffel bag and they did a guy's bear hug. "Great to see you, Deuce."

"I thought you came from some big meeting in New York," Deuce said, indicating Jack's well-worn shirt and jeans.

"I'm the art director. Creatives don't dress up." Jack grinned again. "And I half expected to see you in a Snake Eyes uniform."

Deuce laughed as they started toward the parking lot. "Maybe someday," he said. At Jack's look of surprise, he held up a hand. "A *coach's* uniform. I've got my agent looking around for the right gig."

Saying it out loud made it more palatable. The thought of being around major league baseball and not being a player still felt like lead in the pit of his stomach, but it was the only thing he could do.

"That's a pretty big change in plans, isn't it?" Jack asked. "Who put your head in that direction?"

"You know, you won't believe it when I tell you."

"Shoot."

"Martin Hatcher."

"The Hatchet Man?" Jack hooted with a quick laugh. "Where'd you see him? Stop by the detention hall for old time's sake?"

"Actually, I've spent a bit of time with him down at the field, and he comes in the bar once in a while. He's convinced me to give coaching a shot." Even though he had high-school coaching in mind, the seed had taken hold and given Deuce a direction he needed. "Plus, he's been almost as helpful as you on the project."

Jack slowed his step as they reached the elevator. "We're on for tonight?"

"You bet."

"Does Kendra know yet?"

"I told her we're having a little class reunion, but didn't mention you."

Jack laughed softly. "Little, huh?"

Deuce shook his head. "You know, she's so focused on trying to get this magic number for the investment people, that she's sort of distracted and oblivious."

As the elevator doors whooshed shut in the parking garage, Jack looked hard at Deuce. "This is a pretty major effort on your part, all for her, you know?"

Deuce shrugged, pressing the button for the fourth floor

even though it was already lit. "She deserves it. She's worked really hard. And…" *And I owe her big.* "It'll be good for the bar in the long run. I mean, the whole artists' community and Internet café thing."

Jack's look was dubious at best.

"Seriously," Deuce continued as they reached the parking lot and he indicated the direction to the car. "She's just got her heart in this cyber café and artists' space, she's worked so hard for it, and her ideas, really, are pretty ingenious, but you know how smart she is…"

Jack stood still and stared. Then he turned toward the terminal and squinted, holding his hand over his eyes and looking hard into the distance.

"What is it?" Deuce asked.

"I'm just seeing if there are any airborne farm animals out there."

"What? Why?"

"'Cause don't you think that if you could fall in love, then pigs could fly?"

Grinning, he gave Jack a friendly push on the back. "Are you kidding? Deuce is wild, man."

"Jacks are better." The response was ingrained.

They laughed as Deuce reached the Mercedes and unlocked the trunk with the click of the keychain. He let Jack give him a hard time about the expensive convertible and steered the conversation to cars and work and old times.

He never answered Jack's question.

Kendra hadn't paid too much attention to Deuce's quiet planning of some kind of high-school reunion, expecting that the gathering of old Rock High friends would generate plenty of bar business, but would do nothing to help her get the elusive thirty-percent increase in the Internet café business.

But she remembered him saying that he'd be gone all day to get someone at Logan Airport, and that left her to worry about Newman. The dog wasn't used to total abandonment, so during a quiet hour in the early afternoon, she slipped out of Monroe's to take him for a walk.

The little guy had been delighted with the company, and not thrilled when it came time to say goodbye. He was particularly playful, but it wasn't funny when he snagged her key ring from the chair and bounded up the stairs of Diana's house. Kendra hustled after him, taking the steps two at a time.

"Don't you dare, Newman," she called. "I need those keys."

She heard him scramble down the hallway as she turned the corner, but stopped her chase at the sight of an unmade double bed in the guest room.

Deuce's room. Deuce's bed.

Utterly unable to resist the temptation, she entered the room, immediately picking up his distinct masculine scent, and some kind of sixth sexual sense sent a shiver down her spine. She stared at the impression his head had left on the down pillow, drawn to the bunched-up sheets and comforter, mesmerized by the casually dropped T-shirt and a pair of well-worn sleep pants on the floor next to the bed.

Deuce slept *there*.

Newman barked outside the door, and she heard the keys fall on the floor as he scampered downstairs, evidently done with his silly games.

But she couldn't stop *her* silly games…pulled by some powerful force that compelled her to sit at the edge of Deuce's bed, run her hand over his sheets, maybe take a quick sniff of that pillow.

She didn't know whether to laugh or cry at the dismal depths she'd reached. Mooning over his pillow aroma, for God's sake. Why not just whip out her trusty notebook and inscribe "Mrs. Deuce Monroe" in the margin?

Newman's yelp suddenly turned furious and loud, and Kendra stood to call him. But just as she opened her mouth, the sound of men laughing drifted up the stairs. She froze, and listened. Newman was silent, then she heard the oddest thing.

Her brother.

She closed her eyes, rushing back through time, practically feeling the grates of the heat register pressed to her ear, her heart hammering as she waited for Deuce's voice.

Was her imagination playing some kind of trick on her?

But there it was, the low timbre of a voice she'd know anywhere, anytime. Deuce was having a conversation with his best friend, Jack…in earshot of Kendra.

The years slipped away as she listened.

"I wondered when you'd get back to those flying pigs," Deuce said.

*Flying pigs?* Surely she misunderstood him. She took a few steps to the door, as rapt by his conversation as she had been with his bed.

"It's written all over your face, dude." That was definitely Jack. What was he doing here?

Oh, of course. The *reunion.* He must want to surprise her. Well, the surprise was going to be on him when she skipped into the kitchen and announced—

"You're a goner over her," Jack added, just loud enough for her to hear over her slamming heartbeat. "I can't believe it. Deuce Monroe is in love."

That heartbeat skipped, then stopped. Kendra closed her eyes and gripped the doorjamb. *Deuce is in love?*

"Don't get your pants in a bunch, Jackson," he replied. "She may be your sister, but she's a grown woman."

His...*sister?*

A wave of euphoria and sheer disbelief threatened to unbalance her. Deuce was in love *with her?* Was she hearing this right?

Or was this some really unfair and heartless trick of her imagination and memory? The confession she'd dreamed of hearing through that heating duct for all those years...was it possible? Was she dreaming?

She missed what Jack said because Newman let out a joyful yelp. Someone must have given him a treat.

They laughed at something, and she waited for more. To hear him confirm what she thought she'd heard...that Deuce was in love with her.

"So what are you gonna do about it?" Jack prompted and she made a mental note to kiss him for that later.

Her grip tightened on the wooden frame, her throat so dry she thought she'd choke. What *was* he going to do about it?

*I'm going to...love her. Marry her. Give her nine children.*

"You don't understand." Deuce's voice was low, but clear enough for her to hear. "This situation is a lot more complicated than you realize."

"Because of the bar?"

"Because..."

Kendra held her breath and waited for the explanation.

"Because I have a habit of getting in the way of your sister's happiness."

*Aw, Deuce. You are my happiness.*

She heard the pantry door close and Newman barked,

drowning out Jack's response. Damn if this wasn't exactly like when the heat blasted on and she couldn't hear what they were saying.

"Yeah, that's true," Deuce agreed.

What was true?

"But there's more to it, isn't there?" Jack asked.

Even up the stairs, she could hear Deuce sigh. She imagined him running a hand through his thick hair, his dark eyes clouded over with trouble. "I'm a…reminder of something I think she'd rather forget."

Her stomach clutched as she waited for them to continue. Hadn't he promised her he wouldn't tell Jack the truth?

"No matter what you think you remind her of, Deuce, she's been through worse. Believe me. She's one tough cookie."

They had no idea they were talking about the same thing. About her baby, her loss.

"She deserves to have her dreams, Jack. She wants this big cyber gig and artists' space, and I'm afraid I'll just stand in her way."

Did he really believe that?

"Are you sure you're not just copping out of something real?" Jack asked.

"Nope, I'm sure. I'm just trying to recapture my glory days, and Kendra's trying to build something spectacular. I don't belong in Rockingham anymore. I shouldn't have even come back."

She wanted to call out. *No, no, Deuce. You're wrong.*

"I think you're terrified that something or someone might tame wild Deuce," Jack said.

She heard Deuce laugh softly. "If anyone could ever tame wild Deuce, it's Kendra Locke."

The world tipped sideways and Kendra leaned her face against the cool wood of the doorjamb.

*It's Kendra Locke.*

How many years, how many hours of eavesdropping, how many innings of baseball had she endured just to hear him say that? A distinct rush of exhilaration ricocheted through her.

"But I can't stay here and keep my hands off her. I can't stop thinking about her. I can't stop wanting her."

A lifetime of waiting and listening had come to this.

"So I gotta leave. My agent has some bites from a couple of minor league teams looking for pitching coaches."

The words reverberated as the sliding-glass door opened and closed, Newman's bark now coming from outside. Peering out the window, she saw Deuce and Jack walking toward the beach, tossing a football back and forth with Newman bounding between them.

"I let you walk away once before, Deuce Monroe," she whispered against the glass. "But not again. Not this time."

Scooping the keys from the floor where Newman had left them, she tiptoed down the stairs and out the front door.

She wasn't going back to work today. She had a reunion to go to tonight and she intended to show up in grand style.

If information was power, she had enough to change his plans. It was time to play the game Deuce's way…wild.

# Eleven

**E**very single computer in Monroe's hummed and flashed and zipped through cyberspace, connecting Rock High graduates around the world. Only about forty or fifty attended the reunion in person, but that had never been the genius behind Deuce's idea. What he wanted—and what he got—was a successful cyber reunion.

From his barstool perch, Deuce surveyed the crowd who drank and laughed with gusto, but more than anything, they e-mailed and IM'd and reunited with old friends in two dimensions.

This night alone would yield Kendra her thirty percent increase for the month, then he could leave with a free conscience for what he'd done to her all those years ago.

"Did you hear that?" Jack's easy laugh pulled Deuce back to the present. "Martin knew it was me who painted that mural in the girls' locker room."

Martin's gray eyes twinkled as he tipped his draft to his lips. "I don't think Deuce is listening."

"Sure I am. As a matter of fact, I was just thinking about my own sins of the past."

Jack grinned at the older man. "That was a beautiful mural. But I didn't know you realized the extent of my talent, sir."

"Drop the sir," Deuce warned, forcing his focus on the two men. "He'll nail you."

But while Martin explained that he'd overlooked Jack's locker-room artwork because the baseball team was in the state finals, Deuce's gaze slid once again to the front door. When two young men entered Monroe's, he cursed the disappointment that thudded in his stomach.

Why would he think Kendra would show up tonight? She didn't answer her door or her phone. She was totally missing in action and his fantasies about her "stopping in" to the bar only to realize it was a cyber-reunion set up to benefit her half of the business were just that…fantasies. Like every other thought he'd had about Kendra Locke for the past few weeks.

"I can't believe that, Deuce," Jack said. "Can you?"

"Sorry. What did you say?"

Jack gave him a knowing smirk. "Get your head in the game, dude."

"My head's in the game," he insisted.

"Then listen to the Hatchet Man," Jack said with a sly glance at Martin. "'Cause he's saying something important."

Deuce looked at Martin. "What's that?"

"George Ellis quit the team."

For a moment, Deuce couldn't imagine what that meant. Who was George Ellis and what team did he quit? Then it hit him, more from the expectant look on Martin's face than anything. The Rock High coach and the school baseball team.

"Will he finish the season?" Deuce asked.

"His wife just found out she's pregnant and wants to go home to her family," Martin told him. "George said he'd stay until we have a replacement, but he obviously doesn't want to be away from her that long."

A flash of desire sparked in him. And images of pure bliss followed...coaching Rock High baseball, running the bar at night, married to Kendra and raising some babies of their own.

And then he saw the two men look at each other, as though he'd spoken out loud. Had he?

"My agent's looking for coaching positions with some top teams," he told them, certain the insane thought had been kept to himself. "Sorry."

Martin shrugged. "It was just an idea. I thought there might be something to keep you here."

"There is something to keep him here." Jack looked hard at him. "What the hell's the matter with you, man?"

"I told you, Jack, it's..." The front door open and Deuce looked without thinking. Someone whistled. A loud voice went silent. And Deuce could practically feel his jaw hit his chest with a clunk. "...complicated."

Jack held a beer bottle frozen in midair on its way to his mouth as he stared. "No way," he muttered. "There's no way that's my sister."

Martin beamed. "No reunion is complete without the valedictorian."

Deuce's brain powered down as fast as the computers at night. He tried to think, to comprehend what he saw, but he couldn't do anything but...look.

Black. Leather. Curves. He managed to interpret that much. A sweater cut low and deep. Leather pants, skin-tight and painted over a round backside and long, tight thighs. Black shoes, with mile-high heels and a dozen sexy straps begging to be unfastened. With his teeth.

Swinging her pale blond hair as she looked from the bar to the dozens of computers and over the crowd, Kendra's piercing blue gaze finally landed on him.

Wordlessly, she strutted over, and he could just imagine the tap of those edible high heels on the hardwood. But the music was too loud to hear. Or was that the blood rushing out of his head and down through his suddenly very alert body?

Jack swooped in and saved him by closing his sister in a bear hug. "I thought I'd shock you," he said with a laugh, pulling back to look at her. "But the shock is on me."

She pulled away and gave him a pat on both cheeks, and then another kiss. "Hey Jack, wonderful to see you." She shot a more serious look at Deuce. "It appears I overdressed for the reunion."

He slowly shook his head and didn't even bother to hide his full-body inspection. "Not at all." A grin pulled at his mouth. "You look—" there just wasn't a word to do her justice "—perfect."

Color rose in her cheeks, making her even prettier as she brushed the leather with a casual hand. "You like?"

*Oh yeah.* "I like."

"Why didn't you tell me it was an online event?" she asked, a friendly accusation in her voice.

"I wanted to surprise you."

She laughed lightly, the sound tugging at his heart. Her lips hitched in a sweet, but inviting, smile. "Looks like I'm going to make the extra thirty percent after all."

He nodded, taking in the happiness glimmering in her eyes. "Yep."

Pulling away from her brother she stepped close to Deuce,

a muskier, heavier scent than she normally wore drifting up to him. She rose on her toes, put her mouth against his ear and whispered, "Remind me to thank you properly later on."

Every hair on the back of his head stood straight up. And that wasn't the only thing.

He turned to nearly brush her lips with his. "You're going to have a hard time in the sand with those shoes, Ken-doll."

She curled one long leg around his calf, her heel playfully scraping the denim of his jeans. "I'll take them off."

He closed his eyes and fought the temptation to kiss her. Right there in front of Jack, the Hatchet Man and a few aging classmates. He resisted, but, man, he wanted to.

And then there was that foolish fantasy flash again. Coaching Rock High baseball, keeping an eye on the bar at night, married to Kendra and making love every night until she couldn't walk in those shoes.

He had a really good reason for calling his agent and starting the search for a coaching job. He had a really good reason for letting Kendra realize her dream without him intruding and turning it into his monument to sports. He had a really good reason for keeping his hands off her for the past week and arranging this event so that she made her magic number for the investor.

He knew he did, but for the life of him, good reason had evaporated and was replaced by the need to taste her skin, feel her body and love her every imaginable way and then some.

And if the look in her eyes was any indication, she was feeling the same overpowering need.

Kendra took the ice-cold bottle of beer that Dec Clifford offered and slipped out the back door for fresh air. Scooting up on the hip-high brick wall that lined the parking lot, she inhaled the cool evening air and took a deep drink.

She'd danced until she worked up a sweat, laughed until her face ached, and even shared a warm and funny instant message exchange with none other than Annie Keppler, who'd French-kissed Deuce all those years ago. Annie was married and living in Buffalo.

And Deuce?

He hadn't taken his eyes off Kendra for the entire night. No matter when she caught his gaze, it was returned. All night long, his look had shifted from amused to aroused and everything in between.

The back door creaked as it opened and Deuce appeared in the moonlight.

"Hey lady in leather." He crossed the narrow parking lot to where she sat. "What are you doing out here all alone?"

"Getting air." She held up the beer. "And breaking the rules by bringing a bottle outside."

He walked right in front of her, so his stomach touched her knees.

"Oh yeah?" He put his hands on the leather above her knees, sending fire up her thighs. "I like to break rules."

"That's why they say Deuce is wild."

As easily as he did everything, he gently parted her thighs and slid right into the opening so they were chest to chest. "You look pretty wild yourself tonight, Ken-doll."

She took another drink, then held the bottle to him. "Want some?"

His hands still firmly on her legs, he put his mouth over the top of the bottle, tipped his head and let her give him a slow sip, never breaking eye contact.

Her whole lower half knotted at the sexy move and, without thinking, she wrapped her legs around his waist.

"Why d'ya do it, Deuce?"

He raised his eyebrows. "'Cause I was thirsty?"

"I mean the cyber reunion. The thirty percent. You know if I get that investment money…your dad'll be hard-pressed to keep Monroe's as a sports bar."

"Yeah, I know." He lifted one shoulder. "I give up. It's yours."

"Not like you to be a quitter," she said, carefully setting the beer bottle on the bricks next to her. "Or are you just dying to coach so bad that you're ready to give up on that lifelong dream of owning Monroe's?"

He lifted both eyebrows in surprise. "How'd you know about my coaching?"

"The modern version of a heat register."

He looked warily at her. "Are you serious?"

"Were you?"

His eyes turned smoky dark. "I don't know how much you heard, but, I'm serious, yeah. The bar is yours. I mean, the café. And I'm stepping aside."

Not so long ago, that would have filled her with joy. Tonight, it hurt. "You know, owning Monroe's is not my life-long dream."

"What is?"

She was holding her lifelong dream, he was wrapped in her leather legs at the moment. "You first."

A little smile snagged the corner of his mouth. "Well, not so long ago, my lifelong dream was playing in the major lea-gues. I can't do that, so, I guess my dream has to change."

"That's never easy."

His smile turned tight. "No, it isn't. Okay. Your turn. If owning the Kendra Locke-inspired premier cyber café and artists' performance space isn't your lifelong dream, then what is?"

"You."

She felt the air escape from his chest. "Excuse me?"

"Yep." She nodded, a sudden lightness lifting her heart. "All I've ever wanted to do in my whole life is be with you."

His jaw slackened. "Me?"

She locked her hands around his neck and pulled him closer. "You really didn't read the rest of that journal, did you?"

He shook his head. "I felt bad enough about what I did read."

"Shhh." She put a finger over his lips. "We can't change history. But we can change the future." Leaning forward, she dipped to his mouth and as gently as she could, she kissed him. He eased her closer and she tightened her legs, and let their tongues collide and tangle.

He pulled back enough to look in her eyes, an expression of pure hope and sin. "Let's start right now."

She trailed one finger over his cheek, loving the slightly roughened feel of his beard. "I want to make love to you, Deuce Monroe. And nothing, nothing at all, is going to stop me this time."

Just then the back door opened again and she felt Deuce let out a sigh of frustration.

"Hey Deuce," Jack called. "Someone named Coulter is on the phone for you. Says he's been trying to reach you all day."

Deuce closed his eyes for a second, then turned to Jack. "That's my agent. It can wait till tomorrow." He reached into his pocket and pulled out keys. "Do me a favor, Jackson." He pitched the keys across the parking lot and Jack caught them with an easy snap that came from years of playing baseball together. "Lock up for me when this shindig is over. I have something I have to do."

Jack peered into the shadows where they sat.

"Is Kennie with you?"

"I'll take care of her," Deuce promised. "You can drive my car home. Just handle the bar, okay?"

Kendra leaned forward and whispered, "It's a cyber café."

He slid his hand all the way up her thigh and gave her rear end a mischievous squeeze. Then, his hands still firmly on her backside, he lifted her from the wall and set her on the ground. "Tell me you don't need anything in there," he said huskily. "'Cause I really don't want you to change your mind."

She patted the flat pocket of her pants. "I have a car key and a house key right here. No purse."

He started to tug her toward the street, then froze mid-step. "You're sure, right? I mean, you're sure you want to…repeat history?"

*If anyone could ever tame wild Deuce, it's Kendra Locke.*

She could still hear the honesty and wistfulness in his confession. Sliding her arms around his shoulders, she pulled herself into his chest. His return embrace was automatic and just as powerful.

"I have never been more positive of anything in my life."

Deuce pulled her into him for a lusty kiss before he'd even turned the ignition off. They'd never make it inside, to either house. He was so hard and achy for her, it was a miracle they'd made it home at all. Especially considering that he'd kissed her at every light and was nearly blinded when she reached over and slid her hand up his thigh.

Somehow, they managed to get out of the car and into Diana's house. Newman barked and Kendra grabbed a treat from the pantry to bribe him into silence.

Deuce took her hand and pulled her toward the stairs, pausing only to kiss her again, and skate his hands over her leather-clad backside again. She arched into him with a soft moan.

"Upstairs," he managed to say.

They kissed and caressed and whispered and laughed their way up the steps, and Kendra pushed him into the first bedroom.

Oh, so that's where she'd been when she'd overheard his conversation with Jack. He started to tease her, but she was already pulling off her sweater and all he could manage was to kick the door closed and guide her to the bed while he devoured the black lace bra with his eyes and then his hands and, finally, blissfully, his mouth as she fell backwards onto his bed.

He freed her breasts from the lace, immediately bearing down to taste her flesh, loving how her whole body shuddered when he sucked her nipple deep, deep into his mouth.

He murmured her name and licked the tip into a hardened pebble, and she rewarded him with a writhing, helpless sigh.

Pulling up her leg, he took one sexy shoe in his hand and grinned. "Nice cleats." He slowly unbuckled the strap of one, then the other.

He trailed kisses down her stomach and unzipped the outrageous leather pants. Sliding them over her hips, he discovered nothing but a tiny bit of black satin barely covering her.

"Aw, Kendra, you're killin' me, honey."

With a soft laugh of victory, she tugged at his polo shirt and pulled it over his head. As soon as his chest was bare, he covered her to feel her silky warm skin against his muscles. As he captured her mouth again, she dragged her hands over his stomach and slipped into the waistband of his jeans.

Her fingers closed around him and white lightning shot through his body as she stroked him.

They struggled together to get his pants off, laughing softly at their desperation. Finally, he was down to his boxers. He pushed them off and eased her onto her back.

Taking his erection in her hand, she stroked the length of him. "I love that I can do this to you," she said huskily.

"Every day, all the time," he whispered. "All you have to do is walk into a room and I'm hard."

He gently straddled her and caressed the concave of her stomach, the rise of her breasts, the dip in her throat, the angle of her jaw. He wanted to dive into her, to pound into the heat and warmth of her, but he forced himself to slow down. To look at her.

He'd known this woman since she was a child, he'd basked in the glow of her admiration for years and years, and he'd loved her body once before.

But this was different.

He traced a line from between her breasts, over her stomach, down to the edge of the black triangle of satin that covered her.

This time, this night, something was completely different.

She closed her eyes. He slipped his finger under the fabric, over the soft tuft of hair and onto the wet, swollen nub.

She sucked in a breath as he touched her. He tenderly rubbed her, and sweet torture darkened her face as she sighed and turned her head from side to side. Her breasts rose and fell with each breath.

"Do you like that?" he asked.

She nodded, far away and lost in pleasure.

He leaned over her and eased the little silk patch to one side, revealing the glistening blond hair. She was moist and ready. "And I love what I do to you," he whispered.

She arched in response and he dipped his head to kiss her.

He stroked her once with his tongue. Just once. Easy, slow and deliberate. She tunneled her fingers into his hair, rocked her hips up and asked for more.

Blood pulsed through his head, heating his veins and surging into a potent, aching hard-on.

Her legs were smooth against his face, and warm, as he kissed and suckled her, then he slipped the little thong over her hips so she was as naked as he.

Straddling her again, he pulled open the nightstand drawer and lifted out one foil packet. She watched, taking quick, frayed breaths as he sheathed himself, then lowered himself on top of her.

Once again, she arched upwards and his erection slid between her legs, against her opening.

"Deuce," she whispered as his tip found entry. "I love you."

Her words jolted more blood through him and he entered her almost the moment she spoke.

That's what was different.

"I love you," she repeated, kissing his mouth, his neck, his shoulder as he pulled back and plunged in again.

Everything intensified: the hot, wet walls that enveloped him, the silky curves of her breasts, her sweet confessions, her hungry kisses.

She rose to meet every thrust, and he ground out her name as sweat rolled down his temples and stung his eyes.

Each time, he was deeper into her, lost in the heat, the ecstasy, the pure bliss of her unguarded response. Each time, his body sparked like a flint, his senses overloaded by the womanly smell of her, his head threatening to explode as thoroughly as his body. Each time, pleasure rocked him and stole his breath and brain and heart.

Each time, he was more in love with her. Oh, yeah. That's what was different tonight. He loved her.

And as he realized that, he lost the control he'd barely ever had, finally giving in to the release, spilling into her as she unraveled with a climax as staggering as his.

He collapsed on her, kissing the moisture of her perspiration, letting the heat of their bodies melt together, attempting to get his breath back.

He managed to lift himself from her and look into her eyes.

"I do love you," she whispered, the only other sound the deafening thump of their heartbeats. "I always have and I always will."

Nothing in his life—a life full of glorious moments of victories and success—nothing had ever felt anything quite as complete as hearing those words.

And suddenly he realized that he hadn't come home to find hero-worship at all. He hadn't come home to find glory or admiration or memories of better days. He'd come home to find love and security.

And he had. He held it right here in his arms and he could hold it there forever.

"I love you, Kendra."

She closed her eyes and exhaled as though he'd given her the most precious gift in the world. And yet, he was the one who felt lucky.

Deuce tightened his grip on Kendra as though he thought she'd leap out of bed and run. He should know her better than that by now.

Instead, she slid her leg over his hip and let him pull her so tightly into his chest that she had no idea where she ended and he began. She nuzzled into the dusting of black hair on his chest, inhaling and pressing her cheek to the granite-hard muscle.

He loved her.

"You know what I just realized?" he asked her.

"That you love me?"

He smiled down at her. "Besides that. I realized I came back to Rockingham for all the wrong reasons." He squeezed her again. "It wasn't about running the bar."

She punched him playfully. "You could have fooled me."

"What I wanted," he said slowly, as though the realization was just forming in his mind, "was to figure out who I really was. Without the crowds, without the fame."

"Did you figure it out?"

He smiled and pulled her closer. "I'm in the process."

Somehow, she managed to breathe. Managed to swallow and smile. But then a digital phone beeped "Take Me Out to the Ball Game" and he fell back on his pillow.

"That's my agent's ring," he said, not moving.

"Why don't you put him out of his misery and answer?"

"Because he's going to tell me I got a job coaching in Greenville or Gainesville or somewhere I don't want to go."

The second ring started. "So tell him you're staying here."

He pushed himself up from the pillow and surveyed the floor for his cell phone. "I think I will," he said with finality.

Kendra's toes curled with happiness. She pulled the sheet higher and watched the muscles of Deuce's back tighten as he reached down to pluck the phone out of his jeans pocket.

"Coulter, it's midnight on the east coast and I'm real busy right now. This better be good."

Suddenly, all the air came out of him in one long whoosh. "Are you serious?" he asked, sitting up straighter. "They do?"

He shook his right elbow, then rubbed it. "Well, it's a lot better." He laughed softly. "Maybe by All Star break."

She bit her lip as Deuce listened, then hooted. "They'd actually reinstate my contract? I can be there in May."

She took a deep breath, uncurled her toes and gave in to the way-too-familiar physical pain of heartbreak.

# Twelve

**D**euce tried to concentrate on the instructions Coulter was barking at him about training and timing, but all he could process was the fact that Kendra had scooped up her clothes and disappeared into the bathroom.

Was she leaving?

She couldn't leave. He'd just realized he loved her. He needed to tell her again—to show her again.

"Coulter, can't this wait until tomorrow?" he growled into the phone. "I'm seriously in the middle of something here." Like changing his life.

"Call me first thing in the morning, Deuce," the agent ordered. "We have to go over the fine print of this contract. It's not exactly the cakewalk you had last year."

"I bet it's not." He stared at the bedroom door.

"Some things have changed."

Deuce's gut tightened. "They sure have."

When he hung up, he went straight to the bathroom. "You okay in there, Ken-doll?"

The door swung open.

She was the lady in black leather again, all of that sexy sweetness replaced by the sharp-eyed Mensa candidate who'd fight him for her cyber café.

"I have to work in the morning," she said simply, slipping by him, her gaze never even fluttering over his undressed body.

He managed to grab her elbow. "What's the matter with you?"

Her eyes widened. "I can't spend the night here."

"Can't or won't?" he asked, scrambling to pick up and pull on his boxers. "You don't even know what I talked to him about."

"I don't have to know the details of your contract." She opened the bedroom door. "I've been here before, Deuce. I know the drill."

"Look, I know I have a lousy record, but honestly you don't—"

Newman barked from the kitchen as the sliding glass door opened.

"That's Jack," he said. "You can stay here. He doesn't—"

"Did you miss me, Newman?" A woman's voice traveled up the stairs, and Kendra froze in place.

Not Jack.

"That's Diana." Kendra's face registered the shock he felt.

"Anybody home?" Dad's call was louder, but completely familiar.

Kendra tapped his bare chest. "Get some clothes on. I'll deal with them."

She headed down the steps without looking back. "What are you guys doing home already?"

In thirty seconds, he was dressed and following in her footsteps. The three of them were still hugging and fawning over the dog by the time he got in there.

"Deuce!" Dad seized him in a bear hug immediately.

"What are you doing back so soon?" Deuce asked, returning the hug and gave Diana a quick embrace. "I thought you were in Hawaii."

They looked guiltily at each other. "We never made it."

"No?" Kendra asked. "Why not? You called and said you were on your way."

"We went to Vegas instead," Dad said, a boy's grin breaking across his face. "Show them, Di."

Diana held up her left hand and Deuce blinked at the rock.

"He didn't want to do the honeymoon before the wedding," Diana said. "Who knew your father was such a traditionalist?"

"Oh." Deuce made the sound, knowing he should do better than "oh" but unable. He looked at Kendra. Surely she'd squeal or jump with joy.

But her expression was a blend of torture and surprise. Finally, she reached out for Diana. "Congratulations." Then she threw an arm around Seamus and pulled him into a three-way hug. "I really wanted to dance at your wedding, though."

"We'll have a big party at Monroe's," Diana promised, pulling back to beam at Deuce. "We have so much to celebrate."

"We have even more to celebrate," Deuce said, his gaze sliding to Kendra.

Diana sucked in a little breath. "What is it?"

"I can only think of one thing that could make me any happier." Dad said with conviction. What did he think they were going to announce? "Go ahead, make my day."

"Kendra made her thirty percent."

"Deuce is going back into the majors."

Their simultaneous announcements earned stunned looks from Seamus and Diana.

"Excuse me?" Diana asked.

"Did I hear what I think I heard?"

"He just got the call." Kendra's eyes were bright, and her smile was forced. "They're reinstating his contract."

"Deuce!" Diana exclaimed. "Isn't that wonderful?"

"I don't know," he said, his gaze sliding to Kendra. "Is it?"

He saw her swallow. "I'll let you guys catch up," she said, far too quickly. "And you have Deuce to thank for the thirty-percent windfall. He's…" she paused and looked at him, her blue eyes full of something he'd never seen before. Something so much deeper than hero-worship and adoration. Something that filled him with that same sense of completion he'd felt upstairs when they made love.

He could live for that look.

"He's incredible," she finally said. "There's never been anyone else like him."

"I've always known that." At the sound of his dad's voice, Deuce turned, expecting the old beam of pride. But instead, the Irish eyes were full of sadness and disappointment.

Why wasn't Seamus happy about the majors?

Why wasn't *he?*


Seamus crouched at home plate, a worn catcher's mitt barely hiding the frown he'd worn since they arrived at Rock High field for some practice.

"Why are you separating so late?" he demanded as he threw the ball back to Deuce on the mound.

Deuce shook his right arm, visualized perfect release timing and threw again.

His dad had to dive to catch the far outside pitch. "Why are you striding to the left?"

Deuce rubbed his elbow and caught the toss. Taking a deep breath, he held his glove in front of his face, stared into the strike zone and started his wind-up.

"Why are you curling your arm like that?"

Deuce paused, kicked the rubber and let out a frustrated sigh. Then he looked hard at the man who'd caught more pitches for him than anyone in the major leagues. "Why are you so ticked off at me?"

The return look from Seamus was harsh, but that might have been the weary bones aching as the older man pushed himself into a stand. Most likely it was a dirty look; his dad would never let the pain show.

"I'm not ticked off."

Coming off the mound, Deuce flipped his hat, wiped his brow with his forearm, and resisted the urge to spit. "You've been irritated with me since you got home last night," Deuce said. "You're married, the money's coming in for the café and I'm going back to the majors. Just what does it take to make you happy, Dad?"

That earned him a wry smile. "Same thing it's always taken, son. I want you to be happy. When you're happy, I'm happy."

"Happy is relative," Deuce mused.

Dad just nodded and tossed the extra ball he held, his gaze on the far fence. "Damn nice of you and Jack Locke to arrange that cyber reunion for Kennie," he said slowly. "Guess you really didn't want the bar after all."

So this is where it was going. The bar. "I wanted to help her," he said. "It didn't have anything to do with me not wanting to run Monroe's. I would have been perfectly happy to…"

To what? Marry Kendra and have those nine kids and a lifetime of what they'd had the night before?

Yep.

"I'd have been perfectly happy to run the bar, Dad." Deuce finished the thought by putting his arm on his father's shoulder. "I'm sorry if I disappointed you."

"Not me," he said. "Diana."

"Diana?" Deuce pulled back and peered from under his cap. "How'd I disappoint her?"

"She imagined herself a matchmaker." Dad smiled as they walked to the water pitchers in the dugout. "It was her idea to let you two work it out alone together. In fact, she wanted to make a contest out of it. But I just wanted to let nature take its course."

"Nature took its course," Deuce said quietly.

Dad froze mid-step. "It did?"

"If its course was to make me fall stupidly in love with her, then, yeah. Nature's right on course." It felt good to admit it, he realized, guiding his father to the shade of the dugout.

"But you're going back to Vegas tonight," Dad said, as though he didn't understand. "And that was some lousy goodbye for a woman you love. She waved at you and scooted out the door."

Deuce could still see the look on Kendra's face when she'd said goodbye. All breezy and light. For a moment, he'd thought maybe she was glad he was leaving. As though her admissions of love and lifelong dreams hadn't been real.

If he hadn't seen how she'd looked when he made love to her…if he hadn't heard the truth in her voice when she said she'd loved him, he might not have believed it. But he'd seen and he'd heard and he believed.

"It wouldn't have worked anyway, Dad." He had to try and

believe *that* instead. "We…have some history. Stuff you don't know about."

Dad spun the red lid of a thermos. "I know about the baby, Deuce."

Deuce stared at him. "You do?"

"I got eyes and ears, son. I saw her expression every time she passed that jersey on the wall. That's why I took it down."

"*You* took it down? I thought Diana did."

Dad took a sip of water and swallowed hard. "You're gonna have to stop blaming Diana for everything you don't like around here. She's my wife now."

Deuce sighed. "I didn't know about the baby. She didn't tell me. I had no way of knowing."

"You could have called her."

"You could have called me," Deuce countered.

Dad rolled his eyes. "You just do the opposite of everything I say anyway."

"That's not true. Not always. Okay, most of the time."

"More often than not," Dad said. "And in that case, I felt I needed to butt out."

Deuce dropped on to the bench with a thud. Looking at his dad, he decided it was time to ask the one question he'd never dreamed he'd ask his father. "I'm supposed to get on a plane tonight for Vegas. Tonight." The thought stabbed at him. Not another night with Kendra until…until when? Why should she wait for him? She might think it could be another ten years till he showed up again. Even though he knew with his age, elbow and history, he'd be lucky to get one more year as a reliever.

Then, he'd come home again. And would he destroy her life a third time? "What should I do, Dad?"

He waited for the advice, the sage quote from Mickey

Mantle, the guidance he so desperately needed. He waited, he realized, for someone to tell him it was okay to follow his heart and not his head.

*Come on, Dad. Tell me something.*

*Play to win. Hit it out of the park. Throw a curve when they expect a fastball…*some straightforward baseball analogy to make him understand how he could justify walking away from his last shot at glory…or ignoring the happiness that Kendra offered.

But his father just ran a hand through his mane of white hair and smiled. "Only you know what's important in your life, son. Only you know the answer."

The answer was as loud and clear as an umpire's call.

"If you don't let me in this house this minute I'm going to break the door down." The threat was accompanied by three loud raps at Kendra's door.

Kendra sighed heavily, knowing it was a complete waste to ignore him. She stuffed her new blue notebook under the sofa cushion and padded barefoot to the front door to open it with no small amount of disgust.

"Cut the drama, Jack."

Jack grinned and put his arms on his sister's shoulders. "Why are you ignoring me?"

"Why aren't you sleeping late? You must have been at Monroe's until two or three last night."

"The last e-mail exchange was at two-thirty and I couldn't sleep this morning. Deuce and his dad left to go play baseball, and Diana blew out a few minutes later dressed to beat the world. That left me with a dog who doesn't know how to make coffee." He looked at her little galley kitchen. "Don't make me go to some cyber café for my fix, Ken."

She smiled and tilted her head toward the kitchen. "Come on, I'll make you a cup. What time are you going to the airport?"

"My flight leaves Boston at one, so I should get the heck out of here soon. Will you take me?"

"Isn't Deuce taking you?"

Jack's eyes darkened to a deep sage as he regarded her. "It's a little inconvenient for him to go all the way to Logan Airport twice in one day."

Twice. In one day.

"So, he's leaving today?" She congratulated herself on not allowing a crack in her voice.

"He got on an American flight at six-twenty tonight. His agent wants him in Vegas by tomorrow morning."

"Oh." Kendra managed to scoop the grounds into the coffee filter without spilling a single grain. "Well, sure. I'll take you to the airport."

If she played the timing right, she might never have to see Deuce again. She could take hours returning from the airport in Boston, and by the time she got home, he'd be gone.

"He's in love with you."

Jack's statement jerked her back to reality.

"He's in love with the fact that I'm in love with him," she said. At least, that's how she'd just written it in her brand-new diary, which she was far too old to keep, but much too sad not to. "He's addicted to hero-worship and I give it to him in spades."

"True."

"At least I know who I am and what my weaknesses are," she said, more to herself than her brother. "You know, I was horrified when he showed up here a few weeks ago. So certain he had the power to ruin my life and wreck my world."

"And you showed up in leather pants and wrecked his." Jack laughed softly. "But he was gone long before you put on the battle gear, Ken."

"I don't think so, but you're sweet to try and make me feel better."

Jack plopped his elbows on the counter and looked hard at her. "I'm not trying to make you feel better. I think the guy's nuts if he walks away from you again—"

"Again?" This time her voice did crack.

"He told me about the baby."

Her arms suddenly felt very heavy. "He did?"

"Well, truth be told, I started to tell him about your... history. And then he told me it was his."

"You were very busy this morning," she said, trying for a light tone. Then she closed her eyes for a moment. This was Jack. She didn't have to pretend. "I'm sorry, Jack. I never wanted you to know."

He shrugged. "I managed not to punch his face off, but only because he looked good and truly miserable about it."

She took a step closer to the counter and put her hand over his. "So how do you feel now that you know who the father of that baby was?"

"I feel sad because you and Deuce would make some awesome babies together."

She felt the color rise to her cheeks.

"And you know what else I think, Kendra? I think that if I ever find a woman who loves me as unconditionally as you love him, I would grab hold of her and never, ever let her go."

He flipped his hand and squeezed hers.

"I hope you do, Jack."

"And while I'm doling out brotherly wisdom, here's something else for you to ponder."

Jack was a rebel, but he'd never steered her wrong. Whatever he told her would be true and right. "What is it?"

"We made up all that stuff in the basement because we knew you were listening."

For the first time in hours, she laughed. "I knew that." But not what she heard yesterday. Deuce loved her. He'd admitted it.

"You did not," he countered, sounding very much like the teasing big brother he was. "But it's nice to see you smile."

The fact was, she had her business, her friends, her brother and her integrity. She didn't have Deuce, but she had a lot to smile about.

Since she'd been so creative in avoiding Deuce all day, Kendra's decision to hang around Logan Airport all afternoon and into the evening made no sense at all.

Before Deuce had gotten back to Diana's, she'd packed Jack into her car and they'd taken off for the airport.

Then Jack's flight had been delayed, so she stayed and spent a few more hours with him. Then she dawdled in an airport bookstore, and pretty soon she was hungry, so she had some pizza and then she looked at her watch. It was just past five.

She tried to tell herself she'd just killed some time to avoid the traffic back to the Cape, but who was she kidding?

She'd stayed long enough to say goodbye to Deuce. She had to kiss him one last time, and whisper once more that she loved him.

With a little smile and a pounding heart, she headed toward the main check-in for American. Anyone on Flight 204 to Las Vegas should be in line there right about now.

She understood his decision to play his game, to renew his

contract. Jack said he'd only be a reliever, and this would probably be his last season, but it didn't matter.

For the first time in her life, she felt free. Not of loving Deuce—she always would—but of that desperate feeling that somehow her life was incomplete without him. It wasn't. It was full. So she could certainly be strong enough to wish him well and say goodbye.

She scanned the line for a tall, handsome, powerful man with bedroom eyes and a sexy smile. Her knees weakened as blood rushed to her nerve endings, but she continued walking past the long line of people checking in.

No Deuce.

She slipped outside and studied the people checking in at curbside.

No Deuce.

Back in the terminal, she followed the path from baggage check-in to the entrance to the gates, as far as she could go without a ticket. She watched dozens of passengers walk through security, dozens of men—some tall, some dark, some not bad looking…but no Deuce.

The monitor told her his flight was on time. But she must have missed him. He must have arrived early. Of course, he was anxious to get back to his real field of dreams.

Baseball was still his true love. If he didn't know who he was without the crowds and the competition, then he'd find out next year or the year after. Deuce would never choose a boring life in Rockingham over the major leagues. Even if that boring life included her.

She waited about ten more minutes, then swallowed hard and headed toward the parking lot.

The biggest victory, she decided on the drive home, was the fact that there were no tears this time.

It was time to face one last demon, and it was time to celebrate her life.

Deuce stood at the crest of the sand dune and peered into the darkness. At the far end of West Rock Beach, he saw a faint light, someone holding a flashlight and sitting on a blanket.

Finally, he'd found Kendra.

Why hadn't he thought of coming here first? Instead he'd been all over Rockingham, back and forth to Monroe's and her house with no luck. Her cell phone didn't answer, and Jack's flight had been delayed, but had taken off. He'd checked all that while trying to find her, anxious to tell her of the decision he'd made.

He called her as he approached, not wanting to scare her.

He heard her gasp of surprise in response. "Deuce? Is that you?"

"You sure like to hang out on beaches in the dark, don't you?" he said as he got closer.

She flipped the flashlight off, but he could still see her in the moonlight.

"I'm...what are you doing here? Your flight left hours ago."

"I didn't make it." He reached the blanket and looked down at her. Under the flashlight was a dark-blue notebook with a pen clipped to the cover. He dropped to his knees and looked at her face in the dim light. "You come here often?"

She shook her head, her gaze locked on him. "Except for a picnic the other day, I haven't been here for ten years."

He sat next to her, not too close, but still on the blanket. "What are you doing?"

"I'm celebrating."

*Celebrating?* Well, that was the last answer he expected. "The cyber café and artists' space?"

"No."

"The fact that Seamus and Diana got married?"

"No."

"My reinstatement to the Nevada Snake Eyes?" Please say no.

"Sort of."

He let out a half laugh, half sigh. "You're celebrating with a notebook and pen? No champagne?"

"I'm writing." She picked up the flashlight, and flipped it on, the yellow beam directed at the notebook. "Want to hear?"

Did he? "Go ahead. Hit me."

Very slowly, she picked up the notebook and opened it. She flipped open to the first page.

She cleared her throat and looked at the words.

The year I learned to read, to tie my shoes and to add one-digit numbers, I fell in love with Deuce Monroe.

A completely unexpected and foreign tightness squeezed his throat at the words.

The year I learned the real meaning of life, I lost his child.

He tried to swallow, but it was impossible.

And this year, the year I realized a professional dream, I am finally able to let him go. Really go. Not pretend that he's coming back. Because even if he does,

She stopped and looked at him.

I won't be waiting for him. And it doesn't even make me cry.

He blinked, and felt the moisture on his lids. "Well, then. You must be the only one," he said with a self-conscious laugh.

Eyes wide, she reached over and wiped the tear from his eye. "Now you tell me why you're not on that plane to Las Vegas."

He captured her finger and wrapped his hand around it. "Because I'm not leaving. I'm not taking the job. I'm not letting you go."

Her jaw dropped as she stared at him. "What?"

He tapped the page. "If I go, you won't wait for me and I don't want to live my life without you."

She breathed slowly, evenly, studying his face, taking in his pronouncement. "Deuce, you can't live without baseball."

"I won't. I'm taking the job as the Rock High coach."

"You are?"

He nodded. "And I'm probably going to have to help you at Monroe's."

"You will?"

"'Cause I want nine kids and that'll keep you real busy."

She laughed, but even in the moonlight he could see her tears.

"That's okay, isn't it?"

"You're crazy," she said, shaking her head. "Absolutely nuts."

"About you." He slipped his hand around the nape of her neck and pulled her closer to him. "I love you, Kendra. I love your strength and your intelligence and your ability to stand up to me. And I love that you've loved me your whole life. If you ever stopped, I couldn't stand it."

"I'll never stop, Deuce. I just was willing to let you go if I had to. Willing to be independent and alone, even if I still loved you."

"You can be independent, but not alone. Please not alone. Will you marry me, Kendra Locke? Can I make you Mrs. Monroe?"

She reached down and picked up the pen she'd been writing with. "You know, I've been practicing that signature my whole life. It's about time I get to use it."

Easing her back on the blanket, he tucked her body under his.

"Is that a yes?" he asked, his whole being suspended until he heard what he wanted.

"Well," she said with a sly smile. "It's true that Monroe's has always been run by Monroes."

"Say yes, Kendra." He kissed her eyelids.

"And Seamus does like me better than you."

"Say yes, Kendra." He kissed her cheeks.

"And Martin Hatcher really wants you to coach."

"Say yes, Kendra." He kissed her mouth.

"Yes, Deuce."

Happiness and contentment curled through him as he pulled her body into his. "About those nine kids," he said huskily, his chest tight with a heart that might burst. "We'd better start. Now."

He took her mouth in one long, leisurely kiss, tasting the sweetness of her, filling himself up with it.

"We've had pretty good luck on this beach before." She laughed into his kiss and slid one leg around his. "But I don't want nine kids, Deuce."

"What do you want, Ken-doll?"

"I want you, Seamus."

He pulled her into him and rocked against her, unable to believe that this loving, brilliant, wonderful woman would be his partner for the rest of his life.

"You got me. For life."

"And maybe one little girl."

He put his mouth against her ear and whispered, "As long as she has a good arm, I can work with that."

* * * * *

# MILLS & BOON®
## SuperROMANCE™

## MORE TO TEXAS THAN COWBOYS
### by Roz Denny Fox
*Home To Stay*

Greer Bell is returning to Texas for the first time since she left as a pregnant teenager. She and her young daughter are determined to make a success of their new ranch – and the last thing Greer needs is a romantic entanglement, even with the helpful and handsome Reverend Noah Kelley.

## PARTY OF THREE by Joan Kilby
### *Single Father*

Ben Gillard finally has a chance to build a relationship with his son, instead of being a weekend dad. But he and Danny can't seem to find any common ground. Ben is surprised to find that it is the straitlaced Ally Cummings who can make them a family.

## THE MUMMY QUEST by Lori Handeland
### *The Luchetti Brothers*

Now that Tim Luchetti has found himself the best dad in the world, he needs a mum! Only, picking a wife for Dean is proving harder than he thought. But when Tim ends up in his headteacher's office, he decides Ms O'Connell might just be perfect.

## ALMOST A FAMILY by Roxanne Rustand
### *Blackberry Hill Memorial*

Erin can't believe she has to work with Dr Connor Reynolds – the man her family blames for what happened to her cousin. As well as that, she has to contend with her recent divorce and three children who don't understand why Daddy left. If only she could act as if Connor was simply another colleague…

## On sale from 16th March 2007

*Available at WHSmith, Tesco, ASDA, and all good bookshops*

*www.millsandboon.co.uk*

MILLS & BOON®

# SPECIAL EDITION™

## WORTH FIGHTING FOR
### by Judy Duarte

Single mother Caitlin Rogers knew exactly what her priority was – her little daughter, Emily. So when that relationship was threatened, Caitlin was lucky to be able to count on Brett Tanner, a man with scars in his past who made a family worth fighting for.

## SECOND-TIME LUCKY
### by Laurie Paige
*Canyon Country*

How ironic that family counsellor Caileen Peters was turning to her client Jefferson Aquilon, a foster father, for help with *her* daughter. But Caileen soon found something more in Jeff's arms.

## THE PRODIGAL MD RETURNS
### by Marie Ferrarella
*The Alaskans*

Things were really heating up, when Ben Kerrigan came back after leaving Heather Ryan Kendall at the altar seven years ago. Recently-widowed Heather and her six-year-old daughter had a surprise for the prodigal MD.

**Don't miss out!**
**On sale from 16th March 2007**

*Available at WHSmith, Tesco, ASDA, and all good bookshops*
*www.millsandboon.co.uk*

0307/06

MILLS & BOON

# Modern
### romance™
## Extra

## *Two longer and more passionate stories every month*

### GETTING DOWN TO BUSINESS
*by Ally Blake*

If prim Abbey Parish wants to get sexy playboy and tycoon Flynn Granger on board with her business, she's going to have to loosen up a little... Flynn's impressed with Abbey's ideas, but if he could just get beneath her suited-and-booted persona, he's certain he'll find a wild and sensual woman underneath. Then getting down to business with Abbey would get a whole load more interesting!

### BEDDED BY A BAD BOY *by Heidi Rice*

Monroe Latimer is a drop-dead gorgeous bad boy who doesn't do commitment. One look at Monroe and feisty English girl Jessie Connor knows he's about as Mr Wrong as a guy can get, but there's one big problem. He's sexy as hell, he fires her blood like no other man ever has and his killer blue gaze is focused right on her. His look says he'll bed her – but never wed her... Is Jessie the one who can tame the untameable?

## On sale 6th April 2007

*Available at WHSmith, Tesco, ASDA, and all good bookshops*
*www.millsandboon.co.uk*

# *Regency romance…and revenge by bestselling author Nicola Cornick*

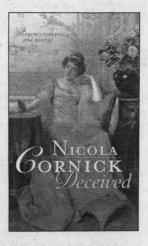

Princess Isabella never imagined it could come to this. Bad enough she faces imprisonment for debts not her own. Even worse that she must make a hasty marriage of convenience with Marcus, the Earl of Stockhaven.

As the London gossips eagerly gather to watch the fun, Isabella struggles to maintain a polite distance in her marriage. But the more Isabella challenges Marcus's iron determination to have a marriage in more than name only, the hotter their passion burns. This time, will it consume them both – or fuel a love greater than they dare dream?

## On sale 16th February 2007

*Available at WHSmith, Tesco, ASDA
and all good bookshops*

# FREE!

## 2 Books
### and a surprise gift!

We would like to take this opportunity to thank you for reading this Mills & Boon® book by offering you the chance to take TWO more specially selected titles from the Desire™ series absolutely FREE! We're also making this offer to introduce you to the benefits of the Mills & Boon® Reader Service™—

- ★ **FREE home delivery**
- ★ **FREE gifts and competitions**
- ★ **FREE monthly Newsletter**
- ★ **Exclusive Reader Service offers**
- ★ **Books available before they're in the shops**

Accepting these FREE books and gift places you under no obligation to buy, you may cancel at any time, even after receiving your free shipment. Simply complete your details below and return the entire page to the address below. You don't even need a stamp!

**YES!** Please send me 2 free Desire books and a surprise gift. I understand that unless you hear from me, I will receive 3 superb new titles every month for just £4.99 each, postage and packing free. I am under no obligation to purchase any books and may cancel my subscription at any time. The free books and gift will be mine to keep in any case.

D7ZEF

Ms/Mrs/Miss/Mr ..................................................Initials ..................................
**BLOCK CAPITALS PLEASE**
Surname ................................................................................................................
Address................................................................................................................
............................................................................................................................
..............................................................................Postcode ..............................

### Send this whole page to:
### UK: FREEPOST CN81, Croydon, CR9 3WZ